ABOMINATION

A NOVEL

E.E. BORTON

authorHOUSE®

AuthorHouse™
1663 Liberty Drive
Bloomington, IN 47403
www.authorhouse.com
Phone: 1-800-839-8640

First published by AuthorHouse   3/16/2011

ISBN: 978-1-4567-2778-9 (e)
ISBN: 978-1-4567-2779-6 (hc)
ISBN: 978-1-4567-2780-2 (sc)

Library of Congress Control Number: 2011900414

Printed in the United States of America

ACKNOWLEDGMENTS

Bringing a world to life in a novel is considered a mostly solitary endeavor. In my case, nothing could be further from the truth. It took a village to create this book and it would've been a more difficult road if not for a special group of people. Thank you seems inadequate.

Crystal, Dave, Tina, Tim, and Anthony, you are the real heroes who chose a thankless job, but are the best at what you do. Nobody will ever be able to take that away from you.

Robin, Z, Hopper, and Gordon, thank you for always believing in me and offering your encouragement and support when I needed it the most – which was often.

Jennifer, Ashley, and Bug, I can't imagine my world without all of you in it.

And to my parents, Kathy and Larry.

There are many others who played an important role in motivating and inspiring me to create the work you're holding in your hand or reading on your screen. Thank you for staying the course and keeping me on it.

CREDITS

Jennifer Ziegenfuss, Editor
Natalie Elzinga, Cover Design
Gordon Wulff, Business Development
Jennifer Hackney, Author Photo

For Jennifer and My Grandfather

CONTENTS

1

PUBLIC PROFILE

HE HATED HIMSELF FOR WHAT he was going to do to her. She did nothing to him except be the perfect choice. She was going to experience excruciating pain and a horrible death in a few hours simply for being blonde, blue-eyed, and young. He leaned in closer to look deeper into his own eyes for answers. A moment later, the bathroom mirror exploded after a bone-crushing punch when the answers didn't come. Not a single shard of glass penetrated his knuckles.

Peter Arrington walked through the broken glass on his bare feet and into the hallway of the abandoned farmhouse in Harrisonburg, Virginia. He arrived in the familiar town two weeks earlier looking for a place to hide from the people looking to end his life. The list grew longer when he discovered the FBI was joining the manhunt. In the back of his mind, he wondered what was taking them so long to stop him.

The FBI wouldn't find him in time to save Laura Ackerman's life. She was dead the moment Peter selected her photo from a list on his computer screen two days earlier. He thought finding the perfect young woman to satisfy his uncontrollable urge would be difficult on the run. He was very wrong. It was as simple as typing a few words in a social networking website. In a matter of seconds, he had dozens to choose from who fit the criteria.

He had no idea why she was the one; she just was. Something electrified in his brain when he scanned the photos and found hers. There were some he considered more beautiful and accessible, but the urge didn't overpower him until he saw her. Two months earlier, he would've been disgusted at the thought of hurting any woman. Two months earlier, he was a proud, decorated, and highly successful United States Marine. Seconds before he destroyed the mirror, he saw a pathetic, weak, and unrecognizable face. He agonized over what he had become, but agonized more not knowing why.

Since the need to satisfy his urge started building momentum two days earlier, he fixated on Laura. She made the mortal mistake of publicly displaying her life for anyone to see who had access to a computer and an internet connection. Everything he needed to stalk his victim from a safe and concealed distance was at his fingertips. Along with over a hundred photos, she announced to the world on a daily basis every move she made. He knew everything about her including where she was going to be later in the evening.

Peter was angry with her for reasons he knew, but he wanted to kill her for reasons he didn't. His anger towards her was based on her obvious lack of understanding that there were bad people out there. His feeling of anger was more paternal than pathologic. Where was her father to demand she stop posting private information about her life? Where was he when she needed him to protect her from the real monsters like the man staring at her photos? But as with every other detail of her life, she wrote to friends about her estranged father who left the family a year earlier. There would be no heroes to save Laura.

Because she had little or no guidance from others who did understand there were monsters out there lurking in the shadows, Laura sealed her fate with her final message. She announced to the world her roommate in the home she rented from her uncle would be out of town for several days. Peter knew exactly where her home was located. A day earlier, he simply waited for her to leave the restaurant where she worked and then followed her home. She ended her last message by writing she was looking forward to a quiet evening with no distractions and a long bubble bath.

Peter steadily paced back and forth through the long hallway in the farmhouse as the sun set behind the rolling Virginia hills. He was losing his battle to suppress the urges and images of tearing into her soft flesh. There were milliseconds of time when he thought of grabbing his gun, holding it up to his head, and pulling the trigger. But as quickly as those thoughts surfaced, they were pushed down again. After less than an hour, even the flashes of welcomed suicide disappeared. Nothing occupied his mind except easing his addiction by putting his hands on Laura. He needed to get closer to her.

She lived eleven miles away in an old one-story ranch house on ten acres. From the numerous photos, he knew he could easily get to her without drawing attention or leaving a witness. Laura's aging uncle couldn't keep up with the dense foliage creeping across the yard toward the house, and neither could she. Thickets of trees lined the property including the long isolated driveway. He knew her nearest neighbor was an old woman who only went outside to get her mail. He read one of her earlier postings stating it didn't matter how loud her Fourth of July party became, the yelling would be a whisper by the time it reached her neighbors.

Peter drove his Jeep Cherokee with tinted windows down the country back roads to the entrance of a closed lumber yard. A poorly kept logging trail, unused for six months, bordered the back of Laura's property. It was three miles from the entrance of the closed business to her home. He parked at the yard and started running down the dirt road in new boots he was only going to wear once. He planned on burying them, and the rest of his clothing, with her.

Even for a conditioned athlete, running fully clothed in heavy boots along a soft dirt road would take at least twenty minutes at a strong pace. Peter was at the edge of her property in ten; he was barely winded. In his original plan, he'd enter the house at two o'clock in the morning when she was more likely to be asleep. Looking at his watch, already battling the urge to get to her, he knew he couldn't wait four more hours.

He stopped his trek through the dense woods when he saw the warm glow of lights through the windows at the back of the house. There was only twenty feet between the last tree and the back door leading to his prize. Peter slowly and expertly maneuvered around the entire perimeter. His Marine training helped him remain concealed and undetected. Laura's car was the only vehicle in the driveway. The young tenants had little use for expensive window coverings which allowed Peter to verify there were no visitors inside. He assumed the only covered window was the bathroom. He took a deep breath thinking of her soaking by candlelight in the tub, oblivious to the danger at her back door.

At that point, Peter no longer cared about why he was there or why he wanted to drain the life out of an innocent girl. In his head, she wasn't innocent. Even though she didn't know he existed, she did something so terrible to him the only way he could recover was to rip her apart. He didn't know what she did either. He only knew he had to do it with his bare hands. A bullet or knife would rob him of the full cleansing effect of the experience. He had to feel each tear, each break, and hear each scream. It was the only way to ease the tormenting and excruciating pain that started as a mild headache two days earlier. And it wouldn't subside until he felt the life leaving her body.

There was enough resistance left inside him to wait outside for a few more minutes. He was hoping it would be enough time for them to find and stop him. He prayed for law enforcement assault teams to flood the woods. He looked up into the clear night sky pleading for helicopters to zero in on his location. But as the minutes passed, so did their opportunity to end him. He erased the thoughts and rose out of the darkness – it was time.

He closed the short distance to the house with blinding speed. Without slowing down, he blasted through the thick wooden door into the kitchen. Debris and splinters peppered the floor and walls as he continued into the hallway to the only room with a covered window. The bathroom door was open, and she was exactly where she posted online she would be: reading a book in a bubble bath.

The sound of the exploding door startled her, but the monster she saw standing in her bathroom terrified her. Laura knocked over several candles lining the tub as she grabbed the sides trying to stand after she heard him crash through the door. Her book was face down in the water between her legs. His ghastly appearance caused her mouth to freeze open, but she remained silent. From his hiding place in her backyard to the doorway in the bathroom, his normal human appearance was replaced by something she had only experienced in the pages of a book. Very much like the one slowly sinking to the bottom of her tub.

Staring at her naked body, Peter was filled with ecstasy laced with rage. He was so close to tasting her that he began to hyperventilate. Still silent, Laura leaned back as if she were trying to force an invisible escape door to open behind her. The door didn't open as Peter stepped towards her, but she finally was able to scream. It was music to his ears.

He knew he couldn't fully enjoy his work at her house. There was the off chance someone might stop by to visit, or her roommate could've cut his trip short. He needed to get her back to the abandoned farmhouse where they'd be alone and free from any interruption. It took every ounce of restraint for Peter not to devour her where she sat. As her screams echoed off every wall in the house, he delivered a nose-breaking punch, rendering her unconscious and quiet. He closed his eyes as he licked her blood off his knuckles. His transformation to an uncaring, unsympathetic, and uncontrollable demon was complete.

2

BUILT TO KILL

AN FBI FUGITIVE RECOVERY TEAM, along with SWAT and sniper units, was assembled in a sheriff's department briefing room. They had been hunting UA Marine Peter Arrington for nearly a month before tracking him to an abandoned farmhouse in Virginia. The agents knew he'd be taking his fourth victim within 12 hours.

"Ladies and gentlemen, my name is Ryan Pearson, and I'm a special agent with the FBI. I'd also like to introduce agents Dallas Chase, Michelle Dobbs, and Thomas Freeman," said Ryan as the three agents rose in the front row. "We're part of a federal task force with only one job: find Peter Arrington."

"Is he the reason we have three missing women in our county that hasn't seen a murder in nine years?" asked local Sheriff Bill Parker in a slow southern drawl.

"Yes, sir," responded Ryan, knowing he wouldn't be a welcomed visitor in the normally quiet town. "We have overwhelming evidence he's the guy responsible."

"Give it to me straight. Are they dead?"

"Until we recover the bodies, I can't say for sure. But I can say, based on the evidence, it's very unlikely they're still alive."

"I gotta tell ya, I find it a little troubling we haven't been allowed access to any of that evidence," said Sheriff Parker.

"Sheriff, you're not going to like my answer, but that information is classified."

"You're right, I don't. We're a close community and we look out for each other. Always have. I know each of those missing girls and their families. I'd like to go to them with something more than it's classified."

"I understand your concern, but –"

"No, sir," interrupted Sheriff Parker. "You don't understand my concern. I tried to get help three months ago, but I couldn't get one damned FBI agent to give me the time of day. Now I've got over twenty of you armed to the teeth and jammed in my briefing room. My boys and I have barely slept since Laura Ackerman went missing three months ago. Who the hell is Peter Arrington?"

"Sheriff, we don't have much time," said Ryan with a stern tone. "Most of your questions will be answered once we have him in custody. But right now we need to focus on stopping him from killing again. And he is going to kill again, Sheriff. According to a fairly regulated timeline of the abductions, he's due. He seems to be a creature of habit. He's also incredibly elusive.

"We believe he's bringing his victims to the farmhouse alive," said Ryan, standing in front of a corkboard displaying photos of each missing girl and a layout of the farmhouse. "He'll spend one day, maybe two, at the house and then he'll disappear. He's taken each victim exactly six weeks apart to the day. We have surveillance teams already posted in the field. If he sticks with his method, he should be returning late this evening."

"Jesus Christ!" blurted Sheriff Parker. "He's out there right now looking for his next victim in my county, and you're going to let him take her? This is bullshit! We need to be warning people, not sitting on our asses. This information needs to be on every television and radio station within a hundred miles. I thought you federal boys would have your shit together. Do you not understand I have an obligation to protect the citizens who elected me to this office?"

Ryan walked to the table where the sheriff and his deputies were sitting. He knelt down beside Parker's chair. He wanted their undivided attention.

"He cuts them until they lose enough blood to where they can't fight, but are still conscious and aware. He wants them to watch his work. He viciously rapes them several times before he starts to disembowel them. Again, he doesn't remove any vital organs that will kill them instantly. He only takes the parts he can play with while they're alive. He'll continue to rape them, but he'll start using objects and tools to do the job. When the anger subsides and he grows tired after a day or two, he'll lie down beside them. He'll hold them like a caring father holds a sick child. He wants to be the last thing they see and feel before they die.

"Our best opportunity to stop him is tonight and in your county. If we hit the streets trying to warn the public and show our cards, he'll know. And if he knows, he'll disappear. Peter Arrington is a fucking ghost. And he's not the Casper kind. He's the kind that comes right out of a nightmare. But disappearing doesn't mean he'll stop killing. What you don't understand is, he has to kill.

"Your jurisdiction stops at the county line. Mine stops at the border of Canada and Mexico. This is a federal case and you were invited to this briefing as a courtesy. If you interrupt me one more time, you and your boys will spend the rest of my visit in your own fucking jail. Is there anything about my tone that makes you believe I'm not serious?"

The sheriff pressed his lips together and leaned back in his chair as he looked at the federal agents surrounding him. He knew he was in no position to argue. He needed to say his piece to look good in front of his deputies, but even they were ready for him to stop talking.

"Get that sick son-of-a-bitch out of my county," said Parker. "The sooner you get rid of him, the sooner I get rid of all of you."

"Deal," said Ryan.

The sheriff and his deputies stood up and walked out of the briefing. There was little they could do to assist the group assembled in the crowded room. Ryan continued the detailed presentation using maps, photographs, and data provided by the surveillance teams.

"My team, Alpha, will breach the rear of the house. Sixty seconds later, Bravo team will enter through the front. Charlie team will cover the rear. Delta, Echo, and Foxtrot teams will take up sniper positions covering the perimeter of the house. If he gets by the entry teams, you have the green light. If you spot him without handcuffs, kill him. Are there any questions from the snipers on the rules of engagement?"

No questions.

"Arrington is a special forces Marine. We have intelligence that there may be sensors around the perimeter and he can possibly intercept our radio communications. The mission will be conducted with absolute radio silence. Remove the batteries from your cell phones and leave them in the vehicles. No exceptions. Alpha is the only team authorized to break silence. We don't expect him to be there when we arrive, but we'll approach and set up as if he was. He'll exploit and make us pay for any mistakes. Check your gear, check it again, and assemble at the vehicles in twenty minutes for a final briefing."

The agents filed out of the room to prepare for the mission. There were no rookies or first timers in the group. Every man and woman was experienced and handpicked for the assault and teams. Each received the call and arrived in the small western Virginia town in less than thirty-six hours. The logistics required to put the group together were impressive. They knew very little about Peter Arrington, but they all felt the sense of urgency to put him behind bars or six feet underground. All of the agents cleared the briefing room except Ryan's team. There were a few items he needed to emphasize to them before the assault.

"I don't think you'll be getting a Christmas card this year from the sheriff, Boss," said Agent Dallas Chase.

"I don't blame him for being pissed," said Ryan, working on his second cup of coffee. "Any other situation and warning the public would be our priority. But even if they barricaded themselves in storm cellars, Arrington would still get to them."

"This guy is no doubt a monster, but he's still just a man," said Agent Thomas Freeman.

"Tom, I wish that statement was true," said Ryan, drawing the team in closer. "The reality is, he isn't."

"I don't spook easy," said Agent Michelle Dobbs, "but I have to admit you're creeping me out a little. So you're telling us Arrington isn't human?"

"For reasons I can't disclose at the moment, I've had to keep specific information about his condition under wraps. Even though we're looking to take him down tonight, I won't be able to answer many of the questions I know you're about to ask."

"His condition?" started Dallas with the questions.

Ryan took a long purposeful drink out of his cup to emphasize his next statement. "That one I can answer. Peter Arrington is faster, stronger, and deadlier than any man we've hunted. And he's the weakest of the four Marines we need to find. All of them have been physically and mentally altered by radical gene therapy treatments over the past two years."

"Okay, now I'm officially creeped out," said Michelle.

"You should be," said Ryan. "The fastest human beings on earth can run almost thirty miles per hour, but only for a few seconds. Arrington was clocked at nearly forty, but he sustained the speed for two minutes. The world record for the bench press is just over 1,000 pounds. Arrington bench pressed 1,200. He did it twice before putting the weight down."

"He doesn't look like a world record sprinter or weight lifter," said Tom. "He's definitely fit, but from his file photos he doesn't look much bigger than you, Boss. No offense."

"None taken," said Ryan. "You also wouldn't be able to tell his eyesight is comparable to a pair of binoculars, or his hearing and sense of smell is comparable to a K-9. His brain processes information at nearly twice the speed of a normal human. For lack of a better term, this guy was built as a super soldier. All of them were."

"They were built?" asked Dallas.

"That's an area where I can't go into much detail," said Ryan.

"Can't or won't?" asked Michelle.

"I can't," responded Ryan. "But mainly because I simply don't know. I promise each of you I'll answer with what I do know, but I'll also tell you if I truly don't."

"Okay, so what can you tell us about how and why they were built?" asked Tom.

"I don't think it shocks any of you that the military has been looking to build a better soldier. Most of the methods they use are strictly regulated by civilian and government oversight committees. Each soldier assigned to the research facility signed consent documents approved by the Department of Health and Human Services as well as the FDA. Both agencies have classified procedures in which civilians don't have access, but the information is mainly related to the individual results. This isn't a new process. It's actually been around for decades.

"As far as the details about how they obtained those incredible results, the scientists at the briefings in D.C. lost me in about ten seconds. They did grab my attention when they started talking about the Marine's capabilities. The military was highly satisfied with the results until the day all four decided to leave the facility."

"You said they voluntarily consented," said Michelle. "Were they confined to the facility?"

"Oddly enough, no," said Ryan. "They weren't lab rats. They had weekends off and took vacations. They went home to visit their families like any other soldier.

"These guys weren't a flight risk. All four were decorated Marines holding Top Secret security clearances. From what I know, they were highly patriotic and highly motivated. Up until the day they disappeared, there were absolutely no indications they were unsatisfied or unhappy with their assignment. They went through constant psychological evaluations. And they passed every time."

"So, what turned them into monsters?" asked Dallas. "One day they're super soldier patriots and then the next they're serial rapists and murderers? Doesn't make sense, Boss."

"No, it doesn't," said Ryan. "Regardless of what synapse misfired in their brains, they're now killers. They're now a serious threat to anyone or anything they come across. Don't get me wrong, I asked the deputy director the same question. He gave me a simple answer. He told me to go find them so we could ask."

"Understood," said Dallas. "I get your point. Enough said."

"Right now we need to focus on Arrington," said Ryan, bringing them back to the mission. "The scientist did tell me there may be a weakness we can exploit. It's one of the reasons we have to wait until he brings his victim back to the farm. They said Arrington will probably be caught up in the moment right before he starts his sadistic game. He'll be more focused on satisfying his urge rather than looking over his shoulder for us. Once he gets her inside, we should be able to move into position at the back of the house without alerting him. We're going to make a quiet entry at the window next to the rear door. They firmly believe it's going to be our only shot at taking him alive."

"He runs forty miles per hour and can lift a small car," said Tom. "How the hell are we going to put cuffs on him?"

"Let me be crystal clear answering that question," said Ryan. "I'm going to ask him once to put his hands on his head. If he doesn't comply, I'm going to shoot him. I'm going to shoot him a lot. He's a deadly weapon regardless if he's holding one. Do any of you have issue with that approach?"

"I very much like that approach, Boss," said Dallas.

"I'd even consider skipping the hands on the head part," said Tom.

"I'm with Tom," responded Michelle.

"Okay," said Ryan. "I need to call the deputy director and give him a status report before we mount up. I'll need the room, please."

With that request, the team left the room and started their final equipment checks with the group outside. Ryan closed the door, took a seat, and looked at his cell phone. He had been hunting Arrington for nearly four months and was confident he would finally be closing his file by sunrise.

But he couldn't overlook his gut feeling that certain aspects about the mission were a little off. He had more questions than answers about why he was hunting U.S. Marines on American soil. Ryan's only point of contact was the deputy director of the FBI. All his information, orders, and reports came and went directly through the deputy's office in Quantico, Virginia. It was a very unorthodox procedure. Agent Ryan Pearson always followed orders with few questions unrelated to successfully completing his assignment. He shook off the uncomfortable feeling and dialed the number which never went to voicemail.

"Director Donaldson, this is Agent Pearson," confirmed Ryan.

"Hello, Ryan. The brief went well?"

"Yes, sir. This will be my final call prior to the raid."

"My prayers are with you, son. I wish I could send you every assault team in the Bureau. How are you and your team holding up?"

"We're good to go, sir. Well rested and well-armed."

"Good to hear. Ryan, I know this has been a strange assignment and you've performed better than I could've hoped. I know I've asked much of you this past month. It can't be easy going after Marines from your old unit. Especially with one of them being your friend."

"Sir, he was an acquaintance, not a friend. And it's just circumstance we went to the same high school. I have no issue with doing the job when the time comes. It won't affect the result if it dictates I put one between his eyes."

"Your ability to do the job has never been a question, Ryan. But I do need to cover a few items again for my own satisfaction."

"Yes, sir."

"After the assault, you and your team are to either take him into custody or put him in a body bag. I have a very strong feeling it'll be the bag. Make every possible effort to limit contact with Arrington to your team only. If any other agent even makes eye contact with him, they're to be quarantined until the Didache team arrives. Are you clear?"

"Yes, sir."

"Do you have any questions?"

"No, sir, but may I speak freely?"

"Of course."

"Sir, I appreciate the sensitive nature of this assignment, but I have to admit I'm having an issue with not being able to provide full disclosure of Arrington's condition to my team."

"Ryan, I can assure you his affliction is not contagious. I wouldn't willingly send any of my agents unprotected into a situation which may expose them to an unknown deadly pathogen. It may not sit easy with you, but you simply have to trust me."

"I do, sir. But I'm about to send nearly two dozen agents into harm's way without being able to explain what they may witness."

"Containment is a priority. Please don't confuse its meaning with cover-up. There are extremely detrimental ramifications if the public was aware at this point. Remember, we still have three out there and no idea where they're hiding. A public panic would greatly reduce our chances of finding them. That may go against conventional wisdom, but everything about these men defies logic. I concur with my boss this is the best course of action we can take. I'm sorry I can't make the situation clearer. I'm still working on understanding it all myself. What I do know is, you're about to save countless innocent lives by taking Peter Arrington down."

"That's the plan, sir."

"Call me the moment you complete the mission. It's critical we allow the scientific team access to the scene as soon as possible to process Arrington. Dead or alive, they believe he'll provide clues to the whereabouts of the other three."

"What about the victim? Am I to quarantine her as well?"

"Absolutely. Anyone having contact with him must be quarantined with the only exception being your team. But as we discussed, all of you are to stay with the scientists until they release you. Understood?"

"Yes, sir. Do you have anything else for me?"

"I do. Good luck and Godspeed, son. Send that monster to hell if he doesn't comply."

"Will do, sir."

3

AND THEN THERE
WERE THREE

THE ASSAULT AND SNIPER TEAMS were dropped off at various entry points nearly a mile away from the target farmhouse. They used satellite imagery to plan routes that focused on avoiding roads, houses, and any human contact. As the sun was setting, the teams arrived at their staging areas surrounding the property.

The snipers created blinds rendering them nearly invisible. A passerby would have to step on one of their heads to know a human was under his feet. Each shooter had a kill zone around the house they were responsible for covering. The zones overlapped, ensuring there wasn't an inch of space left unseen by their high-powered scopes. The technology used in the optics turned pitch black night into clear day. Each sniper passed the time by locking his site on small rodents scurrying back and forth between the dilapidated barn and the abandoned farmhouse.

Assault Team Bravo staged in a wooded area resembling an island on the edge of a dying cornfield. They were less than fifty yards from the front door of the house. It took nearly two hours for them to silently crawl the hundred yards through the open field to reach the cover of the trees. The withered stalks of corn would provide excellent camouflage when the time came to quickly close the distance to the door.

Ryan's team, Alpha, and Charlie team quietly made their way along a shallow creek bed that snaked around to the back of the farm. They'd stay hidden behind the steep bank until nightfall. Once the blanket of darkness covered the landscape, Alpha and Charlie would rise out of the muddy staging area and take positions along the tree line separating the house from the creek. From their vantage point, they could easily spot the target's vehicle approaching the farmhouse. His approach was the signal for all three assault teams to begin moving in closer.

Since radios couldn't be used to transmit execution orders, hand signals were their only option to maintain silence on the approach. Each FBI agent was equipped with the latest generation of military grade night vision goggles (NVGs) with zoom lenses. It was critical Charlie team maintain visual contact with both Alpha and Bravo prior to the raid. When Ryan's team entered the house, Charlie would signal Bravo to move to the front door and start the sixty-second clock. Charlie would then take its position at the back door. The green light for the snipers would be observing the assault team's positioning at the doors.

None of the teams came across any trip wires, motion detectors or other hidden detection equipment which would alert Arrington to their presence. Ryan observed the house from the creek bed and noticed there were several open windows without coverings. If the farmhouse was Arrington's sanctuary to perform his sick ritual, the highly skilled Marine did an unusually poor job of securing his playground. Ryan began to wonder about the intelligence they were working with which pinpointed that particular house as the killer's lair. All indications from the outside were they were staking out an abandoned farm unoccupied by anything except rats and mice. As the hours passed, so did their hopes of putting an end to the nightmare.

Four hours after Alpha and Charlie moved up to the tree line, Ryan observed a faint light on the horizon in the direction of the entrance to the driveway. Moments later, it was clear that a vehicle was approaching the house. It was shortly before two o'clock in the morning.

It took nearly three minutes for the Jeep with tinted windows to make its way down the rarely used half-mile long driveway. The vehicle circled the house once and then stopped less than ten feet from the back door. It was impossible to see inside the Jeep. To Arrington's advantage, the headlights were pointed in the direction of Alpha and Charlie teams' position. Not one agent dared move an inch while the area was illuminated; their NVGs were useless. They'd only amplify the headlights and temporarily blind anyone looking towards the vehicle.

They were essentially pinned down as if someone was firing a heavy machine gun over their heads.

Ryan immediately thought the odds of the vehicle circling around and illuminating the exact area where they were hiding by accident were questionable. Arrington was a super soldier. Ryan suspected their position had been compromised. The one thing which would render them ineffective would be to take away their vision, and Arrington seemed to make that happen. The only agents who could positively identify the man behind the wheel were the snipers who were ordered not to break radio silence under any circumstances. Ryan slowly lifted his hand and poised his finger over the transmit button on his collar microphone. He was going to break silence and order the teams to pull back. As his finger tensed to press the button, the lights on the vehicle went dark. Ryan moved his finger away from the microphone and turned on his NVGs. A green hue filled the screen, and Arrington's face came into focus.

The target was sitting motionless behind the wheel. It was if he was staring directly at Ryan. The agent felt a cold chill invade his body. He was beginning to wonder if the killer was toying with him, daring him to stand up and take his shot. Ryan was still nearly fifty yards away from Arrington, but it wasn't an impossible distance with his assault rifle. For a moment, Ryan hoped one of his snipers would break protocol and end the monster before he even exited the vehicle. But the FBI wasn't in the assassination business. They had to give the killer a chance to surrender. It seemed like a ridiculous policy knowing what the evil bastard was about to do to another innocent woman.

With that thought, Ryan took his gaze off of Arrington and tried to verify there was another person in the vehicle. He only saw the driver still motionless in his seat. Another eerie minute passed before Arrington opened the driver's door and stepped outside. He went out of Ryan's sight for a moment as he raised the hatchback of the Jeep. He came into view again on the other side carrying a bound and gagged woman effortlessly under one arm and a large duffel bag under the other. He entered the house apparently confident he was alone, letting the screen door clap loudly against the frame.

Every muscle in Ryan's body wanted to propel him towards the house. Every second Arrington was out of sight, he could be dealing horrific pain to his powerless victim. He had to calm himself down by remembering the superhuman speed and strength of the Marine. He knew he had to wait until the monster was about to engage in the first act of his sick addiction. He had to wait until Arrington's otherwise razor sharp mind and senses were overloaded with the ecstasy of the moment. It was the only time the soldier would be weak enough to overpower.

The five minutes he waited concealed in the tree line seemed like five hours to Ryan and his team. He looked to his left and right to give a non-verbal signal to the other three that he was about to move. Ryan rose out of his cover and quickly traversed the open area between the staging position and the back door of the farmhouse. Dallas, Michelle, and Tom followed in close quarters with their weapons aimed at the house. The single file line of swiftly moving agents was the signal for Bravo team to advance to the front door. Charlie team followed Alpha once they confirmed Bravo was on the move. Charlie took cover behind the Jeep as Alpha waited for them to set into position. The countdown started. Ryan had sixty seconds to get inside and find the Marine before Bravo team kicked in the front door.

Once again, Ryan was slightly baffled by Arrington's behavior. He had left the back door ajar. The window the team assumed they'd need to breach was also left open. Ryan easily removed the loose screen from the window frame. He quietly placed it on the ground and took a moment to assess the room inside. There were no obvious signs of traps, tripwires or any devices to alert the Marine of an intrusion. There seemed to be no preparation at all.

The agents entered through the window into the large open room and cleared the space in seconds. The only sounds produced by the team were heavy breathing and the occasional creak of the old wooden floors. An archway separated the cleared room from an even larger area which seemed to be a living room. Once cleared, they silently moved into a hallway connecting the front door to the back. The scientist had informed Ryan that, even though Arrington's eyesight was incredibly sharp, he only possessed a slight advantage at night. The geneticist still hadn't discovered how to effectively give the Marines the ability to see in the dark. When Ryan entered the hallway, his NVGs alerted him to a light source emitting from the bottom of a closed door. It was faint, but definitely man made.

With his team behind him and time running out before things were going to get loud, Ryan quietly opened the door. A staircase was revealed leading down to the basement. As he placed his foot on the first step, the light intensified as if a lantern were turned up to maximum brightness. All four agents reached up and slid their NVGs to the top of their helmets. They were nearing the bottom of the stairwell when they heard a woman's voice.

"I'll do anything you want me to do," she said, surprisingly calm. "I promise. Anything. Please just don't kill me. I won't tell anyone."

"I wish I could stop myself," said Arrington, in a surprisingly emotional voice. "I'm sorry. I'm so sorry."

"What's happening to your face?" asked the bound woman. "Oh, my God!"

Ryan hit the last step and raised his weapon towards the voices. In the far corner about twenty yards across the expanse of a wide open room, Arrington was leaning over the victim who was lying in a bed, bound to the posts. At first glance, it looked to Ryan as if he was kissing her cheek. But she began screaming in agony.

"FBI! Show me your hands!" yelled Ryan, moving in closer. The scene was confusing to the agents. The woman was screaming, but the Marine's hands were visible and he wasn't holding a weapon; he wasn't choking her; he wasn't hitting her. At that distance, it still only looked like he was kissing the side of her face.

"Arrington! Back away from her and show me your fucking..."

The instant Ryan saw the blood erupt from the side of her neck he fired three rounds into Arrington's ribcage. The killer's face was too close to the girl for a clean headshot. The Marine tensed his body as the bullets drilled through skin and bone. Dallas also fired a three-round burst into Arrington's back.

In an inhumanly fast and fluid motion, the monster nearly decapitated his victim with what could only be described as claws on a grossly disfigured hand. With his other hand he easily hurled the large king-sized bed at the agents with the victim still tied to the posts. Each dove in a different direction as the bed slammed into the wall behind them. Before they could regain their senses, Arrington was flying up the stairs.

Bravo team had already made entry and was moving through the upstairs hall from the front door when all hell broke loose in the basement. Arrington's momentum propelled him into the wall at the top of the stairs. The lead agent on Bravo team immediately opened fire drilling more bullets into his body. He turned away from the intense gunfire and exploded through the back door and right into Charlie team's advance.

Arrington ran over the first agent; he was the lucky one. The Marine lashed out and tore through the second agent's throat with his clawed hand. A geyser of blood sprayed several feet from the cavernous wound. The doomed man spun several times like a rag doll before dropping dead on the ground. The third in line was powerless to stop the thrust of Arrington's hand punching deep into his abdominal cavity. He was propelled nearly fifteen feet before stopping and bleeding out in seconds. The fourth agent stood his ground and continuously fired his weapon into the monster who quickly turned away from the determined shooter.

The dozens of bullets already inside Arrington managed to slow him down to normal human speed, but he was still able to run towards the open field. One of the countless bullets Charlie and Bravo teams were firing at the killer finally severed his spinal cord. The monster dropped only twenty feet from the cornfield that may have offered him an escape. He pushed himself up with his arms and tried to crawl away from his pursuers. As the lead agent on Bravo team approached, Arrington's head exploded like a watermelon being smashed with a sledgehammer. The impact was so violent that it caused the agents in pursuit to hit the deck; a sniper would be claiming the kill shot.

Ryan and Dallas bolted through the back door seconds after Arrington fell. Tom and Michelle, who were trained medics, stayed with the victim in the basement. A few agents were still on the ground after the sniper shot. Ryan and Dallas kept their weapons aimed at the headless corpse as they approached.

"Bravo and Charlie, do not approach the target," ordered Ryan. "Check on the downed agents. I don't want you to re-enter the house either. We'll clear the rest of the rooms."

Nobody spoke as Ryan gave instructions. They were all baffled on how the Marine took dozens of rounds and stayed on his feet. They were also baffled on how he managed to nearly decapitate one agent and punch a fist-sized hole in the abdomen of another; it was obvious they both died instantly. Ryan and Dallas knelt beside Arrington's body after they were convinced he was truly dead.

"Look at his hands," said Dallas, observing the long fingers with two-inch nails resembling claws.

"I knew there was going to be some deformity, but I think it was slightly understated in the briefing," responded Ryan.

"Slightly understated? Did you see his fucking face in the basement?"

asked Dallas. "He was pale as a ghost. Look at the skin around his neck. He looks like a zombie."

"There wasn't much light down there, but I agree," said Ryan. "You definitely don't see that every day. Could just be blood loss."

"I guess," acknowledged Dallas. "But still."

"I know, Dallas," said Ryan. "I have a few questions myself. Stay here with him until I come back. Nobody gets close. Understand?"

"I don't think that'll be a problem," said Dallas, looking over at the agents huddled around their two downed men.

As ordered earlier, Ryan slid a battery in his cell phone and immediately called the deputy director. He informed him Arrington was dead and the scientists were cleared to enter the property. He returned to the basement to check on Michelle and Tom.

"Is the freak dead?" asked Tom.

"Very," replied Ryan. "Sniper literally took his head off. But he killed two of ours before he went down."

"Damn it," said Tom. "I really thought we had the drop on him. It was like he didn't even know we were there until you interrupted him."

"This poor girl was probably dead before she hit the wall," said Michelle, kneeling over the victim. "She's nearly decapitated. Did he have a hatchet or a knife?"

"Not that I saw," said Ryan. "But his fingernails are about two inches long. When he rose up, I just saw blood pumping out of her neck."

"They weren't joking about his speed and strength," said Michelle.

"No, they weren't," said Ryan. "We need to assemble outside and wait for the forensic team. There's nothing we can do for her now."

"Boss?"

"Yeah, Tom."

"Take a quick look down here before you go up. I cleared the other rooms when you and Dallas were upstairs. You're going to want to see what's in there."

"Not a word to anyone else about what we saw, Tom," said Ryan in a commanding tone. "You either, Michelle. This stays with us for now, okay?"

"Got it," responded both as they left the basement.

Ryan stood alone next to the woman still bound to the broken bed. Her lifeless eyes were only half closed. He clenched his teeth and thought if they had entered the house one minute earlier, she may have survived.

There was a sense of guilt for not advancing on Arrington as soon as he stepped out of the Jeep.

He turned away from the woman to take a closer look at the monster's torture chamber. The only light source in the basement was an oil lamp on a nightstand. Ryan's mind briefly wandered to the file folders containing photos from Arrington's first murder scene in New York. He expected to see a table covered with the tools he would've used to rape and disembowel his prize. He imagined pools of blood on the floor and organs sitting like trophies in glass jars lining the shelves.

Arrington's first victim was discovered in the furnace room of a steel mill that went out of business years ago. The beautiful 23-year-old medical student from Syracuse University died on a filthy floor after experiencing what could only be described as unimaginable pain. He kept her alive for two days as he repeatedly raped and tortured her. The autopsy revealed he started IVs and gave her fluids to combat shock and keep her aware. There were only trace amounts of painkillers and anesthetics. His intent wasn't to relieve her agony. It was for her to see and feel as much as possible without passing out.

Forensics also proved he curled up beside her and held the victim close in the final moments of her young, promising life. Those final moments came after she received a deep cut starting at her breastbone and ending below her navel; the mattress was soaked in her blood. The report stated not all of her organs were recovered from the scene. Ryan fully expected to discover them somewhere near where he was standing.

He removed the high-powered flashlight from the end of his weapon. As he lit up the large room, the reality of Arrington's torture chamber was completely different from the photos in the case files. It was meticulously clean and in order.

Ryan deducted he must have moved the entire contents of one of the upstairs bedrooms down to the basement. Each piece of furniture was carefully cleaned and restored to its original condition. There were no medieval tools lined up on top of the dressers and no jars containing the organs of past victims. He turned to look at the bed Arrington used as a weapon. Other than the blood from the victim's neck wound, the sheets were pristine. He looked down at his feet and noticed the lack of dirt on the old farmhouse's concrete basement floor. He turned his light upward and couldn't find one cobweb attached to any corner of the room. There was no dust on any of the flat surfaces. Had he been anywhere else, Ryan would've thought of the room as cozy and comfortable. The exact opposite of anything he expected to see.

He noticed a door at the far end of the room. As he opened it, he was hit with a slight breeze of stale air. It was a large unfinished space with a dirt floor. His light illuminated tall stacks of old wooden produce crates lined up against the walls. Ryan noticed a gap between two stacks. As he approached, he observed an opening had recently been created through the wall. When he lit up the darkness on the other side, he saw four graves. Three were covered with mounds of settling dirt. The fourth was still open.

Anyone walking through that hole in the wall would've instantly recognized the mounds as graves. Not because of the shape or recently disturbed earth, but because each was marked with a wooden cross bearing a name. The first cross had the name Laura Ackerman and the date she was murdered. The same woman Sheriff Bill Parker mentioned during the brief the previous morning.

Against the specific orders of the deputy director, Ryan used the camera on his phone to take several pictures of the gruesome cemetery. He took several more of the adjoining rooms before he heard the rotors of approaching helicopters. He left the crime scene and regrouped with the agents outside. The two aircraft landed as flashing blue strobes and headlights from several fast moving vehicles were visible approaching the farmhouse.

4

DoUBT

THREE BLACK SUVs WITH TINTED windows stopped only a few feet from Arrington's headless body. The doors opened quickly on the first two, spilling out nearly a dozen heavily armed security personnel forming a perimeter around the corpse. Ryan noticed more security personnel deploying from helicopters in a field next to the house.

One of the new arrivals approached Arrington with his weapon ready and reached down to check for a pulse. It seemed a little odd since he was missing his head, but after what they just experienced, Ryan understood the caution. The trooper squeezed the talk button on his radio and announced the target was indeed dead. The doors on the third SUV opened and four men in black coveralls carrying large tackle boxes walked up to Ryan and his team.

"I need to speak with Special Agent Ryan Pearson," said the first set of coveralls.

"That would be me."

"Agent Pearson, my name is Scott Wilson. I'm a biochemist with the Michaels Laboratory assigned to the Didache program. I'm here to recover the body of Peter Arrington and debrief your team. I'm assuming containment was difficult?"

"I've been expecting you, Scott," said Ryan, slightly irritated. "Your Didache project pet gave us one hell of a fight. He killed two of my agents before a sniper put him down. Containment wasn't a priority once we figured out shooting him with little bullets wasn't working. I believe almost everyone here put their eyes on him. So to answer your question, yes, containment was difficult."

"I'm sorry," said Scott in a disarming tone.

"Excuse me?" asked Ryan, a little puzzled.

"The agents you lost. I'm sorry, Ryan. I promise you we'll take good care of them. Once we finish processing the area, we'll be taking them to an airstrip about six miles from here. The deputy director is making arrangements to get them home."

"I appreciate that, Scott. What about the rest of my guys?"

"Bravo and Charlie teams will go by ground in the vehicles to the airstrip for debriefing. We've taken over a small hangar there as a command post. We'll send the sniper teams by helicopter once they come in from the field. You, Dallas, Michelle, and Tom need to stay with us for a little while longer. You should be out of here in about an hour."

Bravo and Charlie teams were immediately whisked away in the vehicles. Ryan and his team took off their tactical gear and huddled around the remaining SUV. They watched as the forensic team poked and took photographs of Arrington's body.

"How many bullets do you think we put in him?" asked Dallas.

"Enough," responded Ryan curtly.

"I mean, you told us he was fast and strong," continued Dallas. "You didn't say anything about being bullet proof. That information may have helped down there in the basement."

"You think I knew?" asked Ryan, stepping closer to Dallas.

"No, Boss. That's not what I meant. I meant *they* could've told us. I mean told you so you could've told us. Fuck, I don't know. I'll shut up now."

"It's okay, Dallas. I'm sorry. I know what you meant. I'm not happy with the way this turned out either. I've never lost an agent under my command. Tonight I lost two. Believe me when I say I have more questions than answers. I seem to be somewhat limited with what I can ask and what I have to accept without question. Do you understand?"

"I do. I understand I wouldn't want your job," said Dallas, lightening the mood.

"Did you take a good look around down there?" asked Tom, changing the subject.

"I did," responded Ryan. "It didn't look anything like I expected."

"You told me and Michelle not to talk to anyone about it, but I figured it was okay to talk to each other."

"Speak freely," said Ryan sensing Tom had something he wanted to say.

"We both have extensive backgrounds in behavioral science with serial killers. Nothing down there fits Arrington's profile evaluation we received from Quantico. Serial killers tend to escalate with their violence and frequency of attacks. Arrington seems to have deescalated, and he sticks to a concrete schedule."

"Deescalated?" asked Ryan. "He killed three people in 15 seconds. How is that deescalating?"

"I have no doubt he was going to kill the victim, but there were no indications he was going to brutalize and torture her," continued Tom. "My point is, the crime scene here is a polar opposite from the Syracuse murder. As far as the violence we witnessed, I believe it was solely a reaction to our presence."

"Is it really that big a deal if his methods have changed?" asked Ryan. "We all watched him nearly cut her head off. Some of the details of the environment may seem odd, but there's no denying he's our guy."

"I wouldn't think twice about it if it wasn't such a radical change, Boss. Take away the fact Quantico pointed us in this direction, and I'd bet this farm we're looking at two different killers."

"Also," interrupted Michelle, "No serial killer since recordkeeping began has ever clearly marked the grave of a victim. Many have left hints and even taunted police to find where they've hidden the bodies, but none have ever marked the burial site with a cross and the victim's name. That shows an uncharacteristic degree of remorse. There were absolutely no signs of remorse or guilt in Syracuse. If a murderer is going to display those types of emotions, it's usually with the first victim. Everything about this crime scene screams different M.O. and different guy."

"Listen," said Ryan, "Nothing about what we're doing here can be categorized or compared with previous cases. We've entered a strange new territory, and I need you to start thinking outside the box. Dump all your conventional wisdom about how these four killers are supposed to act."

"Dump our conventional wisdom?" asked Tom, perplexed. "With the lack of credible information we have on these guys, what are we supposed to use? A crystal ball?"

"That's enough, Tom," replied Ryan, sternly. "I can assure you the information I'm passing to you is credible. It may not be as much as you'd like, but it's all we have. You guys need to stand fast while I go talk to the guys in the black coveralls."

"Of course," said Tom, relenting.

Ryan walked away from the team and headed for the front door of the farmhouse. He wanted to end the questions coming from his own team without having to order them to back off. He hated having to dodge their legitimate concerns. Michelle was the first to voice her opinion about Ryan's demeanor.

"What's wrong with him?" asked Michelle. "You know we're right, Tom."

"I'm not sure what's wrong. He did seem to dismiss our observations rather quickly. That's not like him."

"He has his reasons," injected Dallas quickly. "He'll let us know when we need to know."

"I think I just figured out who's the teacher's pet," said Michelle with a smirk.

"All that and a sense of humor, too. Weird that you're still single, huh?" replied Dallas. "Whatever reason he has for being elusive is probably because he just lost two agents. I think you'd be a little off, too."

"All the more reason not to be elusive, wouldn't you think?" said Michelle.

"Look," said Tom, attempting to keep the peace. "He was just as surprised as we were down in the basement. Dallas is right. He's never lost anyone in the line. We need to give him a little space to sort things out. And Michelle, Ryan sorts things out better than anyone else I know. That includes us."

As Ryan attempted to re-enter the farmhouse, he was challenged at the door by two armed guards.

"I'm sorry, sir, but I can't let you inside."

"Are you FBI?" asked Ryan.

"No, sir, I'm not. But we've been given orders not to let anyone enter other than the scientists."

"Would it be too much trouble if you brought one of them to me?"

"No, sir, no trouble at all."

The guard turned quickly and disappeared into the house. Ryan stared at the other guard who didn't make eye contact. He carefully sized up the sentry. His stance, weapons, and posture led Ryan to believe he was military, or at least former military. Everything that had happened since he fired the first rounds into Arrington generated more questions. His patience was wearing thinner with each passing minute. Being denied access to his crime scene wasn't helping. Scott Wilson, the man who seemed to be in charge, reappeared with the guard.

"Again, I apologize, Agent Pearson," said Scott. "They're under strict orders not to let anyone inside without my permission."

"Could I bother you for a moment of your time?" asked Ryan condescendingly.

"Absolutely," replied Scott, walking with Ryan to the side of the farmhouse.

"I have no idea what's going on here, and I know you're not going to tell me. So I won't insult you and ask. But I have a funny feeling in a couple minutes you're going to tell me in which direction I need to go in order to find the other three Marines. And without question, I'll go. How you obtained the information doesn't concern me. What does concern me is that I know you have information which may help me keep my team alive when we do find them. Help me do a better job than what I did for my guys being zipped up in those body bags."

Scott looked over at the slain agents and then turned his gaze upward toward the night sky. Ryan couldn't put his finger on it, but he felt the scientist wanted to tell him more than he was allowed. He had a feeling Scott was being ordered from above to produce the maximum amount of damage control possible. Ryan understood his position because he was in the same one.

"For the record, Ryan, the only chance you had here tonight was to take him when he was in his most vulnerable state. You did everything right. If you went a moment too soon, or too late, I'd be putting all of you in body bags. I'm not exaggerating."

"What happened to Arrington, Scott? He was a decorated Marine with a spotless record. They all were. Now they're heartless rapists and killers? What the fuck happened to them?"

"I can't tell you what happened because I really don't know. I just know what they are now. My job is to show up after you finish yours and clean up the mess. You're right about me telling you where to go next, but I was made aware only a few hours ago. You're not the only people looking for them, but you are the only people with the legitimate authority to stop them."

"What's with all the armed goons? You have more firepower here than I do."

"These soldiers are here to protect us."

"So they are military," deducted Ryan.

"Some of them are Marines assigned to the lab. Most of the others are former military hired by our company as security."

"What are they protecting you from?"

"I've already told you more than I'm allowed. I shouldn't be talking to you at all. Do you understand?"

"I do, Scott. Do you understand innocent people are dying and will continue to die until we find the other three? Now, what are these troops protecting you from?"

"That *is* what they're protecting us from."

"The other three? Are they close?"

"As you just found out, it would only take one of them to wreak havoc. We believe they're communicating with each other. We just don't know exactly how. This is going to sound weird, but –"

"After what I just saw, I bet it won't."

"All indications are they can communicate through other than conventional means."

"Scott," said Ryan, growing irritated, "Just spit it out."

"We think they can feel when another is in distress or needs help," said Scott, pausing for the reaction.

"Telepathy? Are you kidding me?"

"Actually, I'm not. And it's not so much telepathy as a keen intuitive sense something is wrong. There have been numerous studies on the ability of identical twins to communicate nonverbally when they're separated. You're just going to have to take my word on this one. We don't really have the time right now for a lengthy discussion."

"But these guys aren't identical twins."

"In many ways they are."

"You're killing me with this cryptic shit."

"I'm sorry, Ryan."

"That's also the third time you've apologized to me. Why can't you just tell me exactly what we're dealing with? I understand we don't want to create a public panic, but aren't we on the same team here? I'm not asking you to go into detail about the science or what may have went wrong in the lab. But remember, I'm the guy kicking in the doors and taking all the risks. The least you could do is tell me exactly what's on the other side of those doors."

"Monsters. That's the simplest way I can put it. I'm almost positive they've murdered at least twenty women over the past six months. We've only discovered eight. They're not going to stop killing, either, because they can't. It's now their nature. A nature I don't believe they were born with."

"Scott, I couldn't care less if they were born with it or not. The more I know about them, the faster I can put an end to this. That's all I care about."

"I want this to end as well, Ryan. I didn't sign on for this shit. The only reason I'm here is because I understand how dangerous those men are. The information I gave you put one of them down. You don't realize this now, but you need me. If I tell you too much, they'll take me off this team. I guess you're just going to have to trust me."

"Trust is earned, Scott. Give me something."

The scientist paused and again looked up at the night sky. It was as if he were looking for guidance about what he could give Ryan that wouldn't jeopardize his position. He brought his eyes back down to Ryan's.

"Kristina Anderson," he finally said.

"That's it? A name?"

"She's a civilian geneticist that worked with all four Marines since day one of the project. She quit the lab six months ago and took a teaching position at Johns Hopkins University in Baltimore. She's a dear friend, Ryan. Be careful how you reach out to her. Because of her background, they're probably keeping an eye on her."

"They?" asked Ryan. "Who are they?"

"You're on your own with that one. I can't tell you."

"I understand," said Ryan.

"I don't think you really do, but you will. There's one more thing, and you're not going to like it."

"I'm all ears."

"Any digging you do on your own, keep it to yourself. Your boss and my boss are running the show here. Anything you tell yours, you can be sure he's telling mine."

"You want me to do this behind his back? You do realize he's the Deputy Director of the FBI?"

"Trust goes both ways. Talk to Kristina first. If you still think I'm being paranoid, then feel free to tell your boss everything we talked about."

Another man in black coveralls turned the corner, startling Scott.

He immediately changed the subject and his tone. Ryan picked up on his diversion.

"Agent Pearson, for the last time, I need you to remain with your team. There's no way I can allow you back into the house. If you continue to disrupt our work, I can call your boss who will explain I'm the one in charge of this crime scene. Do I make myself clear?"

"Are you okay, Mr. Wilson?" asked the other scientist. "We're about ready to wrap it up down there and we need your help."

"We're done here. Right, Agent Pearson?"

"Apparently we are," said Ryan, walking back to his team.

He leaned against the SUV without saying a word. Each member of the group could tell the wheels were turning inside his head.

"Looks like the sniper teams have made it back," said Dallas, noticing the six men approaching the helicopters. "I wonder which one fired the money shot. I'd like to buy that guy a few drinks."

"I don't think we need to worry about radio silence anymore," said Ryan.

"Got it," replied Dallas. He pressed the talk button on his radio.

"Delta this is Alpha. Do you copy, over?"

"This is Delta, go ahead," replied the lead sniper, climbing into the chopper.

"That was a hell of a shot. Who gets the case of beer on this one?" asked Dallas.

"Say again?"

"Which one of you took down the target?"

"Foxtrot One squeezed off two rounds, but he says he missed by a mile. We were trying to figure out which one of you cowboys took his head off with the shotgun. We saw his head come apart, but it wasn't us, over."

"Really? I don't think anyone down here was carrying a –"

Ryan reached over and pushed the radio microphone away from Dallas's mouth. He immediately knew why his teams were being separated. It had nothing to do with containment of exposure to Arrington. It had everything to do with preventing anyone from comparing notes. The puppet masters wanted to make sure none of the pieces of the puzzle were put together. Ryan needed to figure out who was pulling the strings. He already suspected who might be pulling his.

Over a mile away, another black SUV was creeping down a dirt road without headlights. The driver was scanning the tree line wearing NVGs. A faint infrared strobe light invisible to the naked eye caught his attention. When the truck stopped, four men rose from their camouflaged position. Two were carrying high powered .50 caliber sniper rifles. They quietly climbed into the waiting vehicle.

"Nice work, Alex," said the driver.

"The Feds made it easy," he replied.

5

PUPPETS

THE ONLY PEOPLE ON THE planet Ryan felt he could trust were standing next to him. Dallas still had a puzzled look on his face as to why his boss prematurely ended his conversation with the sniper team. Tom and Michelle were staring at the ground trying to make sense of the inconsistencies of Arrington's behavior. All three were wondering why Ryan seemed distant and dismissive of their observations. He was beginning to wonder the same thing when his phone alerted him to an incoming call from the deputy director.

"Ryan, we just received a videotape from the Terrebonne Parish Sheriff's Department in Louisiana. It shows Richard Elliot abducting a young woman from a supermarket parking lot yesterday. We have subsequent data that he may have taken her to a location in the Lower Ninth Ward in New Orleans. We believe we've contained exposure, so any local police or press interference should be minimal. I'm sending a plane over to you now. It should be there in about an hour."

"Yes, sir," responded Ryan. "We should be finished here shortly. I'll brief the team."

"I hate this part, but we both know she's already dead. I want the same setup as the Harrisonburg mission. Find his kill house, set up surveillance and wait for him to return with the next victim. I'll put together the assault and sniper teams and get them to you as soon as possible. You'll have the full cooperation and assets of the New Orleans field office, but the same rules of containment apply

there as well. All of the files and reports on Elliot will be on the plane. Call me when you get settled in down there."

"Yes, sir."

It took a tremendous amount of restraint for Ryan not to ask the questions he needed answered. But he also knew, if he asked, he'd probably be pulled from the team as Scott warned. He didn't completely mistrust Deputy Director Donaldson, but he was certainly more cautious about voicing his concerns.

Ryan pulled his team in close to give them the news that they were heading to New Orleans to take down the second UA Marine. "Okay, guys," started Ryan. "Looks like our next monster, Richard Elliot, made a few mistakes. They have him on video abducting a woman in South Louisiana."

"Where exactly?" asked Michelle.

"He said Terrebonne Parish."

"I have family there," she said with obvious concern. "My sister lives in Houma. It's a small town in Terrebonne Parish. She's twenty-five and –"

"Use discretion if you need to contact her," said Ryan immediately.

"Thanks, Boss," said Michelle, quickly grabbing the phone from Ryan's outstretched hand.

"Thought we were supposed to leave those behind," smiled Tom, referencing Ryan's cell phone.

"The rules are for you guys."

"Boss, goon squad approaching," said Dallas. Michelle discreetly palmed the phone and slid it in her pocket.

"Agent Pearson, we have evidence Richard Elliot may be –"

"In New Orleans," said Ryan, finishing Scott's sentence.

"Yes. We're done here. I'll be taking you and your team to the airport now."

"We need to recover our vehicles from town. We'll drive ourselves from there," insisted Ryan.

"Of course," said Scott without an argument.

Ryan took the passenger seat next to Scott as his team filed into the back. As soon as they pulled onto the main road from the long dirt driveway, Scott handed Ryan a small piece of folded paper and nodded for him to read it. Feeling like a schoolboy being handed a secret note in class, Ryan carefully unfolded the paper. *No questions. They're listening and have been since day one. They're already heading to New Orleans to shadow your team. I don't know exactly who they are. Figure it out and you may get some answers. Be extremely careful!*

Ryan finished reading the note and looked over at Scott. The scientist glanced over just in time to see him stuff the note in his mouth and start chewing. Scott quickly returned his eyes to the road, but a slight smile was growing on his face. A few moments later, he began to laugh out loud. Ryan joined him. Not another word was spoken during the ride into town.

"Thanks for the lift," said Ryan, stepping out of the truck with his team.

"It's the least I could do. Your plane will be landing shortly. The sooner you get started down there, the better. Elliot has the same capabilities and temperament as Arrington, but he also has the same weakness. I know you learned a hard lesson at the farmhouse, but it'll help you deal with Elliot. I'll see you after you take him. Good luck, Ryan. Good luck to all of you."

"Thanks, Scott. You take care of yourself as well," said Ryan. The SUV pulled out of the sheriff's department parking lot, leaving the agents alone for the first time since they entered Arrington's hideout.

"So, are you two friends now?" asked Dallas.

"He's got a job to do just like us. I think he's doing the best he can under the circumstances," said Ryan.

"Speaking of circumstances," added Tom, "I can't shake the thought that Arrington was just reacting to us –"

"Not now, Tom," said Ryan, cutting him off. "I'm going inside to talk to the sheriff. Stow the gear and grab us some coffee from the café across the street. I won't be long."

"Sure," said Tom, feeling like a scolded child. "We'll make it quick."

Ryan walked inside the office as his team crossed the street. He knocked on the sheriff's door which was already open.

"Good morning, Sheriff Parker," said Ryan, moving inside and closing the door behind him.

"Hopefully it is, Agent Pearson. How'd it go last night?"

"Arrington's dead. A sniper took him down after he killed his victim and two of my agents. We were a few seconds too late to save her. I'm sorry."

"What are you sorry about? She did her job, right? Being the bait? She served her purpose and you got your man. Now you can write your reports, receive your attaboys from D.C., and ride off into the sunset. Me, I've got another home to add to my list of places I have to go to devastate a family."

He stood there silently taking his lumps from the sheriff. He knew he was the most appropriate target for him to aim his anger. It wasn't the first time Ryan had to be the punching bag, and it certainly didn't look like it was going to be the last.

"I also wanted you to know we found the other three missing girls in graves underneath the house. I don't know when their bodies will be released to their families. I imagine it'll be a few days, maybe even a week."

"Well, me and my boys will just sit around, drink some moonshine, and spit tobacco until then."

"I am sorry, Sheriff. For what it's worth, I don't believe they were raped or tortured. I think they died very quickly and in little pain. I know it's not much, but it may offer some consolation to the families."

"It isn't worth shit," said Parker. "They're still dead and we'll probably never know why. And you're sure as hell aren't going to tell us. So, please, stop pretending to give a crap about what happened here."

"That's where you're very wrong," said Ryan, running out of cheeks. "If I didn't give a crap, I would've just left town after we finished. Nobody told me to come here and see you. I told you the men I'm hunting are out of your worst nightmare. I wasn't being melodramatic."

"Agent Pearson, you may be surprised at what kind of nightmares I have. You made the mistake of assuming I'm some hayseed born in a barn who stumbled into this job. I was a homicide detective in Chicago for fifteen years. The truth is, I was born and raised here. After seeing the worst parts of what people were capable of doing to each other up there, I couldn't wait to get back to this small, slow town. This accent is from my memory, and I use it to make folks around here more comfortable talking to me. I'm not the redneck you think I am.

"I was elected sheriff after I returned because the locals thought they'd be safer with a man of my experience watching over their town. All they see now is a weak man powerless to protect their daughters from a monster. A monster that took another one of their innocent girls and two of your best federal agents with him. This town will never be the same again, Agent Pearson. Forgive me if I wanted to give the families answers to questions they should be allowed to ask.

"Do you have any children?" asked Sheriff Parker.

"No, I don't. I've never been married, either."

"Well, if you did have a daughter, wouldn't you want to know why someone murdered her? Wouldn't you want to put your hands on the animal that did it?"

The sheriff's questions hit Ryan hard. Of course he would want to know why. Of course he would want to put his hands on the animal that did it. The families did deserve to know what happened to their daughters. Ryan started to feel anger towards everything and everyone associated with the manhunt he was chosen to lead. Ryan pulled up a chair close to the sheriff's desk.

"What I'm going to tell you can't leave this office until I find the other three fugitives. You have to give me your word."

"My God, the other three," gasped the sheriff. "Yes, you have my word."

———

Across the street at the café, Tom, Michelle, and Dallas waited for Ryan to return to the car.

"Tom, I'm sure he has his reasons," said Dallas, defending his long-time boss and friend.

"I'm sure he does," said Tom. "I'm just not used to him shutting me up. Sure, sometimes I ramble, but I can't seem to finish the first sentence before he slams the door on me. Actually, on any of us."

"He's been acting odd since the first day he told us to pack our bags," added Michelle. "On every other manhunt, he's inundated us with the smallest details of the targets. He pushes us to find answers, and if we can't, he pushes harder until we do. I mean, think of the countless hours of all four of us sitting around a table full of files, photos, and reports, bouncing questions and ideas off of each other."

"We've never come across anything like this in our careers, Michelle," said Dallas. "Maybe he's just at a loss right now. Maybe he needs us to give him a little space while he figures out what the hell is going on instead of bombarding him with theories."

"Why change what's worked for years?" asked Michelle. "You can't just simply dismiss our combined experience and tell us to think outside of the box. I'm sorry, Dallas. But none of this, including his behavior, makes sense to me. And figuring out behavior is what I do."

"So what do you want to do?" asked Dallas, becoming frustrated with the mutiny. "Put him in the corner and demand he pay attention to us? Tell him whatever he's thinking is wrong and we're right? He's earned more from us than that."

"Christ, Dallas, that's not what I mean," said Michelle.

"I have to say I agree with Michelle," added Tom.

"Thank you, Tom."

"Not with everything," said Tom, bursting her bubble. "Mainly with the part about none of this making sense."

"My turn to say thanks, Tom," sneered Dallas, sticking his tongue out at Michelle.

"Seriously," responded Michelle. "You just stuck your tongue out at me?"

"It could've been worse," laughed Tom. "Kidding aside, I also agree we've always worked as a close team on all our assignments. On this one, he's keeping us at arm's length. It's as if he doesn't want us to get too involved, which is ridiculous. He cuts all of us off before we can say a word and –"

"Fuck me," interrupted Dallas. "That's it."

"This should be good," said Michelle.

Dallas put his finger up to his mouth as he grabbed a napkin from the table. He scribbled one word and showed Tom and Michelle.

Bugs.

The sheriff stared at Ryan in disbelief at the revelation that four UA Marines simultaneously turned into serial killers. He was taking a risk telling the story, but Ryan was confident the listening devices were embedded in the team's cell phones and gear. Both Ryan and Dallas had extensive training in surveillance and, more importantly, counter-surveillance. Training they received courtesy of the FBI and the military.

"We have a lead on the whereabouts of one of the other Marines. We have a plane waiting for us at the airfield," continued Ryan. "I'm not sure when I'll be back. I'm afraid the families are going to have to wait a little longer for their answers. But I promise you I will come back."

"I appreciate you trusting me with this, Ryan. That took guts. It stays with me until I hear from you," said the sheriff as Ryan rose to his feet.

"Thank you, Sheriff. I need to go now."

"Of course. Good luck, Agent Pearson."

"I believe I'll need it," said Ryan as he turned to leave.

"One more thing, if you don't mind?" asked the sheriff. "What were the names of the two agents that were killed?"

"Patrick Barron and Frank Hansen."

"Patrick and Frank," repeated the sheriff, committing their names to memory. "I'm sure they were fine men. Their souls and families will be in my prayers, too."

"You're a good man, Sheriff. I owe you an apology for throwing my weight around during the briefing. I'm not normally so impatient. When I figure this mess out, I'd consider it an honor to sit around, drink moonshine, and spit tobacco with you and your boys."

"Wouldn't that be something?" chuckled the sheriff. "I have to admit, I believe you would've thrown me in my own jail. Do you mind if I borrow that line when my deputies screw up?"

"Not at all."

The two men shook hands and Ryan returned to the car. His team filed out of the café carrying large cups of coffee. Dallas was the first to reach him and handed him a cup and the folded napkin.

"I've been getting a lot of these lately," said Ryan, unfolding the note.

"Sorry it took us so long. There was a line at the cash register," said Dallas with a smile.

"Did you get in touch with your sister, Michelle?" asked Ryan.

"I did. She's fine."

"Houma, Louisiana," said Tom. "I knew I recognized the name. It's the setting for the 'Swamp Thing' comic book series?"

"I never would've pegged you for a comic book reader," said Michelle.

"Love them," said Tom. "Every week as a kid I'd spend my entire allowance at the corner drugstore. Soda pop and comic books were my Saturday routine. Sadly, the files I read now contain the real monsters that are out there."

"Well, maybe we'll run into the Swamp Thing down in the bayou," said Dallas. "You could ask him to help us find our monster."

The team arrived at the airport and boarded the Learjet that would take them into the hunting grounds of Richard Elliot. He was also a highly decorated and patriotic Marine who volunteered to become a better soldier through genetic experimentation. His record was spotless until the day he and the others decided to walk away from the lab in Maine and become a ruthless band of murderers.

During the flight to New Orleans, the only team member remaining awake was Ryan. A folder with red stripes marked "Classified" was in the seat next to him. He didn't bother to open Elliot's file and bury himself in the pages filled with horrific images and reports. Instead, he sat quietly looking out the window as the world slowly passed underneath.

6

ZYDECo

THE AIRCRAFT LANDED EARLY IN the afternoon at Louis Armstrong International Airport in New Orleans. The team was met by agents from the local field office. They were given vehicles and escorted to one of the FBI's safe houses located on St. Charles Avenue near the French Quarter. The local agents had no idea why Ryan and his team were visiting their city. They were told to accommodate and provide them with any equipment, information, and support they requested without question.

During the thirty-minute drive, all four agents remained silent. Hardly a word had been spoken since they boarded the plane in Virginia. Each was trying to anticipate Ryan's next move. But Ryan wasn't thinking about the complexity of the situation he needed to sort out. He brought his thoughts down to a very basic human level. He was thinking about Sheriff Parker driving down a country road carrying the weight of having to tell a mother and father their daughter was dead. He had to tell them their daughter was murdered by a U.S. Marine.

Ryan wasn't so naïve to think the chaos of the world owed anyone an explanation for the horror it could produce, but the chaos he found himself in wasn't one of those situations. The answers were out there to be found. As the vehicles pulled into the driveway of the safe house, he made his decision. He wasn't going to let the sheriff go down that country road alone.

"Let's get all the gear inside," said Ryan. "We're taking tonight off.

It's been a while since I've been in the Quarter, and I think we all could use a drink."

"Sounds like an excellent plan," said Dallas, knowing the real reason for the break.

He knew the reason because he had worked with Ryan for over six years. Dallas started his career with the FBI after serving four years with the Marine Corps. Both he and Ryan were stationed at Camp Lejeune, North Carolina, but their paths never crossed. Dallas was assigned to the Marine Special Operations Support Group while Ryan was assigned with the 2nd Marine Special Operations Battalion. The same Battalion of the four killers he was hunting. Dallas knew that was no coincidence. Ryan knew as well.

As a Marine, Dallas's specialty was counterterrorism and surveillance. After his initial training with the FBI, his abilities earned him immediate assignment to the elite Hostage Rescue Team (HRT) based out of Quantico, Virginia. He excelled in both planting and detecting hidden surveillance devices, but his forte was finding foreign and domestic terrorist groups operating within the United States.

While with HRT, Dallas had been the newest addition to Ryan's already established team. He immediately recognized what made Ryan stand out from the crowd. He was simply relentless and a natural born leader. Ryan recognized Dallas's abilities as well. When Ryan was selected to lead an Inland Regional Apprehension Team (IRAT), he requested Dallas join him to chase down the country's most wanted fugitives. He accepted the job on the spot.

In a departure from the normal job description of an IRAT team, Ryan's group would work closely with the FBI's Behavioral Science Division, also located at Quantico. It only took a few days for Ryan to understand his team would be charged with hunting the most elusive and dangerous killers who found themselves on the FBI's Most Wanted list.

Ryan and Dallas possessed the skill set necessary to plan and execute an arrest warrant in almost any environment, but both lacked the experience needed to profile and track their prey. Another positive characteristic of Ryan's leadership ability was the self-awareness to identify his weaknesses. To compensate, he surrounded himself with agents that would bring strengths he didn't possess to the team. And two of the strongest profilers were Michelle Dobbs and Tom Freeman.

The fact that they also had experience working in the field made them too appealing to pass up.

Before they knew what hit them, they were kicking in doors and practicing assault tactics with Ryan and Dallas. It was less of an invite and more of a draft when they joined the IRAT team. They didn't put up much of a fight, knowing they'd still be intimately involved with behavioral science. They both found the idea of applying their skills in the field and putting the bad guys in handcuffs very appealing. Ryan succeeded in creating a highly tenacious and effective group that cleared cases with impressive speed.

Dallas, Michelle, and Tom were wondering when their old leader would be returning to the team. They didn't have to wait long for their answer. After Ryan made a phone call to the deputy director to make him aware of their short break, he hailed a cab and disappeared for over two hours. When he returned to the safe house, he had the cabbie wait out front.

"Are you guys ready?" asked Ryan.

"Yep," responded Dallas, patting a small leather bag over his shoulder.

"And it matches your shoes," added Michelle.

"And my eyes," said Dallas. "You don't win best-dressed agent by ignoring the details."

"You're absolutely hopeless," said Michelle, closing the door behind them.

"Where are we headed?" asked Tom.

"A quiet little place where I like to relax and think," answered Ryan.

After a short ride, the cab dropped the agents off on Canal Street. There was still daylight illuminating the Quarter, but it was already filled with loud groups of tourists and locals getting a head start on the evening's festivities. Most were carrying large plastic cups full of beverages that could power a dragster. About a block away from Ryan's "quiet little place" on the corner of Canal and Bourbon streets, they could hear the distinct piano accordion from the Zydeco band playing inside.

There was a decent crowd already forming in the bar, but they managed to grab a table in a slightly quieter corner facing the front entrance. Without saying a word, they all dropped their cell phones in the bag Dallas carried. He removed a small plastic case from the bag before he asked the bartender to hold it behind the bar.

Ryan and Dallas then excused themselves to go to the restroom. When they entered, Dallas removed a small device from the case, and Ryan assumed the position of a traveler getting the wand at an airport security checkpoint. Dallas quickly scanned his boss with the RF receiver and no spikes were detected. He removed a second device from the case and pressed the power button to activate the unit. If he missed any bugs, the transmission frequency would be scrambled as long as Ryan stayed with ten feet of the jamming device. The unit was compact and powerful, resembling a walkie-talkie, but only had enough battery life to remain effective for thirty minutes. They returned to the table as the drinks arrived.

"When in Rome," said Tom, picking up his glass. The rest of the team followed the cue. Ryan wasted no time starting the conversation.

"First, I want to apologize to all three of you," said Ryan. "I report to and take my orders from Deputy Director Donaldson. From the beginning, I was instructed to give you enough information to keep you safe and nothing more. Any requests for support from you guys was very detailed and scripted. It's a complete departure from the way we normally operate. When you offered anything more, I didn't have much choice but to ignore you. When you started putting things together and I suspected someone else was listening, I didn't have much choice but to cut you off. And for that I am sorry. I especially owe you an apology, Tom."

"I had a feeling something else was distracting you," said Tom. "No apologies necessary now that we know you were under some hefty constraints. So where do we go from here?"

"I know where I'm going, but what I need to make clear is that I'm not telling you three to come with me," said Ryan. "I'm only asking. Before you answer, it's important each of you understand a few things. You should know me well enough not feel any pressure to do something beyond your level of comfort. If you decide to walk away from this, I'll completely understand."

"Enough with the disclaimers, Boss," said Dallas. "We're in."

"You have no idea how premature that statement might be," said Ryan. "I'll start with what I know. Donaldson called me in his office a few months ago and handed me four files. Those files contained the dossiers and crime scene information similar to what I was allowed to disclose before we hit Arrington. There were two scientists in attendance from the Michaels Lab in Maine during our meeting. They gave me very little information about the nature of the research and experiments they were conducting on the Marines. They basically told me they were super soldiers with greatly enhanced capabilities. But after what we experienced in Harrisonburg, they seemed to have left out a few important details. I strongly believe understanding those details could've helped me keep our agents alive. Needless to say, I'm a little pissed."

"Obviously, their strength and speed are enhanced, but I wouldn't go so far as to say their mental capabilities were as well," said Michelle. "At least not in Arrington's case. The fact that he basically let us walk into the farmhouse undetected doesn't lend weight to his mental strength."

"They told me he was the weakest of the four men," responded Ryan. "They emphasized his physical abilities were much stronger than his mental. The other three scored much higher on the cognitive testing. I'm not saying he was an idiot, but based on their scale, he was less formidable."

"After what he did to our agents with his bare hands, they have an incredibly skewed definition of less formidable," said Tom.

"Exactly," responded Ryan. "Somebody knew. But whether or not that somebody was Deputy Director Donaldson remains to be discovered. And that brings me to what I don't know.

"I'm having a hard time swallowing the assumption that he's intentionally holding back information that could've prevented unnecessary deaths. I do, or did, trust him. Now I'm not so sure. I need to find out. But even if his office is compromised, my plan is to continue with the mission. We all witnessed Arrington killing that woman. Regardless of how they turned, we need to stop them."

"What's the plan?" asked Dallas.

"The plan is, you and I are going to find out who put that bullet in Arrington's head," started Ryan. "I'm thinking it was a .50 caliber sniper round. Our snipers weren't using rifles with that type of ammunition. That has military written all over it. I'm also thinking they're a part of the same group Scott eluded was shadowing us. Again, I can't confirm if the deputy director is the one giving up our location and plans. Hell, I don't even know if I can trust Scott, but oddly enough, he's the only one that seems to be pointing me in the right direction. He also gave me the name of a scientist we need to track down. She may have some answers for us, but she's not the priority at the moment."

"I didn't find any bugs on us or our gear," said Dallas. "I'll check our cell phones before we leave. I can guarantee our safe house is wired in every corner, but every FBI safe house is tapped. I should be able to determine if the devices are ours or someone else's."

"Okay, before we go any further," said Ryan, "We'll have to conduct our investigation as if we're cut off from the resources of the Bureau. That means I don't intend to report our methods or findings. We have to dumb it down and leave no trail for anyone to follow. And to make it more interesting, we still have to make the deputy director believe we're following his orders as normal without question.

"What I just asked of you is grounds for your dismissal from the FBI or even criminal charges. I'll take full responsibility for anything I ask of you, but know you may suffer consequences for sticking around."

"Ryan, I'm in agreement with Dallas," said Tom. "Disclaimers aren't necessary. I can't speak for Michelle, but I'm pissed, too. It could've easily been us that Arrington ripped apart. Not to mention we had to stand by and watch him kill an innocent girl. If I had known more about what we were dealing with, I never would've let him take her into the house."

"Actually, Tom is speaking for me and quite well," said Michelle. "I don't like being used. It feels like we were set up. If you're right about the other group shadowing us, it seems we're taking all the risks flushing out the target so they can kill it from a mile away. I wouldn't mind getting my hands on the assholes looking at me as expendable. Of course I'm in."

"Thank you, Michelle," said Ryan. "I promise I'll try to give you that opportunity to put your hands on them. I feel sorry for the guy making the mistake of looking at you as a defenseless girl."

"Many have, but not one of them will again," she added with a slight smile. "What do you need me to do?"

"It's actually what I need you and Tom to do," said Ryan. "I need you to start with a clean slate profiling the remaining three. You can begin with the several photos I took with my phone of the Virginia crime scene. I had a feeling they'd come in handy. I also need you to look at the files I'm not supposed to show you. I want you to work up a second profile focusing on who created them. We all know Arrington's file didn't fit what we saw, but I'm not sure it was completely fabricated. I suspect the Syracuse killing may not have been one of his. What it should do is give us another angle to possibly identify the other group crashing our party."

"Reverse engineering a serial killer's profile," said Tom. "That's an interesting approach. You basically want us to figure out the artist who painted the fake picture of Arrington."

"I do," emphasized Ryan. "But even that takes a back burner to working up an accurate profile on Richard Elliot. The second order from Donaldson I'm going to ignore is not finding him before he has a chance to take another victim. We'll let the deputy director believe we're following the designed plan of allowing Elliot to abduct her and then assaulting his hideout afterwards. I'm no longer a fan of waiting to take them down while they're preoccupied with killing."

"That makes much more sense," said Michelle. "I don't ever want to see that again. I can't shake the feeling we used that poor girl as bait."

"I can't either," affirmed Ryan. "While you're digging for information, Dallas and I will be focusing on identifying the unknown players. I'm hoping it's just another FBI team Donaldson sent as our backup, but my gut tells me we're going to find something more sinister. I believe the other players are military, or ex-military. And if I'm right, those may be the real animals we're hunting. Not only did they break the law by conducting a mission within our borders, but they assassinated a U.S. citizen. It doesn't matter what Arrington did; the Constitution guarantees him the right to face his accusers and stand trial. It's impossible for me to ignore that."

"This got complicated pretty fast, didn't it, Boss?" observed Dallas.

"Yes, it did," confirmed Ryan. "And we're going to try and sort it out just as fast."

The team ordered another round of drinks. Dallas retrieved the bag containing their cell phones from the bartender. He scanned each and then took them apart to look for listening devices. He found nothing.

"These are clean," said Dallas. "It doesn't mean they haven't been listening to our conversations. They could've easily cloned them, which would also give them our constant location using the embedded GPS chips."

Ryan handed each member on his team a cell phone and USB flash drive. "Not with these."

"That would explain your little trip today," said Tom.

"You don't chase fugitives all over the country and not learn a few things from the bad guys about how to evade the good guys," explained Ryan. "The cell phones are untraceable, and the GPS tracking chips have been removed.

"The flash drives are for our laptops. They'll give us internet access anywhere without identifying our IP address or our location. There are also several links to criminal databases, including NCIC. Phony access codes and login information will automatically be populated when you open the links. Again, all of it's untraceable."

"You have phony access codes and user data for classified information the FBI maintains?" asked Michelle, somewhat perplexed.

"I have a guy," responded Ryan with a smile.

The team finished their drinks and returned to the safe house. Dallas scanned each room and found the standard number of cameras and listening devices. All of them were hardwired to one room upstairs full of video screens and tape recorders. Dallas didn't find one active device either transmitting or receiving data. Ryan recognized it as standard operating procedure for an FBI safe house. There were no indications that another group was listening in on the team. Ryan requested Dallas do a second sweep, and again, the results were negative. The agents could speak freely in one room upstairs. It was the only space without windows.

The lack of bugs in the safe house didn't make Ryan less suspicious. All it did was add weight to the suspicion that the Deputy Director of the FBI was feeding information to the unknown group. There was no need for them to risk being exposed by physically following Ryan's team or attempting to plant bugs in their path. All they had to do was wait for the deputy director to tell them when and where to go to murder the fugitive Marines.

Ryan needed to create a plan that would expose the group without their knowledge. He also couldn't alert the deputy director of his mistrust. Dallas was right. It was getting complicated fast.

7

TREASURE ISLAND

RYAN WOKE EARLY WITH RENEWED determination after some much needed sleep. He hoped a morning run would set the tone for the day. An hour later, he found himself pacing back and forth in the small windowless room of the safe house. Dallas was the first to join him and handed him a cup of coffee.

"Thank you."

"Were you up all night?" asked Dallas.

"No, I wanted to get a jump on the day. The problem is the day jumped on me with more questions I can't seem to answer."

"We'll try to take care of some of that today, Boss. Now that the cat's out of the bag, you can utilize our world-class skills," he said with a smirk. "Well, at least Michelle and Tom's skills. I'll kick the shit out of a door for you, though."

Ryan smiled at Dallas, knowing he was kidding about his lack of investigative skills. Dallas was responsible on numerous occasions for putting puzzles together and putting very bad people behind bars. But he hit the bull's-eye about his door kicking ability. Ryan couldn't think of anyone else he would want beside him in a fight. As tenacious as Ryan was about finding fugitives, Dallas was equally tenacious when it came time to put hands on them.

In the freshman year of the IRAT team, the group was hunting a militia leader in Utah. He was wanted for the murder of a U.S. Marshal and the attempted murder of two others. The compound was located on the edge of Wasatch Mountain State Park, which is one of the largest in the region. The lifelong woodsman fugitive who grew up in the area slipped away from the initial grasp of the assault team and disappeared into the Herber Valley. Dallas didn't hesitate to follow. For two days, he never stopped moving. Bad weather grounded any air support, and no one was prepared with the gear normally carried on a wilderness manhunt – no one except Dallas.

Ryan remembered the looks and chuckles other agency officers gave Dallas when he showed up at the Sunday morning briefing wearing forty pounds of equipment, including a pouch containing NVGs. Dallas's core philosophy was to be better prepared and equipped than the guys he was going after. Everyone stopped laughing after Utah.

At the start of the pursuit into the woods, fourteen agents went in with Dallas. It didn't take long for the first officer to collapse trying to keep up. One by one, he'd radio the position of another exhausted officer that gave up the pursuit. A support group of marshals carrying food, water, and medical supplies would scoop up the cold, dehydrated, hungry, ankle sprained, and all around miserable professional man hunters. At the end of the second day, the weather finally cleared. Thirty-two miles into the dense heart of the state park, helicopters retrieved a smiling Dallas and his not-so-happy prize from a river bank.

"Do you really think the deputy director is feeding information to another group?" asked Dallas.

"I send all my reports as well as our movements only to him," said Ryan. "I know that doesn't mean he's intentionally leaking information or even knows it's happening. But until I know for sure it isn't him, I have to treat him like it is."

"Any idea how we can find out?"

"I do, but before we set that plan in motion, you and I have to go on a little trip."

"I love trips," said Dallas. "Where to?"

"Baltimore."

"What's in Baltimore?" asked Tom, joining them in the secure room.

"Kristina Anderson," replied Ryan. "I need you and Michelle to work up a quick and dirty background on her. According to Scott, she's on staff at Johns Hopkins University. I need as much information about her daily routine as possible."

"Consider it done," replied Tom. "Will I be using our new gadgets to gather the data?"

"What data?" asked Michelle, walking in the room and taking Dallas's coffee out of his hand. "What are you boys up to?"

"Those two boys are going to Baltimore to visit Kristina Anderson," explained Tom. "And you and I are going to stay behind and put her life under a microscope."

"Sweet," said Michelle. "I love digging up dirt on unsuspecting civilians."

"Our trip and your digging will be under the radar," said Ryan. "Your profiling and hunting Elliot can be out in the open, but Kristina needs to stay a ghost. Dallas and I will be leaving our company phones behind so it looks like we never left New Orleans. My guy cloned my number into my untraceable phone, so if the deputy director calls, the GPS will show me in this room. But you guys are free to move around the city."

"Okay," replied Michelle. "When are you leaving?"

"This afternoon, so I'll need a dash of speed on her itinerary for the next few days. But for right now, I want you both to talk to me about Peter Arrington. You know, the subjects I cut you off on earlier."

"Sure," said Tom, going first. "Back at the farmhouse, I was making the point that the crime scene didn't look anything like the others. Arrington created a comfortable space to work on his victims in the basement. It was meticulously cleaned, and the furniture was arranged to mimic a woman's bedroom. It seems to me he wanted them to have some comforts of home.

"In Syracuse, the scene resembled a sadistic torture chamber. There was no attempt made by the killer for comfort. The degree of brutality suggested an extremely elevated level of anger. The ritual was about inflicting pain and prolonging suffering until the anger apparently subsided. Like I said, I'd stake my reputation on Arrington not being responsible for Syracuse.

"As far as him killing the woman in front of us and our two agents, I believe it was his reaction to being cornered. I'm not saying he was going to let her live, but all indications were it was less about torture and pain and more about being powerless to stop himself from hurting her. If you remember, before he knew we were there, he apologized to her and told her they made him that way. I'd sure like to figure out who *they* are."

"I agree with Tom," added Michelle. "The Syracuse killer left her body to decompose out in the open after he repeatedly raped and then disemboweled her. Once he was finished with his ritual, he simply left without even trying to hide his work. Arrington buried his victims and marked the graves with their names on crosses. That would indicate he felt some sense of remorse or even guilt for what he did to them. And like I said, no serial killers on record have ever marked the graves of their victims in that way."

"Unfortunately, we're not going to know for sure how he killed the other three he buried in the basement unless we get ahold of the autopsy reports," said Ryan.

"Those would speak volumes as to his method and frame of mind during the killings," said Tom. "If we could find a way to get our hands on those reports, I'd know without a shadow of a doubt if Arrington was responsible for Syracuse. I'd also know a hell of a lot more about the killer who actually is responsible."

"I might have a way to get ahold of those findings," said Ryan.

"Let me guess, you have another guy?" asked Michelle.

"I just might. I'll see if I can reach out to him while I'm in Baltimore."

"What about the reverse engineering of the profiles?" asked Ryan. "Any clues on who or what created them?"

"Well, it took very little time for us to figure out they weren't fabricated," answered Tom.

"You just told me it wasn't Arrington in Syracuse."

"Correct," said Tom.

"English, please," pleaded Ryan.

"The information in each of their files is real," explained Tom. "The crime scene photos, the police reports, witness accounts, and even the coroner's reports are all real. The interesting part is, I believe they're all the same killer. All the data points to one guy."

"We fully expected the information in the reports to be fabricated," added Michelle. "A made-up crime scene, a fake police officer making a fake report, and so on. But they seem to be legitimate. From a profiling standpoint, it's as if they carbon copied one suspect four times. Now, taking what we know about Arrington, we can rule him out as the suspect. That narrows it down to Richard Elliot, Derek Mathews or Joshua Bell as the man behind the murders. Well, at least the killings in these files."

"Okay," exhaled Ryan. "Working off what we do know, we can

establish we have at least two killers. Arrington being one, and the other being the unidentified suspect responsible for the murders in these reports."

"What I don't get is why somebody wants us to believe Arrington is responsible for Syracuse." said Dallas.

"I believe it's because they wanted to make us angry," replied Ryan. "And it worked. I focused most of my energy on locating Arrington and very little on figuring out why he's killing. They want us to discover where he is, not what he is."

"No offense, Boss," said Dallas. "But you make that sound like a bad thing. I really don't give a shit which part of his brain misfired. I just wanted to stop him, and if it meant killing him, then so be it. After we get the rest of them off the streets, we'll let the Toms and Michelles of the world pore over the reports to determine what made good men turn into bad ones."

"Because we're not hired thugs, Dallas," replied Ryan. "I personally put three bullets into Peter Arrington and gave the order to kill him if he tried to escape. If I'm going to kill a human being, I need to know why. You should want to know why. I'm not a hit man for the government and neither are any of you."

"I don't like getting played either, but the bottom line is that Arrington won't be cutting the throats of any more women," said Dallas.

"But the other three will be," said Tom. "If we could've interrogated Arrington instead of cutting him down, he may have disclosed some information that would've helped us find the others. Establishing a pattern allows us to anticipate movement, and there's always a pattern. Even seemingly random events or taking victims based on opportunity versus stalking are patterns. The more we know about them, the more we'll know about how to stop them."

"That's the reason you and I are going to Baltimore," said Ryan. "According to Scott, Kristina Anderson worked with all four Marines since the program's inception. I believe she'll be able to shed some light on their progression from squeaky clean soldiers into what they are now. I'm also hoping she'll be able to tell us another way to go at Elliot instead of waiting for him to take another victim."

"That part I get," said Dallas. "I don't see going toe-to-toe with any of them as a smart option. Other than carrying a rocket launcher, we don't have much of an advantage in a straight shootout. Imagine the damage Arrington could've done if he had gotten ahold of a weapon."

"Not that taking Arrington was easy, but I have a feeling the others are going to be much more difficult," continued Ryan. "Scott alluded to the possibility that all four are somehow communicating with each other. If they know we're closing in on them, they're going to be better prepared. I don't think the others will be leaving any doors open for us like Arrington."

"Understood," replied Dallas. "What's the plan in Baltimore?"

"I'll figure that out on the way there, but we need to check in at the field office before we head to the airport. I want us to be seen by the local feds before we disappear."

For the rest of the morning and early afternoon, the team pored over the stacks of files, and Michelle began digging into Kristina Anderson's life. Tom drove Ryan and Dallas to the field office for some face time with the New Orleans feds. After the visit, he dropped them off in a questionable part of town near the airport. Ryan instructed Dallas to wait for him in an even more questionable corner bar while he met with his unknown contact in the city. He returned less than an hour later with the fake IDs used to purchase the plane tickets.

They easily passed through airport security as Michelle started sending information on Kristina's daily routine to Ryan's phone. By the time they landed at Baltimore Washington International Airport, he and Dallas had already started working out a plan to make contact with her.

They checked into a hotel room near the East Campus of Johns Hopkins University where Kristina Anderson was a tenured professor at the medical school. She lived a few blocks away from campus in a modest house. Some of the files sent by Michelle were too large to download on Ryan's phone, so he used his laptop to retrieve the data.

"I've never seen so many acronyms after a name," confessed Dallas. "PhD, ScD, MD, MPH. I'm surprised she doesn't have an MPG. Earning one undergraduate degree nearly killed me. How old is this lady?"

"Thirty-six, never married, no kids and lives alone," responded Ryan, reading her file.

"Thirty-six?" emphasized Dallas. "How is that possible?"

"I'm not sure, but I'm guessing she has a house full of cats."

"No kidding," replied Dallas. "Do you have a photo?"

"Yeah, I'm downloading it with her itinerary now," said Ryan. "Whoa. This can't be right."

"Let me see," said Dallas, standing over Ryan's shoulder. "That's a 'Wow,' not a 'Whoa,' Boss. How old is she in that photo?"

"It was taken two months ago at a university dinner."

"That is one beautiful mind," said Dallas.

"Hey, there's a note from Michelle under the photo," chuckled Ryan. "'Tell Dallas he doesn't have a chance.'"

"Obviously, she's never seen me work," gloated Dallas.

"Obviously, she has," responded Ryan quickly. "You and Michelle remind me of two third-grade kids pulling each other's hair."

"That's crazy talk, Boss," said Dallas, defending himself. "There is no mutual attraction there whatsoever. She's not even my type."

"Mutual attraction?" asked Ryan, cocking his head at Dallas. "I was just talking about the bickering. You just got busted, sailor."

"Anyway," said Dallas, turning red and changing the subject, "The itinerary Michelle put together shows Anderson teaching a class until six tonight. According to her purchasing habits, she religiously stops by a bookstore after class called Drusilla's. It's about two miles from the medical school. She doesn't own a car, but has a Metro card she normally uses for the train between seven-thirty and eight."

"Good," said Ryan. "That gives us plenty of time to check out the area before we meet her."

"I take it you'll make contact with her in the bookstore?" asked Dallas.

"Yeah, that's my brilliant plan. I'm just going to walk up to her and ask a few questions. I should know fairly quickly if she can help us. I want you outside looking for anyone that may be following her."

"Are we expecting company?"

"I really have no idea," admitted Ryan. "But nothing surprises me lately."

"This traveling under the radar is exciting, Boss. But I have to admit I don't like the idea of being unarmed."

"I thought your mind was your deadliest weapon?"

"Oh, it is. And it's telling me we need to head out."

Dallas drove the car rented with the credit card that accompanied his fake ID. He dropped Ryan off a few blocks away from the bookstore which was located on Antique Row in the cultural district of Baltimore. It was shortly after seven when he entered Drusilla's. He was a little surprised to discover the quaint store housed antiquarian, rare, and out-of-print books. Its main specialty seemed to be children's books, folklore, and fairy tales. With Kristina's advanced education, he expected her to frequent a bookstore filled with textbooks and research material far beyond his own comprehension.

Ryan walked nearly every inch of the store to locate blind spots and possible exits. He needed to make every effort to conceal his identity from anyone watching from outside. One public entrance and only two windows gave him the distinct advantage of eyeballing anyone walking into the store. He picked up a copy of Grimm's Fairy Tales and took a seat at a table with a direct line of sight to the front door. Before he started reading, Ryan transmitted Kristina's photos and other key information to his unidentified source in New Orleans. Forty-five minutes later, the bell chimed over the front door as Kristina Anderson walked into Drusilla's.

With her dark brown hair pulled tight in a ponytail and oversized reading glasses sliding down her nose, the brilliant doctor's face lit up, resembling a kid walking into a candy store. She was greeted by an elderly woman rearranging books on a shelf who looked just as excited to see her. She immediately dropped what she was doing and quickly ducked behind the counter.

Kristina wore a drab suit jacket and skirt with plain shoes that added only half inch to her already respectable height. Even with the obvious attempt to dress down, she was strikingly beautiful.

"It came in this morning," said the elderly woman, handing Kristina a package. They both were bubbling with excitement.

The young professor gingerly opened the package and carefully picked up the rare book. "First edition, first issue of *Treasure Island*. I can't believe this is mine, Emma."

"Oh, it's beautiful, sweetie," admired Emma. "I know you've been waiting a very long time for this one."

"My father started reading this to me when I was seven years old," reminisced Kristina. "He'd come bouncing into my room after work and read to me until my mom would remind him of the time. After they tucked me in, he'd sneak back in and finish the chapter. He'd always say the book wasn't ready to say goodnight."

"He sounds like a wonderful man," said Emma.

"Oh, he really was amazing," said Kristina. "He read to me almost every night. When he became too sick to even hold a book, I began reading to him. He never stopped smiling while I fumbled through the words. We didn't have enough time left to finish *Treasure Island*. I think that's why I wanted the first edition. Whenever I open it, I can hear his voice and see his face as if he were still sitting on the side of my bed."

"Stop it, child, before you have me ruining this book with tears," said Emma, sniffling. "How about I put on some tea and we turn a few pages?"

"That sounds perfect, Emma. Thank you. I'll be at my usual spot."

"Be back in a jiffy," said Emma, disappearing into the stockroom.

Kristina stood for a moment at the counter holding the book close to her chest. She closed her eyes and inhaled deeply. Ryan overheard her conversation and knew she was somewhere far away hugging her father. For a brief moment, he thought about leaving the bookstore unnoticed and finding another way to get his answers. He didn't want to bring the ugly reality of his world crashing into the peaceful daydream of hers. But that moment passed when he thought of the women who would be dying soon if he didn't get those answers.

"Dr. Anderson," said Ryan, startling her.

"Yes," she said, quickly returning the treasure to its box.

"I'm sorry to disturb you. My name is Ryan Pearson," he said, producing his credentials. "I'm a special agent with the FBI. I was hoping to have a few minutes of your time."

"In regards to...?"

"Your work with the Marines at the Michaels Laboratory in Maine," said Ryan, wasting no time.

"I'm sorry, Agent Pearson. I can't openly discuss any of my work at the lab. But you should already know that."

"Scott Wilson gave me your name as somebody who could help answer a few questions," said Ryan. "I understand this is an unusual setting to approach you, but I'm under some severe time constraints."

"Scott Wilson? Is he okay?"

"Yes, ma'am. You could say we're working together. Why would you ask if he's okay?"

"He's a dear friend and I have my reasons," said Kristina. "Some of those reasons being why I left the program. I am sorry, but I really can't talk about our work. If you'll excuse me, I have a little reading to do."

"Dr. Anderson, it's my turn to apologize."

"For disturbing me?"

"For having to tell you Peter Arrington was shot and killed by federal agents two days ago. He was wanted for the murder of three women in Virginia and one in New York. He killed one of his victims in front of me before I could stop him and murdered two of my agents with his bare hands. Right now we're closing in on Richard Elliot who is also wanted for killing three women and will kill another very soon. After we find him, we're going after Derek Mathews and Joshua Bell for the same crimes.

"Dr. Anderson," pleaded Ryan. "I've been assigned to hunt these four Marines and bring them in dead or alive. I'm trying like hell to find a way to do that without killing them or letting them kill anyone else. For some reason, I'm being kept in the dark about why these four men went from being model soldiers to brutal rapists and killers. I need help, and Scott seems to think you're the one to ask."

Kristina stared blankly at Ryan for several seconds. He knew he fired some unbelievable words in her face, but he felt there was little choice. She closed the box around her book and tucked it under her arm. Without saying a word, she slowly walked over to a table and took a seat.

"Peter is dead?"

"He is," said Ryan. "You don't know me, but I hope you believe I had no choice."

"Did you know him?" asked Kristina.

"Only what I read in the files. That's why I'm here. I need to get to know all of them."

"So you can shoot them, too?"

"So I don't have to."

Kristina looked into Ryan's eyes after what he said. He could see tears forming in hers.

"Peter was a sweetheart," she said. "On most days, I forgot he was a special forces Marine. He had a baby face and was always so polite. He'd talk for hours about his family and growing up in Virginia. Did you know he was the only son with four sisters?"

"Doesn't make sense, him raping and killing innocent women, does it?" asked Ryan.

"You have no idea how ridiculous that sounds, Agent Pearson. No idea."

"Then help me understand how ridiculous it is, Dr. Anderson. Because what isn't ridiculous to me is that they've turned into monsters. The men you speak fondly of who were assigned to your project are now serial killers."

"You mean the five," said Kristina, correcting Ryan.

"Arrington, Elliot, Mathews and Bell," counted Ryan. "That's four."

"Alex Tifton," she said. "There were five Marines assigned to the Didache Project. They all received the exact same gene therapy treatments. They did everything together. Eat, sleep, train, and even go out together. When you saw one coming, you knew the other four were close behind. They were like brothers."

"Excuse me," said Ryan, feeling his phone vibrating on his hip.

"Boss, two players outside," said Dallas. "Dark blue minivan. They're definitely not pros. I saw them coming a mile away. They're creeping up a few parking spaces every couple minutes and are fixated on your front door. They're definitely scoping the doc."

"Good work," replied Ryan, closing his phone.

"Dr. Anderson, will you help me? Please."

Before she answered, Ryan felt his phone vibrate again. There was no need to take the call. He knew they were about to have company.

8

CHoW

THE BELL RANG OVER THE front door signaling to the storekeeper she had more customers. She stepped out of the stockroom, concentrating on not spilling the two cups of hot tea. Her attempt was useless as the two men carelessly pushed her aside while frantically looking down the rows of antique books. As the scalding water spilled over her hands, one of the men quickly returned, grabbing her by the throat.

"Where is she?" he yelled in her terrified face.

"I – I don't know who you're talking about," responded Emma. "Please, you're hurting me."

"Dr. Anderson," he yelled. "I know she's in here! Where the fuck is she, old lady?"

"Hey, back door is open," shouted the other man. "She's running down the alley! Bring the car around!"

The man gripping Emma's throat coldly looked into her eyes and purposefully squeezed harder before he finally released her. As she slumped crying to the ground, attempting to catch her breath, the bell over the front door jingled again. The man turned his head to give a viscous glare at the new customer, but was greeted with a blinding heavy punch crushing his nose. His knees buckled as the unexpected and painful shock to his system dropped him beside Emma. His eyes were unable to focus as he was pulled to his feet, spun around, and pinned against the wall. A muscular arm wrapped around his throat in a choke hold.

"I bet you didn't expect this to happen while beating up this nice lady, did you, shithead?" asked Dallas, whispering in his ear. "Answer one question and I won't choke the life out of you. Who do you work for?"

"Fuck y—"

Before he could finish his answer, Dallas choked the life out of him. Well, at least temporarily as he lay unconscious on the floor. Dallas searched him and took his wallet, cell phone, and gun.

The other man darted into the alley after spotting Kristina running toward the street. He was in full stride when the metal trash can lid magically appeared, stopping his face while his legs kept running. If the metal lid didn't take care of the problem, the brick alleyway did when the back of his head made contact. The entire event was so violent Ryan had to check his pulse to make sure he didn't kill him.

"That's gonna leave a mark, Boss," said Dallas, coming through the back door of the bookstore.

"Did the other one see your face?" asked Ryan.

"If he did, he won't remember it. He had the old lady by the throat when I came up behind him. Looks like these guys want the doc pretty bad. They were just sitting in the van when this one answered his phone. They bolted out of the truck as soon as he hung up, like someone ordered them to taker her. What kind of asshole chokes an old lady?"

"The kind that doesn't care who they hurt," replied Ryan.

Kristina heard Dallas's last sentence and ran back into the store before Ryan could stop her. Dallas held up a roll of duct tape he picked up out of the stockroom. "Are we taking them with us?" asked Dallas, tapping his finger on the roll of tape.

"No, but we're taking her. Use the whole roll on these jerks and stuff them in that dumpster. Did you find anything on your guy?"

"Yeah, I've got his wallet, phone, and gun."

"Well, that's good news. You got your gun now," smiled Ryan.

"You should get a holster for that trash can lid," laughed Dallas. "That was very Starsky and Hutch."

"Thank you. Have Michelle dump both their phones and run their IDs," said Ryan. "I want to know where that order came from. I'll go get Dr. Anderson while you tape up our friends."

Ryan walked back inside the store where Kristina was attending to Emma.

"Are you two okay?" asked Ryan.

"I'm fine, but she needs to be seen in an E.R. She has high blood pressure and broke her hip last year. Who were those animals?"

"I don't know. But I do know they were coming for you and not her."

"Why?"

"I don't know that, either," said Ryan. "You need to come with us."

"This is all a bit much, Agent Pearson."

"Please, call me Ryan."

"I can't leave her here, Ryan. She may have internal injuries."

"Call an ambulance, but as soon as we hear the sirens, we need to head out the back. I can't be seen here and certainly not with you."

"You're an FBI agent. You're not supposed to be the one running."

"I'm not running, Dr. Anderson. I believe we have a mole in the Bureau. Right now, the guys calling the shots think I'm in New Orleans hunting Elliot. If they know I'm operating under the radar to find the truth, they'll pull me off this case. And if they do, more innocent people are going to die. I hate to say this because I've been hearing it thrown around too much lately, but I have to ask you to trust me."

"Kristina." she said, quietly stroking Emma's silver hair.

"I'm sorry?"

"Call me Kristina."

"Okay, Kristina. We need to get back to New Orleans. The other half of my team is there looking for Elliot. You'll be safer there while we find out who came after you and why."

"Boss," said Dallas, motioning Ryan away from the women. "We need to move. How are we going to get her to New Orleans? We can't just stroll into the airport. These goons aren't too sharp, but they'll probably have the airports covered. As soon as her name hits the ticketing system, she's done. It's an eighteen-hour drive, so we need to get rolling."

"We can't waste eighteen hours," said Ryan. "We'll drive south to Richmond, Virginia tonight. It's about a three-hour trip. That should put a little distance between us and them."

"What's in Richmond?"

"Hopefully a plane."

"How did you – never mind."

Emma persuaded Kristina to let her stand. She walked without pain to her seat behind the counter. She was shaken, but was aware they weren't after her.

"Why do they want to hurt you?" asked Emma with a trembling voice.

"I don't know," replied Kristina. "These men are FBI agents. I have to go with them so we can find out. An ambulance is on the way. I can't have you argue with me right now, so will you promise me you'll go to the hospital?"

"Yes, child, I'll go. You have to leave now?"

"I do. I can't explain why, but I promise to get in touch with you as soon as I can."

"Be careful, sweetie."

"One more thing."

"I'm listening."

"Tell the medics and the police two men tried to mug you, but a good samaritan chased them off. Don't mention I was in here or the FBI agents. I'll explain that later, too."

"Okay. I can do that."

"I'll see you again soon," said Kristina, hugging Emma before leaving.

During the three-hour drive, Ryan brought Kristina up to speed on the events of the past several months. She sat quietly, taking in every word. Ryan worried he was overwhelming her with the details of the killings, but he wanted her to know everything. He wanted her to trust him.

They arrived at Hanover County Airport located fourteen miles north of Richmond and boarded a small Learjet. Less than two hours later, they landed in New Orleans. Tom and Michelle gave each other puzzled looks as Ryan, Dallas, and Kristina piled into the back of the sedan.

"Sorry, guys," said Ryan. "I didn't want to pass any compromising information over the airwaves. Tom, Michelle, this is Dr. Anderson."

"Welcome aboard, Dr. Anderson," greeted Tom.

"Please, call me Kristina."

"Not a chance, huh?" said Dallas, smiling at Michelle.

"We'll be dropping you and Michelle off at a house two blocks from ours," said Ryan. "She'll be staying with you tonight. It's safe, but tomorrow Dallas will be reinforcing the locks and installing a security system. You'll have a keychain panic button that'll put us at your front door in less than forty-five seconds.

"Kristina, it's very important you understand you cannot leave that house for any reason. You can't call home. You can't let anyone know where you are. That means no e-mails and no checking in at work. Do you understand?"

"I do."

"Okay, good."

Ryan's phone alerted him to an incoming call from Deputy Director Donaldson. "Quiet, please."

"Ryan, we've just received information that one of the scientists who resigned from the project has gone off the grid. Her name is Dr. Kristina Anderson, and her last known location as of yesterday was Baltimore. There's evidence she's in a relationship with Joshua Bell and has been in close contact with him since the first killing. If we find her, we'll probably find him and Derek. We believe she's the one responsible for their condition.

Scott Wilson is on his way to see you now. His team is also in New Orleans and should be at the house in a few minutes. He worked with her and thinks he may be able to help us locate her. I want your team to consider her just as dangerous as the monsters she created."

"Yes, sir," responded Ryan. "Do you have any idea where she might be heading?"

"Elliot and the other Marines are still your priority, Ryan. Get what you can from Scott and keep an eye out for her, but don't concern yourself with finding her. I have a team of agents leaving Quantico now to hunt her down."

"Understood," replied Ryan, ending the call. "Step on it, Tom. We're going to have visitors at the house in a few minutes."

Kristina and Michelle quickly exited the vehicle and entered the scientist's new home. The rest of the team arrived back at the FBI safe house less than two minutes before two familiar black SUVs screeched to a stop. Four heavily armed security personnel jumped out of the first vehicle as Scott and another man darted out of theirs. A third SUV parked behind the house unloaded four more troops, effectively sealing the perimeter. Scott banged on the door continuously until Dallas opened it.

"Where's Ryan?" Scott demanded.

"He's upstairs, but –"

"You stay here," said Scott to his companion. "I need to speak with Ryan alone."

Dallas escorted Scott to the windowless room where Ryan was sitting at the table. He closed the door behind them.

"I said I need to speak to Ryan alone," repeated Scott with emphasis.

"It's okay, Scott. He's one of the good guys."

"Really? Because I thought you were one of the good guys, Ryan. What the fuck did you do? I gave her name to you as a sign of trust, and you literally handed her over to them! I told you she was a friend and to be careful! What kind of idiot are you?"

"Hold on, Slick," said Dallas. "Easy with who you're calling an idiot. We didn't give up your girlfriend."

"She's not my girlfriend, you ape. She's someone I care very much about, and you two goons probably got her killed. I don't know where she is, and your boss is sending a team of headhunters after her. So not only are the bad guys looking to shut her up, but you've got the so-called good guys doing the same. You couldn't have fucked this up better if you were actually trying! You're right, Dallas. I take back my idiot comment because I'm the fucking idiot for trusting you!"

"What are you, Scott? A buck forty?" patronized Dallas. "Are you going to shank me with your slide rule?"

"You really are an ape," said Scott, trying to stand his ground.

"Well, Dallas," interrupted Ryan. "Do you think he's one of them?"

"I hope not, Boss. He's a little wolverine. I really think he'd take a shot at both of us right now."

"You think this is funny?" said Scott, taking an aggressive step toward Dallas.

"Scott, we have her," said Ryan, saving his life.

"What?" asked Scott, halting his advance and turning his attention to Ryan.

"We made contact with her yesterday evening in Baltimore," explained Ryan. "While we were having a nice conversation, two thugs were tailing her like you suspected. They received an order from someone and they tried to take her. They're probably still duct taped in a dumpster."

"So she's okay?" asked Scott, needing more clarification. "Where is she?"

"She's fine. One of my people is with her now. I hope you understand I can't tell you exactly where."

"No, no, I understand," said Scott, calming down and taking a seat at the table. "I'm sorry for getting so upset. You don't know how much she doesn't deserve to be involved in all this."

"Actually, I do," said Ryan. "The fact that my boss wants her out of the picture makes you one of the few I believe. With that phone call, he effectively removed all doubt he can't be trusted. I still don't know how involved he might be in any conspiracy, but I certainly can't let him know I have Kristina."

"This is getting out of control, Ryan," said Scott. "I'm looking over my shoulder every second of every day. I can't trust my own people, the military or the federal government. If the second most powerful man in the FBI is in on this, how do we fight that? How do we end this?"

"Scott, listen to me," said Ryan in a calming voice. "You're doing great. I just need you to hold it together a little while longer. I'll sort this out. But I need you to tell me everything you know. I need to know what happened to those Marines at the lab. I need to know why they're killing."

"Ryan, I don't know what happened to them," said Scott. "I really don't. I have theories, but absolutely no evidence. I wasn't a part of the Didache Project. I was working on a different project, trying to figure out ways to make their metabolism more efficient."

"Then why did they choose you to lead the forensics team in Virginia?" asked Ryan. "Do you have a background in crime scene investigation?"

"I told you at the farmhouse, I'm here to clean up after you guys," explained Scott. "That's what we do. Those Marines are property of the U.S. Military. Let me put it to you this way: those four men are the most expensive weapons ever created in the history of warfare. You could build a fleet of nuclear submarines with the amount of government funding allocated to genetic research over the past ten years. Most of that money has been awarded to the Michaels Laboratory. Losing one microscope slide of their DNA would constitute a catastrophic breach of national security. It's my job to recover every drop of blood or piece of tissue they leave behind. I have nothing to do with the actual investigation."

"So who's collecting evidence and feeding us information about where to go to next?" asked Dallas.

"There's another team that travels with us, but we never speak," said Scott. "I mean not a word. No 'good morning,' no 'how's the family,' no 'fuck you.' They poke around as we recover biological material. Every once in a while, they'll get on their cell phones, but I don't know who's in charge. Well, I mean I don't know for sure."

"Okay, understanding you don't know for sure, who do you think it is?" baited Ryan.

"Ask Kristina about Colonel Marcus Brown," conceded Scott. "He's the Marine military liaison and the commanding officer of every soldier at the lab. I've only bumped into him in the hallways. Kristina worked very closely with him. She's not a fan."

"Will do," said Ryan. "Hang in there, buddy."

"Easier said than done. You don't know these guys."

"That's going to change very soon."

"Scott, what are the chances of you getting ahold of the autopsy reports from the three women Arrington buried in the basement in Virginia?"

"Actually, pretty good," said Scott. "The bodies were taken back to the lab in Maine. They're basically being scrubbed for any biological material left behind, like Arrington's saliva, hair or blood. We use the reports to identify wounds that may contain material. I'll make copies and try to get them to you in the next few days."

"Perfect, thank you."

"I need to go," said Scott. "Please tell Kristina I'm sorry. I hope she understands why I'm doing this."

"Consider it done."

As soon as Scott appeared in the doorway, the security detail quickly scanned the area and then returned to the vehicles. The small convoy turned the corner and headed for the interstate. They sped by two intoxicated tourists hugging the walls, still clutching their large cups of dragster fuel. Their numerous Mardi Gras beads glistened as the headlights from the vehicles lit up the corner and then disappeared down Canal Street.

"Quite a bit of activity tonight at the feds clubhouse," said Joshua Bell.

"Scott looked pissed," said Derek Mathews, guzzling the rest of his soda.

"Easy on that pop, Derek. You don't want to rot your teeth."

"You're hilarious."

"I didn't see the female agent go into the house," mentioned Joshua. "I wonder where she disappeared."

"Is that important?" asked Derek.

"No, not really. We'll deal with her and the rest of them later."

"I just wish there was another way," said Derek, lowering his eyes to the ground.

"There isn't," replied Joshua. "I don't want to sacrifice him either. But when we give them Richard, the only one that can get close to us will be

Alex. And when we remove him from the equation, we'll make them all pay for what they did to us."

"Richard goes fast," demanded Derek. "We need to make sure of that. I don't want him feeling the agony Peter did."

"Okay. We'll make sure," said Joshua, "But either way, you and I are going to feel it. There's no getting around that."

"I don't want to get around it," said Derek, becoming angry. "I want to remember how it feels. I want to remember when I'm making all of them feel it, too."

"It's about time you started coming around, Derek. I have to admit I was beginning to worry you might soften up like the others."

"Don't worry about me. Those bastards deserve everything we're going to give them."

"Good, brother. That's what I like to hear. Now, all this talk of a reckoning is making me hungry. Let's go grab someone to eat."

9

WHAT'S UP, DOC?

MICHELLE HEARD THE HEAVY FOOTSTEPS of a man on the front porch. She put her hand on her weapon as she approached the door. The smoked glass made it difficult for her to identify the visitor. A light knock and a whisper lowered her guard.

"It would help if you'd call before strolling over here," said Michelle.

"Sorry," said Ryan. "Is she awake?"

"I don't think she'll be sleeping anytime soon. I can't blame her for being a little rattled. She told me about you making her run down an alley as bait so you could TKO the bad guy. A trash can lid?"

"Yeah."

"Nice touch," said Michelle, walking him into the living room where Kristina was sitting.

"How are you holding up?" asked Ryan.

"I wish I knew how Emma was doing. She must be scared to death."

"Michelle?"

"I'm on it, Boss," said Michelle, grabbing her untraceable phone and walking into the kitchen.

"Scott Wilson was here a few minutes ago. He wanted me to tell you he was sorry you became involved. He seems to be genuinely worried about you."

"He was always worrying about me. Most of the men in my life do worry. I think they see me as frail and easily breakable. I'm not a weak person, Ryan."

"I don't believe you are, Kristina. But I can see where others would want to protect you from the ugly things that are out there."

"That sounded a little patronizing," she said.

"Not my intent. We could all use a little protecting every now and then. It's why I need your help. But I'm not here now to ask you questions. I just wanted to make sure you were okay and as comfortable as possible under these circumstances."

"I'm fine, really. I am a little tired, though."

"I know it won't be easy, but try to get some sleep," said Ryan as Michelle returned.

"Good news, Kristina. Emma was released from the E.R. shortly after you left Richmond. She had a little bruising around her neck, but she's fine."

"She's going to be worried sick about me. Is there any way –"

"I'm sorry, there isn't," interrupted Ryan. "The men after you will be watching her every move and listening to every word she says. If you contact her, you'll unwittingly put her in harm's way. She'll be in more danger if she knows where you are."

"Is this where you tell me to trust you again?" asked Kristina.

"I'm afraid so."

"If anything else happens to her, I won't be the only person I can't forgive. After I lost my mother, Emma is the closest thing to family I have left."

"Try to get some rest. We'll be starting early."

Michelle walked Ryan to the door. "Do you think she'll try to contact her?"

"I don't think so, but you need to make sure she doesn't."

"What did you do with her phone?" asked Michelle.

"We threw it away," smiled Ryan as he left.

———

"Yes, I'm sure. According to the GPS in her phone, you're right on top of it."

"Okay, but we don't see her out in the open – wait."

The men heard rustling in the dumpster a few feet away. One held up his finger to his mouth as he pulled his weapon.

"Stand by. We may have found her hiding place," he whispered into his radio.

One man held his gun on the large container as the other quickly flipped open the lid. Pointing his flashlight into the garbage, he looked down to see their two missing associates bound and covered in blood. On the severely swollen face of one, a cell phone was duct taped to his forehead.

"Fuck," said the man holding the gun.

"What's your status, Blue Team? Do you have her?"

"Negative. But we did find her phone and Red Team."

———

"Colonel, we've got a problem," said Alex Tifton, walking in to the secure operations center at the Michaels Laboratory in Bar Harbor, Maine. "Dr. Anderson slipped away, but she seems to have acquired some help."

"How do you know?" asked Colonel Marcus Brown.

"Two men from Red Team were just found beaten half to death, bound, and thrown in a dumpster with her cell phone taped to one of their foreheads. I don't think she did that."

"Jesus Christ," said the Colonel, rubbing his temples. "Those civilian security people are about fucking useless. We should've picked her up the same day we rounded up the other scientists. What I should've done was sent you. I knew this would bite us on the ass. If she talks and somebody with half a brain puts two and two together, that's the end of us."

"Who could've taken her?" asked Alex.

"It's not Ryan's team. They never left New Orleans. Besides, the deputy director would've told us. It's obviously not us, so who else would be looking for her?" asked the Colonel.

"You think Joshua or Derek took her, sir?"

"At this point, I'm hoping it was them. They want to kill everyone who had any involvement in the Didache Project. That includes you and me. We have the other three scientists secured here, so they may have simply chosen the easiest target as their first. No telling what's going through their sick minds."

"Does this change our plan?"

"Not the end result, but we do need to speed things up," said the Colonel. "I want you to head to New Orleans tomorrow alone. I'll let you know how to bring Elliot out in the open for the feds. If you can give me another head shot like Arrington's, we'll have this mess cleaned up in a few weeks instead of months. Go get your gear ready. I have to make a few phone calls."

"Will do, sir."

———

As the sun was peeking over the horizon, Kristina walked downstairs in search of a cup of coffee. She was wafted by an aroma of French vanilla when she reached the landing. She was also startled by Dallas who was moving quickly through the hallway.

"Morning, Doc," greeted Dallas. "I hope I didn't wake you?"

"No, I'm usually an early riser, but I'll give you a million dollars for that cup of coffee."

"Here you go," said Dallas, laughing as he handed her his cup. "Haven't taken a sip, and it's on Uncle Sam. Ryan brought it over a few minutes ago."

"Is he here already?"

"Yeah, he's on the back porch with Michelle and Tom. I'm going to be running around the house for a little bit installing your security system. Go ahead and take this," said Dallas, handing her a small device resembling a remote keyless entry for a car. "There's only one button. When you press it, an alert will be sent to our phones, along with GPS locating data. We'll test it before I leave."

"That's very James Bond," said Kristina, walking toward the back porch. "Good morning," she said to the agents sitting outside on the deck.

"Go back inside," said Ryan, standing quickly and startling her.

"Sorry," she said, closing the door.

Michelle pressed her lips together and started shaking her head as Ryan returned to his seat. "That was a little harsh."

"What was?" asked Ryan, oblivious.

"She's had a rough couple of days because of you," explained Michelle.

"Because of me?" said Ryan, looking puzzled.

"Yeah, because of you," she repeated. "Let me break it down for you. You, a stranger with a badge, show up while she's having a nice visit with a friend in a bookstore. You tell her four of her former patients have turned into raping killers. Two goons try to kidnap her and put her friend in the hospital. You then tell her she can't go home or contact anyone and drag her to New Orleans without even a toothbrush or a change of underwear. You ask her to voluntarily turn her life upside down and she does. After all that, she comes outside with a smile and a good morning to us. And what do you do? Bark at her like a child to go back inside while the adults talk."

"Well, you certainly put me in my place," said Ryan.

"You're welcome. And Dallas makes fun of *me* for being single?"

"Thanks for the guidance," said Ryan with a smile. "I need to talk to her alone for a few minutes. I'll come get you when we finish so she can help you with the profiles. Tom, would you mind running out and grabbing some breakfast for us?"

"My pleasure," said Tom.

Ryan walked into the kitchen and found Kristina sitting at the table reading a newspaper. She didn't raise her head to look at him while he warmed up his coffee. He grabbed his notebook and files and sat at the other end of the table.

"How did you sleep?" started Ryan.

"I slept," she responded, not raising her nose from the paper.

"Tom's going to grab us some breakfast. He's pretty good at covering the basics, but if there's anything special you'd like, I can let him know."

"I'm sure whatever he gets will be fine."

"Kristina, I'm sorry for snapping at you," said Ryan, sensing her irritation. "But we can't run the risk of anyone seeing you here, not even on the back porch. You came out with a smile and I ruined it pretty quickly. Sometimes I can be a little insensitive. I am sorry."

"I understand," said Kristina, finally looking at him. "Your delivery sucks, but I understand."

"Thank you. I'd like you to take a look at these files," said Ryan, sliding the stack of folders toward her. "I have to warn you, they're very graphic."

She opened the first folder labeled with Peter Arrington's name. Her eyes opened wide and she took a deep breath to maintain her composure. A wallet-sized photograph of Arrington was paper clipped to an 8x10 photo that captured the shredded body of the young woman killed in Syracuse. She flipped through a few more pages and then closed the folder.

"He didn't do that," she sighed. "He's incapable. I worked with him almost every day for years. He did not kill that girl."

"He's killed men in combat, Kristina. I also witnessed him cut the throat of a woman he kidnapped and tied to a bed. When we tried to stop him, he ripped apart two of my agents with his bare hands. I assure you he's capable."

"When he and the other four were chosen as test subjects, they had to go through an intense psychological evaluation," said Kristina. "They had to have certain characteristics most people don't possess. I understand he had to kill in combat, but he hated it. He truly hated it more than the others. He didn't become a Marine to kill; he became a Marine because he's from a long line of Marines. It's what the men in his family do. We talked for hours about his wartime experiences. He had a kind heart and was a good man. You're trying to tell me he just snapped?"

"They all did. All except Alex Tifton. There's no doubt they've snapped. The proof is in front of you. I was hoping you could tell me why. I was also hoping you could tell me why Alex didn't."

"I still can't believe Peter was capable of what you're showing me. It really doesn't make any sense."

"Would any of them be capable?" asked Ryan. "Because I don't believe Peter killed that woman in Syracuse either, but I do believe one of them did. If you had to choose, who would it be?"

"Ryan, it's just my opinion," replied Kristina. "You can't take my word for it. I mean, I'm a scientist, not an FBI agent."

"I understand. But you know more about these men than we do. So right now I'm just asking for your best guess."

"Joshua Bell," answered Kristina. "He was different from the others. He was much more aggressive and would even bully the security guards posted in the lab. Sometimes he tried to make it look like a joke, but he would provoke them so he could show off his abilities. One guard had enough and took a step toward him. Before any of us could say a word, he had him on the ground. I thought he was going to kill him. Derek knelt down and whispered something in his ear and Joshua let go. He helped the terrified man to his feet and started laughing as if he was playing around. But we all knew differently. If Derek hadn't had been there, I think he'd have really hurt the guard."

"I received a phone call right before we arrived at the house last night from my boss," said Ryan. "You had a pretty rough day, so I didn't tell you the reason for the call. I wanted you to get some rest."

"Okay, I'm rested. Go ahead."

"You're wanted in connection with these murders," said Ryan.

"You're joking, right?"

"I'm afraid not. I was informed you were in a relationship with Joshua for several months and you may know his location. I was also told you may be assisting them in some way because of that relationship. Now, I obviously don't believe that's the case. But I was wondering why they might have chosen to name Joshua as your boyfriend."

"It wasn't for his lack of trying, Ryan. That's another reason why I suspect he's responsible for the brutality in those photos. There was hardly a session that went by where he didn't try to make a move. After several turndowns, he seemed to get easily angry with me. He'd say things that made me uncomfortable, but I never reported it. I just wrote it off as some kind of Marine bravado, but I did make sure we were never alone. I can only describe it as a creepy feeling."

"Did the others make advances toward you or any other women at the lab?" asked Ryan.

"No, not at all," she responded. "I even think Derek picked up on the situation and kept a closer eye on me."

"How so?"

"Well, he also made sure Joshua and I were never alone. Like I told you, most of the men around me think I'm frail. I guess Derek was no different. Peter, Richard, and Alex thought the same. They'd look after me like big brothers."

"Did you guys ever go off the compound?"

"Once," replied Kristina. "It was my birthday, and they wanted to take me to dinner. Other than the creepy vibe from Joshua, they really were great guys. We had a few drinks at the bar after dinner, and if a guy even looked at me, he had five big Marines circling him. I don't have any siblings. It was kind of sweet the way they looked out for me."

"Well, you're about to have another group of guys looking out for you," said Ryan. "My team and I can't risk exposing you by hanging around. There's a possibility the bad guys may try to keep an eye on us as well."

"Another group of FBI agents?"

"No," said Ryan. "A close friend of mine from my Marine days now owns a security firm. They're all ex-military and mainly do contract work for the government overseas. He's the man responsible for the jet that picked us up in Richmond, the security system Dallas is installing, and a few other critical items. I trust him with my life. He knows everything, including you being wanted by my own agency. His team will be here later this evening."

Tom returned to the house with several bags of breakfast food. Ryan brought him and Michelle up to speed on the conversation he was having with Kristina. He instructed them to spend the rest of the morning with her working on Richard Elliot's profile. Dallas completed the security system installation and tested her panic button. Everything was in working order. The entire group sat at the dining room table, attempting to enjoy the meal.

"Oh, I almost forgot," said Ryan, taking his last bites. "Scott wanted me to ask you about Colonel Marcus Brown. He said you weren't a big fan."

"No, I wasn't," she said. "He's another one of the reasons why I left the project. And it's not because of what he did to me. It's because of what he was doing to them. I'd hear the speeches and pep talks he'd give them when it came time for them to sign waivers on a new round of experimental therapy."

"Waivers?" asked Dallas.

"Yes. They have to consent to every new procedure we introduce. There are guidelines to human testing set up by the U.S. Department of Health and Human Services. The Michaels Laboratory itself was subject to unscheduled visits by investigators from a Congressional Oversight Committee. We operated under very strict rules and regulations. Colonel Brown did everything in his power to bypass those rules. He wanted maximum results in much shorter periods of time."

"Dallas, let's do a little digging and find out more about the security group assigned to the lab," said Ryan. "Michelle, any luck on the phone records and IDs from our two dumpster divers in Baltimore?"

"Not yet," responded Michelle. "It usually takes a few hours, but add a couple more since I'm circumventing normal channels at the Bureau. I should have an answer shortly."

"Good," said Ryan. "We need to know who they are and who's giving the orders. Tom, I'd like for you to stay with Kristina and go over some of the more technical questions about her work at the lab. You're the biggest nerd on the team, so I need you to absorb it and then dumb it down for me when I get back. Also, get a preliminary profile created on Elliot. He still needs to be our primary focus while we're conducting our own investigations on the side."

"Will do, Boss."

"Let's keep our eyes and ears open," said Ryan. "I have a funny feeling this town is going to get more crowded the closer we get to Elliot. I want to know who everyone is that decides to show up at the party."

10

UNQUENCHABLE

RICHARD ELLIOT WAS ON HIS knees with his head over a large bucket quickly filling with blood. The average human body holds roughly ten pints. He consumed over six of hers. His own body was rejecting the massive amount of metallic tasting liquid refusing to settle in his stomach. A final wave of nausea passed through and he rolled onto the floor exhausted after wiping his mouth with a crimson rag. He forced himself to look over at the drained body of his last meal.

The burst of endorphins and adrenaline which coursed through his veins as he tore into her flesh were subsiding. The reality of what he did to the beautiful young woman was replacing the euphoria of the kill. Richard began convulsing and crying as he looked into her lifeless blue eyes only a few feet away.

He saw the large hole in the side of her neck where he ripped through her skin with his teeth to start his feeding. He kept her alive as long as possible so her beating heart would force the blood out of her body and into his. When her heart mercifully stopped, he sucked harder to bring more fluid to the wound. After the first source was depleted, he used his clawed hands to punch into her abdominal cavity to remove her blood engorged liver. With his insatiable thirst still unsatisfied, he used rags to absorb any fluid left inside her open torso and squeezed the last few ounces of her into his mouth.

He didn't disembowel and consume her out of unbridled rage or sick ritual. In the chaos of his mind, her body was just a vessel that held the substance he craved. In the chaos of his mind, the woman he abducted was merely a container. If he was a junkie, she was a porcelain doll stuffed with heroin. But what he craved was the blood running through her veins.

As he lay at her side crying, he welcomed the pain shooting through every electrified nerve as his grotesque clawed hands and fangs began receding back into his body. The swollen blue veins under the pale skin of his face and neck started disappearing beneath the surface. It would take several minutes for his features to return to their familiar human color and tone. His fangs retracted quickly into the roof of his mouth, but it would take another several minutes for the elongated bones of his fingers to be reabsorbed into his hands. The process was excruciating.

After thirty minutes, he slowly rose to his feet, unable to look directly at her anymore. He took his false teeth out of a small plastic container and pushed them into place. The people responsible for his transformation didn't take into account that the spaces needed for the fangs to fully deploy were already occupied by teeth. During the first mutation, the pain was so intense the teeth had to immediately be removed. Shortly after the first episode, they tried to remove the fangs. They grew back stronger four weeks later.

Richard pulled himself together and walked into the backyard of the abandoned house located in the middle of the still deserted Lower Ninth Ward in New Orleans. When the levees failed during Hurricane Katrina, the house he eventually turned into his lair was under six feet of water. Even though there were efforts to rebuild the devastated area, Richard was isolated for over a mile in every direction. Curfews were still in effect, and it was only on a rare occasion a patrol car or survey crew passed within a hundred yards. His keen senses greatly enhanced by the genetic alterations alerted him to any presence. Richard could easily avoid detection and was free from any interruption for weeks at a time.

Under a full moon, he walked into the shack behind the house. He lit a small lantern inside the musty building. He reached down and pulled up plywood covering the dirt floor. Richard started digging the fourth hole located beside the three already occupied graves of his other victims. An overwhelming sense of guilt surged through him with every thrust of the shovel into the hard earth. There was little remorse while he selected, hunted, abducted, and drained the life out of his defenseless prey. The guilt and remorse didn't manifest itself until after he satisfied his uncontrollable urge to feed.

On the same day every six weeks, Richard Elliot would wake up shaking like a junkie needing a fix. No other emotion or craving would occupy his mind except the desire to taste human blood. Even the powerful daily quest for self-preservation escaped his thoughts as he focused on his addiction. It was an addiction he wasn't born with or acquired a taste for over the years. It was an addiction created at the Michaels Laboratory and delivered to his brain stem by a manufactured virus.

The brain cells associated with primordial survival instincts were manipulated and altered by a single session of DNA therapy. Along with the addiction, altered DNA making a soldier incapable of surrendering to an enemy or suicide was uploaded into each of the four hunted Marines. In spite of efforts by each soldier, they couldn't suppress the urge to feed or succumb to the guilt associated with the killing of innocent women. They were incapable of ending their own lives. They were told the effects of the genetic mutations were irreversible.

He finished digging the shallow grave and returned to the gruesome scene inside the house. Wrapping his victim carefully in a white sheet, Richard carried her out to the shack. He gently laid her in the fresh grave and quietly said a prayer. He asked for forgiveness for what he had done. He also asked God to take him and send him deep into Hell where he belonged. After the prayer, he placed the bucket he had filled with her blood at her feet, and began shoveling dirt over her body. He made quick work of the chore and returned to the house to clean his killing room. He wasn't worried about leaving evidence behind proving he was a murderer. Richard simply didn't want any reminders of what he did...again.

As with Peter Arrington, Richard's keen senses were dulled while engrossed in his bloodlust. During the phase, his ability to sense the presence of the other genetically altered Marines was greatly reduced. When he finally felt the tingling sensation alerting him to the unexpected visitor, the Marine almost invisible in his black camouflage had his gun sights dialed in to the space between Richard Elliot's eyes.

"Thank you, God," whispered Richard less than a second before the large caliber bullet penetrated his skull, answering his prayer.

Alex picked up the shell casing as he waited for Colonel Brown to answer his phone. "It's done, sir."

"Excellent work, Marine. Is the girl there?"

"I waited for him to finish burying her with the others."

"Good. God rest their poor souls. Stage the scene and get out of there quickly. I'll give you a few minutes before I notify Scott Wilson. He'll be bringing the feds, so it has to look like the real thing."

"Yes, sir."

"Are you picking up anything on the location of Derek or Joshua?"

"Nothing yet. I still have the feeling they're together, but I can't seem to nail down their location. When I arrived, I sensed they'd been here recently, but I have no idea where they went after. I don't know how they're doing it, but they're getting better at covering their tracks. They seem to be much stronger than the others."

"Don't worry about it, son. We'll let the FBI figure out where they are. Get yourself back up here as soon as possible."

———

"Michelle, it's been almost three days," said Ryan, stretching in his chair. "Please tell me you have something."

"I do," she said, entering the room. "Trying to work under the radar and without Bureau resources is a pain in the ass."

"I know," said Ryan, trying not to show his frustration. "So what did you find out?"

"The two goons in Baltimore that tried to take Kristina are contract security employees for the Michaels Lab. The company is called Safeguards and the lab is their only contract. All of them are ex-military or police and all are handled by Colonel Marcus Brown. The two guys you and Dallas put in the dumpster were Army Intelligence prior to taking the civilian job."

"No surprise there," said Ryan. "Any luck on tracing their last phone call?"

"They must know the same guy you do," answered Michelle. "I can tell you which cell towers the call hit in Maryland, but the number on the other side is untraceable."

"Shit," sighed Ryan. "We've been in New Orleans four days, and all we know about the other players is that they're connected to the lab." He stood and walked around the table covered in folders and photos. "Are the guys on their way back?"

"They should be here shortly," said Michelle. "They left the bayou over an hour ago. In the last message I received from Dallas, he was whining about the mosquitoes. Tom's probably ready to shoot him."

"Are we any closer to finding a lead on Elliot?" asked Ryan.

"Tom said he put together a decent profile from the folks he talked with around his hometown. He believes we need to start canvassing some of the closed off areas near the levees. They're still basically ghost towns, and Elliot is very familiar with the Lower Ninth Ward. He spent a few summers with his uncle who owned a business and a couple of houses down there before the flood."

"That makes sense," said Ryan. "We'll head out there in the morning. Have you been over to check on Kristina?"

"I told the team watching her to let me know if she needed anything, but they haven't called. Do you want me to go over there?"

"No, I'll go. Besides, I'm sure Dallas would rather be greeted by you after his long trip instead of me."

"What's that supposed to mean?" asked Michelle, cocking her head.

"You guys crack me up," said Ryan, walking out of the room. "I'll be back in a few."

Ryan called the team watching over Kristina to alert them he was heading their way. The group of professionals scanned the area to make sure nobody was tailing Ryan as he approached. He used the back door to avoid the illumination of the street lamp exposing the front yard. He was surprised to see his old friend who owned the security company sitting at the kitchen table.

"Hey, Steve," greeted Ryan. "What brings you out here and away from your big house on the river?"

"Making sure my guys impress the feds," said Steve Kramer. "It's not every day I get to watch your back, Ryan."

"Once again, I can't thank you enough for your help. I don't know too many people who would send a jet to me in the middle of the night with no explanation, not to mention handing over one of your rental properties to hide a fugitive."

"Well, luckily, you only need to know one," said Steve. "You pulled my ass out of the fire once or twice when we were overseas, so no need to thank me. How are things on your end?"

"Confusing," answered Ryan. "I'm no closer to finding Elliot than

I was when we arrived. I still don't know if my boss is a mole and I'm currently harboring a fugitive. Other than that, things are going well."

"You'll work it out, buddy. Let me know if I can help in any of those areas."

"You're doing plenty. Besides, you're harboring a fugitive as well. Speaking of which, how's she doing?"

"All she has really asked for are books. She has her nose buried in one just about every time I see her. I have to admit she's handling everything very well. She always greets me and my guys with a bright smile and pleasant conversation. I also have to admit she's very easy on the eyes."

"No argument there," said Ryan. "I'm going to check in on her. Is she in her room?"

"Yep. Reading."

Ryan walked upstairs and lightly knocked on her door. Kristina greeted him with one of her bright smiles. He silently agreed with Steve again. She was very easy on the eyes.

"Ryan, how are you?"

"I'm supposed to be asking you that question."

"I'm doing okay. Please, come in and have a seat."

"I don't want to interrupt your reading."

"At this point, any interruption is welcomed."

"So really, how are you doing?" asked Ryan.

"Really, I'm okay," she said, sitting on the corner of the bed. "I mean, going outside and feeling sunshine on my face would be nice, but I understand that's not a good idea."

"I think that can be arranged. I'm sorry we've had to keep you in lockdown these past few days. Until I work out a couple of issues, it really is safer for you in here."

"The isolation is a bit unnerving, but I can handle it. Are you any closer to finding Richard?"

"We have a few places we're going to look over tomorrow morning. Tom and Dallas have spent the last couple of days walking through alligator infested swamps talking to his friends and family. We'll find him soon."

"I hope you do," said Kristina without a smile. "I can't get the images of those girls from the files out of my head. Knowing three more might meet the same fate breaks my heart. I just wish I knew why."

"I'm working on that, too" said Ryan. "That's the question keeping me up at night."

"I can't imagine how hard this must be for you," she said with a disarming tone, "Not being able to trust anyone while you're looking for those answers. And knowing if you don't find them, more people could die. That's an incredible amount of pressure."

"I need to know what happened to them," said Ryan, leaning forward in his chair. "It should be impossible for me to look at them as victims, but I can't help feeling in some way they are. I simply can't accept they woke up one day wanting to be serial killers. How is that possible?"

Kristina sat for a moment looking at Ryan who had his eyes turned down to the floor. She knew he had risked a great deal to find her in the hopes of getting those answers. She decided it was time to give them. She decided to trust him.

"Not only is it possible, but probable," said Kristina, immediately grabbing his attention.

"Probable?"

"I told you one of the reasons why I left the Didache Project was because Colonel Brown was pressuring us to bypass the rules. There was another reason."

"Please continue," said Ryan. "Anything would help at this point."

"When I was asked to participate in the project, it was a scientist's dream come true. The Michaels Lab has unlimited funding and is on the cutting edge of genetic research. They're able to pick and choose the brightest minds in the field. That was the lure. After I accepted the position, I quickly discovered the reason why they had unlimited funding. They were under contract by the U.S. military to genetically enhance a soldier's ability in the field. The lab had several departments that actually did research in other areas, but the military side, the Didache Project, was their bread and butter."

"That doesn't sound very sinister," said Ryan. "In fact, I can support efforts to make soldiers more capable in combat. If I had a squad of Arringtons, more of my men may have survived the war."

"I agree with you," said Kristina. "I'm not opposed to making them faster, stronger, or even bulletproof. I'm not a bleeding heart liberal who believes all wars can be avoided by diplomatic intervention. What I am opposed to is genetically altering their behavior."

"You're going to have to dumb that one down for me. Genetically altered behavior?"

"How many of the men and women came back from the Gulf Wars clinically diagnosed with Post Traumatic Stress Disorder? Most of those diagnosed never saw a day of combat or even fired their weapon at the enemy. They suffered from PTSD because of what they saw and felt. They didn't know how to cope with the horrific images stamped into their memories of the aftermath. The burning bodies hanging out of tanks or laying on the side of the road. The women and children caught in the crossfire smoldering in each others' arms. Do you remember a course at the academy that taught you how to deal with those situations?"

"No," said Ryan. "I don't think anything can prepare you for those moments."

"But more importantly to the fat cats sitting thousands of miles away, what was the total cost of having to treat those soldiers with PTSD once it was recognized as a clinical illness?"

"My guess would be billions in treatment as well as a ton of lost man hours," offered Ryan.

"Exactly, billions for just PTSD," acknowledged Kristina. "Now, add the cost of all the psychological disorders recognized as a result of soldiers going into combat. And not only the diagnosed disorders, but the undiagnosed disorders. How many men did you know that suffered from depression, separation anxiety, loneliness, guilt, remorse, doubt, or even anger? How many did you know nearly paralyzed by fear? All those emotional factors are commonplace for the average soldier. All those emotional factors make a soldier less effective in the field.

"We were working on making them physically stronger as warriors. Colonel Brown wanted us to work on making them mentally stronger as well. And not just mentally stronger, but incapable of suffering from those common emotional stresses associated with being human."

"He wanted you to build the perfect killing machines," said Ryan. "A fearless warrior."

"No offense to your Marine background, but that's what every branch tries to do starting on the first day of boot camp," continued Kristina. "They want to tear you down emotionally and physically so they can rebuild and mold you into a killing machine that won't hesitate in combat. But they also want to build servicemen and women who will follow orders from above without question or doubt. Imagine if they could accomplish that goal every single time with just one session of gene therapy."

"It would be a very valuable pill," said Ryan.

"That's an understatement," said Kristina. "It wouldn't be as easy as giving them a pill, but you're in the ballpark. All that would be needed is a sample of their DNA. We'd then introduce the altered DNA in the form of a virus that would target specific cells in the brain that are linked to specific behaviors. The transformation would start within hours and be completed within two weeks."

"How close were you to creating it?"

"Uncomfortably close for me. I left the program a few weeks before the first round of trials."

"Human trials?"

"No," clarified Kristina. "We start the process on computer models. We had several programs designed to mimic human DNA and the reactions to any modifications. Once the models showed the desired result, we would upload the modified DNA into pigs. Believe it or not, they have the closest anatomy to a human of any animal, including primates."

"How do you modify the behavior of a pig?" asked Ryan.

"That I don't know. I left before they finished."

"How many other scientists were working on the Didache Project?"

"There were close to thirty with varying levels of skill, but there were four of us that spearheaded the research. The others mainly acted as technicians building the live samples and uploading them into the virus."

"So the other three are still there?"

"I believe they are, but Scott would know for sure," answered Kristina. "All three had IQs off the charts and their first PhDs before their twentieth birthdays."

"When did you get yours, if you don't mind me asking?"

"I was a late bloomer. My first was at twenty-two. Ryan, those guys have the answers."

Ryan looked at his buzzing phone. "I'm sorry, I need to take this." He stood up and walked into the hallway for privacy. It was Deputy Director Donaldson. A few moments later he returned to Kristina's room.

"They found Richard Elliot in an abandoned house in the Ninth Ward. I'm sorry, Kristina. It looks like he committed suicide."

"Oh, my God," whispered Kristina. "Ryan, we did that to him."

"No, Kristina, you didn't," said Ryan, trying to console her. "But I promise you I'm going to find out who did. I'll be back soon."

"I'll wait here," she said with a forced smile.

11

HARD TO SWALLOW

DEREK AND JOSHUA WERE WALKING back to their hotel room when the familiar wave of nearly unbearable pain hit them simultaneously. When Ryan put the first bullets into Peter Arrington, the pain started in their ribcages. As each subsequent bullet entered their doomed comrade, they felt each penetration. Nineteen rounds went into Arrington before the headshot ended his life.

They both ducked into an alleyway as the full force of the killing reached them. Joshua leaned against a brick wall to brace himself while Derek dropped to his hands and knees. They were both growling while clenching their teeth to keep from screaming in agony.

When the agents killed Arrington, the episode lasted nearly a minute. When Alex Tifton killed Richard Elliot, the episode only lasted fifteen seconds. Derek received his wish that Richard would die quickly. As blood dripped onto the ground from their noses, both men looked at each other, puzzled.

"It had to be Alex," said Joshua. "The feds didn't have time to mobilize their assault teams."

"How could he kill him?" asked Derek. "Those two were like brothers."

"They may have been like brothers, but the Colonel is more like Alex's father," explained Joshua. "That weak mind would do anything dear old dad told him to do."

"Alex just added himself to the list of people I'm going to kill slowly," said Derek.

"That list is getting pretty long," said Joshua.

"Not one name on it doesn't deserve to be there," said Derek. "The Colonel being on the top of that list. His brainiac puppet scientists who did this to us and the fucking fed hitmen that killed Peter are close behind. They all deserve to be on it."

"Patience, my young angry friend," said Joshua. "We didn't expect Alex to jump the gun and take Richard, but that only tells us the Colonel is getting sloppy. He's starting to panic. He's going to send every one of his henchmen, including Alex, and the feds to come after us in Atlanta. And when he does, we're going to show up at his front door in Maine. We'll arrive with a smile and plenty of time to work on him and every other white coat at the lab. Anyone that could even come close to slowing us down will be a thousand miles away chasing our fucking ghosts. Once we cut the head off the snake, Alex will be shitting his pants and running scared. It'll make doing him much sweeter."

"What's the plan after, Joshua? What the fuck are we going to do? Where are we going to go? They'll just keep sending guys after us."

"And we'll send them right back in fucking body bags. But we'll be doing it from a Caribbean island I plan on calling Joshualand. And every six weeks the natives will bring me a virgin sacrifice to keep their new god happy. Because they know what will happen if they don't."

"Jesus Christ, Joshua!" said Derek, taking a step back from him. "You want to stay this way? You want to keep killing women and tearing them apart? You want to keep puking up their blood? I've taken your sick comments and jokes with a grain of salt because I thought that's how you were coping with this, but now I wonder. I'm wondering if you like being this way."

Joshua took two steps closer to Derek. He didn't move towards him as an aggressor, he moved in closer so he could hold his undivided attention. Regardless of the intent, Derek stood his ground. He didn't always agree with Joshua's methods or ideology, but he knew the only way to destroy the people that destroyed them was as a team.

"It doesn't matter if I like being this way or not," said Joshua in a lowered voice. "I am what they made me and I can't change that. Even they can't change that. Either we accept what we are, or we end each other right now," said Joshua, offering his pistol to Derek. "I didn't enjoy killing those women, and I threw up their blood just like you. I tried to stop myself just like you. And just like you, I couldn't. So get off your high fucking horse and let's finish what they started. After they're gone, we'll figure out what to do next."

Derek reached out and pushed the pistol toward the ground. "Then stop acting like you enjoy this so much. Stop making me wonder what's going on in your head."

"That I can do, Derek. I didn't know it was bothering you so much. You're right, I do joke around because I don't know how else to deal with this. I'm sorry. You and I need to stick together. Running scared is what got Peter and Richard killed. We didn't ask for this, but they gave it to us anyway. Let's start giving a little back."

"Okay," said Derek. "We need to go home. Even those idiots should figure out it's where we're heading."

Ryan and Michelle arrived at the house where Richard Elliot had been hiding for months. Scott Wilson's team was there waiting for them. Ryan immediately noticed Scott looked nervous.

"Agent Pearson, Agent Dobbs," greeted Scott.

"This was a suicide?" asked Ryan.

"Apparently," said Scott. "The local police received an anonymous call that someone was squatting in the area. They saw a light coming from a shack behind this house. This place hasn't had electricity for years. They discovered four graves in the shack. One of them is very fresh. They found Richard inside the house. We haven't touched anything. We were waiting for you to get here."

"Well, that's quite a departure from the Virginia scene," said Ryan. "You guys wouldn't even let me in the door and handed me my hat as soon as you arrived."

"We're under orders to allow you to verify his identity and that he's dead. And that's all we'll need from you," said Scott, making a show in front of his team. "When you accomplish the task, you're to leave the scene so we can process the area. My men will accompany you inside. I need to make a phone call."

"Then I guess we need to get started," said Ryan.

The agents walked into the small house with four men dressed in black coveralls following close behind. They headed to the largest room dimly lit by battery-powered lanterns.

"Any chance we could get more light in here?" asked Ryan to one of his escorts.

"No, sir."

Ryan chuckled at his new friend as he and Michelle approached Richard's body positioned in a chair. A shotgun was between his legs, and what was left of his head was draped over the back of the chair. His brain, bone fragments, tissue, and blood covered the wall and ceiling behind him. The blast greatly distorted and reduced the anatomy of Richard's head, but there was enough left for a positive ID.

"Would you agree that's Richard Elliot?" asked Ryan's escort.

"I do."

"Would you agree Richard Elliot is dead?" asked the escort, writing down Ryan's response to the first question.

"I do."

"Thank you, Agent Pearson," he said, writing down the second answer. "Would you please wait outside while we process the scene?"

"Could we do this over the phone next time?" asked Ryan.

"No, sir. We needed you for this very important phase of the investigative process. And now we're finished with you."

Ryan took a step toward the young man wearing black coveralls. As the FBI agent towered nearly five inches over him, the young man tried to take a step backward. The wall prevented his retreat. "You have no idea how wrong you are, kid."

Ryan turned and walked out of the room.

"I think he likes you," added Michelle before she followed.

As they cleared the front porch, Scott Wilson passed them without a word. Dallas and Tom arrived on the scene and met Ryan in front of the house.

"What did we miss?" asked Dallas.

"One of the worst staged suicides I've seen in a while," said Ryan.

"Did you miss me?" asked Dallas as Michelle caught up.

"You were gone?" replied Michelle.

"Why do you think it was staged?" asked Tom.

"The obvious tells were his finger still on the trigger and the shotgun still between his legs," said Michelle. "The recoil would've at least knocked his finger away and probably the gun as well."

"He was also sitting in an old wooden chair in the middle of the room," added Ryan. "The shockwave from the blast would've laid him out on the floor. Of course, the second blood spatter that was poorly concealing the first helped a little, too. Unless he killed himself twice, I'd say he had some help."

"Like I said, these guys aren't pros," said Dallas. "And neither is Scott."

"Scott?" asked Ryan.

"When we pulled up, he was standing beside your car like a kid caught with his hand in the cookie jar," continued Tom. "He saw it was us and quickly headed toward the house. There was a large white envelope sitting in plain sight with your name on it. We tucked it under your seat."

"Did anyone else see him?"

"I don't think so," said Dallas. "All eyes were on us when we turned the corner. I killed the headlights as soon as I recognized Scott. I figured he was leaving another note. I don't think he went to spy school."

"No, I don't believe he did," said Ryan. "He's spooked about something. Okay, let's head back to the house and open our gift from Scott."

As they left the crime scene, Ryan dialed the director's number.

"Is he dead?"

"Yes, sir. Looks like he did it himself after he buried his last victim."

"I wish Derek and Joshua had followed his example, but they decided to take two more women instead. I just received a call from the Atlanta Field Office. Two bodies were discovered off a jogging trail at a state park a few hours ago. Both victims have our guys written all over them. We discovered two more went missing exactly six weeks ago just outside of the city. We're digging deeper to see if any others have gone missing in the past few months. It's our worst nightmare, but it looks like they're working together."

"Any news on the whereabouts of Dr. Anderson?"

"Nothing concrete, but we're assuming she's with Joshua in Georgia. I'm sending a plane that should be there in a few hours. You need to hit the ground running."

"Yes, sir," acknowledged Ryan, ending the call.

"We need to pack up the house and get ready to move."

"Where are we headed?" asked Dallas.

"Atlanta."

"Your home town."

"Sort of. I went to high school there my junior and senior year. I left for Virginia the week after I graduated. Our buddy Derek went to the same school as me, but he was a freshman when I was a senior. He actually grew up there. It's a little west of Atlanta. But we do actually know some of the same people."

"Yeah, I figured that's why they grabbed you up pretty quickly when this thing broke," said Dallas. "It's also kind of weird he joined the Marines and ended up in your old unit. It's like he was trying to follow in your footsteps."

"Lucky me," said Ryan.

They arrived back at the safe house and immediately headed for the windowless room. Everyone wanted to get a look at the autopsy reports from each of Peter Arrington's victims. The similarities and patterns were obvious as soon as the files were spread out on the table.

"They're all blond with blue eyes," observed Tom. "Between 120 and 140 pounds. All very attractive young women."

"And all killed the same way," continued Michelle. "Large holes in their necks apparently from bites. Larger holes in the abdomen with –"

"With organs missing," finished Ryan.

"He's eating them?" asked Dallas with a grimace.

"And bleeding them dry," continued Tom. "Each victim is also missing about two-thirds of her blood volume. Some of the organs were returned inside the abdominal cavity with bite marks, but very little missing tissue; however, they were drained of blood as well."

"You're telling me they're fucking vampires?" asked Dallas, holding the painful expression.

"No, I'm not telling you they're vampires, Dallas," clarified Tom. "Vampires don't exist. What I am telling you is that he's taking their blood. We just don't know why."

"Cannibalism isn't breaking news," added Michelle. "Those types of serial killers are rare, but unlike vampires, they do exist."

"Many, if not most, serial killers take some type of trophy from their victims," said Tom. "Physically holding on to something belonging to the deceased helps them remember and relive the moment. Some take objects such as a driver's license, jewelry or keys. A lesser number actually take parts ranging from snippets of hair to the entire head. I don't know of any who have taken such a large volume of blood, but I'm not willing to rule out anything at this point.

"More than likely it's being kept in a container of some kind and not ingested. Even a small amount of human blood is at least extremely irritating to the digestive tract. Ingesting a large amount would surely make them violently ill."

"What's interesting is that, even though the wounds are large and numerous, there seems to be little indication of anger or rage."

"Once again, Tom, you're losing me," said Dallas.

"Like that's hard to do?" jabbed Michelle with a smile.

"Seriously, he bit a hole in her neck, chewed on her liver, and drained her blood. How is that not an indication of anger or rage?"

"Take wild animals as an example for perspective," started Tom. "I'm sure you've seen countless National Geographic episodes showing lions hunting prey in Africa."

"Now I'm with you," said Dallas.

"When most people see the lion take down an antelope, all they hear is the roar and see the violence of the kill. What they don't see is that it's all about efficiency and self-preservation. It has nothing to do with anger. The lion goes for the throat because it's the fastest way to cut off air to the lungs and blood to the brain. Going for the throat quickly disables the prey. It may look like a defenseless animal, but if the lion didn't kill it quickly, the antelope has very powerful legs and sharp hooves that could tear the lion open. My point is, wild animals have no desire to inflict pain on their prey. They kill for survival."

"Arrington killed those women for survival?" asked Dallas.

"In his mind, maybe," said Michelle. "But what Tom is saying is that Arrington's primary focus was blood, not pain. Killers are violent. They get off on the control and the pain they inflict on the victim. The wounds on these women seem to be created with the sole function of efficiently extracting their blood."

"Absolutely," said Tom. "The only other injuries listed are ligature marks on the wrists and ankles. But even those are mild. They weren't bound so tight as to cut off circulation. They were bound to keep them stationary. There's no other bruising or abrasions on their bodies. There's hardly a scratch on them other than the neck and abdomen wounds."

"It makes sense the first wound would be a major artery in the neck," said Michelle. "It's the easiest to access with a bite. It would've supplied a tremendous volume before the heart stopped. And when it did stop pumping, it makes sense he would go for the organs engorged with blood, like the liver."

"This is all fascinating stuff, really," said Dallas. "But what are we trying to accomplish here? Is what you're talking about going to help us find the others? There are two more monsters out there we need to find and stop before they kill again. Does it really matter how or why they're doing it? I'd just like to know where they are so we can scratch the last two off the list."

"I understand what you're saying, Dallas," said Ryan.

"You do?" asked Michelle.

"I do. But, Dallas, what we've accomplished here is figuring out Arrington didn't brutally rape and murder that woman in Syracuse. But people wanted us to believe he did. That tells me without a shadow of doubt we're in the middle of a conspiracy, and we're being used like puppets to cover it up. The more we find out about these monsters they obviously want us to kill, the closer I get to finding out who's pulling our strings."

"I agree with you, Ryan," said Tom. "This goes much deeper than just apprehending four UA Marines on a killing spree. We know they were genetically altered at the lab to make them super soldiers and something went wrong. I can wrap my head around one man snapping, but not four at the same time. What we need to figure out is what happened to them and who did it. We have our theories, but proving it is going to be incredibly difficult."

"It will be unless we can find the scientists who put their hands on them," said Ryan. "Kristina told me there were three main players at the lab. They were working on some high-speed creepy stuff before she left. Those are the guys with the answers."

"Being the guys with the answers, they're going to be on short leashes by the guys who don't want them talking," said Dallas. "How do we get to them?"

"It won't be easy, but we already have a guy on the inside," said Ryan with a grin.

12.

UNIT 731

THE TEAM PACKED ITS GEAR and was ready to move in less than thirty minutes. They still had over an hour before the plane would arrive to take them to Atlanta. Ryan walked out onto the back porch for some air. After a few minutes, Tom joined him on the deck.

"You need some alone time, Boss?" asked Tom.

"No," said Ryan. "Just out here finding myself asking the same question over and over."

"What's that?"

"Why? Why would they do that to those Marines? Why did they turn them into monsters and then turn them loose on the public? And then once that happened, why use us to hunt and kill them?"

"Tough questions, Ryan. But some of those answers can be found in the history of biomedical human research. I'm sure you're familiar with the atrocities committed by the Nazis and the Japanese Army during the thirties and forties, but are you familiar with our own?"

"No, but that's why I have your big brain on the team. You have to compensate for my little one."

"I know you're not serious," said Tom. "Anyway, in 1932, the U.S. Public Health Service recruited 400 underprivileged African-Americans with syphilis to participate in a study. They called it the Tuskegee Syphilis Experiment, and its main purpose was to study the untreated progression of the disease. Now, at the time, there was no known cure. Where it became a serious question of ethics was when penicillin was discovered in 1940. It did effectively cure the disease, but it wasn't administered to the Tuskegee recruits. The U.S. Government basically let those people suffer and die even though a cure was available. They continued the experiment until 1974 when someone finally blew the whistle and leaked the project to the press. By then the victims included the men who died, their wives who contracted the disease, and their children who were born with congenital syphilis. All of that happened under the direct supervision of Uncle Sam."

"That's barbaric," said Ryan. "You're right, I didn't know."

"And really, that's just the tip of the iceberg. But if there's a bright side to that dark time in our history, it would be the immediate formation of the Office for Human Research Protections, or OHRP. Those are the guys providing the ethical oversight which mirrors the powers and responsibilities of the FDA. Those are the guys that are keeping an eye on what's happening at the Michaels Laboratory. Like Kristina told us, the Marines had to sign consent forms before any procedure could be performed on them. Those consent forms are mandated and reviewed by the OHRP."

"Obviously, they're not keeping that close of an eye on the lab," said Ryan.

"Obviously," said Tom. "But the OHRP is a very small department within the much larger Department of Health and Human Services. They probably have no idea something went wrong. And even if they did, they may not know the extent. And even if they knew the extent, the individuals or group responsible may not even be prosecuted."

"Not prosecuted?" asked Ryan, perplexed. "People have been murdered. How could they possibly not be prosecuted?"

"From 1932 until the end of World War II, Unit 731 of the Japanese Army conducted gruesome experiments on thousands of prisoners," continued Tom. "It included vivisection, which means dissecting them while they were still alive. They were opened up and exposed to numerous deadly bacteria and viruses so the scientists could watch the deterioration of the internal organs and tissues. The unit was headed by Shiro Ishi who was a lieutenant general and microbiologist. After the Japanese surrender in 1945, General Douglas MacArthur offered immunity from any prosecution to Ishi and his entire unit. All they had to do was turn over the results of those experiments. And, of course, they did."

"That's insane," said Ryan. "Our government condoned the murdering of our own POWs?"

"Now, that's where it gets a little tricky," said Tom. "They didn't condone it, but they understood the value of the data in those results. It catapulted our own discovery of vaccinations and treatments which has arguably saved millions of American lives and even more around the world."

"Tom, you can't seriously believe the ends justified the means."

"Not at all, Ryan. I'm just warning you what we've stumbled across in this case may not see the outcome you're looking for. We're going down a very slippery slope, and I worry that you're sliding down it faster than you need to be."

"You don't think I should concern myself with finding those answers, do you?"

"I think we should concern ourselves more with stopping Derek and Joshua," said Tom.

"What are you really trying to tell me, Tom?" asked Ryan with a disarming smile.

"I saw the way you reacted when you lost the two agents at the farmhouse. And the way you reacted is the way a good leader should. You felt responsible. But you also felt responsible for the woman Arrington killed in front of us. And neither situation was your fault."

"Tom, I'm not cutting you off this time. Just say what's on your mind."

"I don't think it's a good idea to split up again and go to Maine looking for the other scientists. I think we may be putting the cart before the horse. Dallas may not completely understand the science or the politics involved, but he does understand the importance of stopping the other two. Powerful agencies and billions of dollars are at stake if it's discovered our own military created serial killers in a lab and then proceeded to unleash them onto the public. If we tip our hand now we're on to them, we're out of the game. And there isn't a better team out there that plays this game.

"I know you want those answers so you can go back to the families of the victims, including the two agents that died, and give them closure. I want the same thing, but there's more at stake now. We're getting a little overwhelmed here, and our resources are at critical mass. What would happen to Kristina if we were pulled from the case? Who would protect her? Would she have to run and hide forever?"

"Okay, Tom," conceded Ryan. "Okay. We'll focus on finding Derek and Joshua. All of us."

"I hope you understand –"

"Tom," Interrupted Ryan. "I do. And thank you. It's another reason why I put you on this team."

"What's that?" asked Tom.

"Helping me to keep my priorities in order. I appreciate that, Tom. I really do."

"Anytime, Boss."

"Speaking of our little hostage, I need to go talk to Kristina. We'll head to the airport when I get back. Our plane should be there shortly."

"Understood."

Ryan made his way back to the house Kristina had called home for nearly a week. He started laughing to himself as he approached the back door. He started laughing after he thought about leaving her in New Orleans with the security team Steve had assigned to the house. He needed her help in Atlanta, but he also knew she'd be safer the farther away she was from the action. Both Derek and Joshua would be there, and he also knew Colonel Brown was going to send every thug he had on his payroll. Knowing another FBI team was probably on its way to Georgia with the sole purpose of hunting her down, Ryan had to think hard about dragging her back into harm's way. He was laughing because he realized he had become another one of those men in her life who wanted to protect her.

He walked in the house and found Steve sitting in the same spot at the kitchen table reading a book. "Nobody can accuse you of not being vigilant. Alison would kill me if she knew I was the reason you weren't home."

"No, she's probably going to kill you for being in town and not stopping by to see her or the kids," said Steve.

"Are you going to turn me in?"

"Not if you promise to come back and visit them for more than a few minutes."

"Deal."

"How'd it go out there?" asked Steve.

"Staged suicide, but the end result is that we're done here. They're pointing us to Atlanta where it looks like Derek and Joshua are in cahoots. We're leaving in a few. Is that a fresh pot of coffee?"

"Very. I'll take a cup, too."

He poured their coffees and sat with him at the table. Steve put his book down. Ryan noticed the title. It was Kristina's beloved copy of *Treasure Island*.

"I see she's got you hooked on the classics," said Ryan.

"Yo-ho-ho and a bottle of rum," sang Steve. "Did you know this is a first edition?" he said, patting the cover.

"I know she has a significant connection with it," said Ryan. "I overheard her talking about how her father read it to her when she was a child."

"Yeah, she mentioned that after handing it over to me. She said I looked bored sitting down here by myself, and it would keep me company. This book is probably worth close to 20,000 dollars, and she just handed it over so I could enjoy it."

"Sounds like you two are getting along well."

"Oh, we are," said Steve with a sly smile. "Especially when she found out you and I have a long history together."

"I'm not sure what that means."

"It means Alison's right, you are hopeless. But it also means Kristina is a very sweet girl. I think being so intelligent, driven, and beautiful intimidates most people, but especially men. How somebody hasn't swept her off her feet is beyond me. Anyway, there's just something about her that makes you want to look after her."

"You're not kidding," said Ryan. "When the bad guy was chasing after her in the alley, I probably didn't need to smash his face in with a metal trash can lid. But I wanted him to feel it, you know? I wanted him to remember that moment."

"Have you ever tried candy or flowers, buddy?" asked Steve.

"You're a funny guy. Listen, I hate to ask for any more favors, but –"

"Consider it done," said Steve, anticipating the question. "I have an office in Atlanta with some great guys running the show. They'll set up a secure house before she arrives. We'll look after her here for a couple of days while you get settled in. If they want her, they'll have to get through us. And that ain't easy, my friend."

"No, I imagine it isn't," said Ryan. "Thank you. Uncle Sam will be cutting you some checks if I don't get myself killed or sent to prison when this is over."

"Who do you think paid for the houses and the jet?"

"Good point."

"She's still awake. You should tell her you're leaving and return this with my thanks," said Steve, handing him the book. "I'm going to head home shortly."

Ryan and Steve talked for a few more minutes and finished their coffees before he headed upstairs to Kristina's room. He stopped short of her doorway and looked at the cover of the book. Most people wouldn't let something so expensive out of their sight, but she gladly gave it to a virtual stranger so he could enjoy its pages. He thought about the men in Baltimore who tried to hurt her, and it made him angry. He shook off the emotion and knocked on the open door.

"You should really try to get some sleep," he said.

"I can say the same for you."

"Well, that probably won't be happening anytime soon. We believe Derek and Joshua are together in Atlanta. My team and I will be leaving for Georgia shortly. Oh, Steve asked me to return this with his thanks," said Ryan, handing her the book.

She stroked the cover gently and sat quietly for a moment. "I love where these stories can take you. After only a few pages, I'm sailing with Captain Flint and Long John Silver along the Spanish Main. For a few hours, I can escape with the characters to the wonderful chaos of their world and leave the confusion of mine."

"That does sound appealing," said Ryan.

"I do have to admit," said Kristina with a smile, "I can't remember ever having so much time to just sit and read. When I don't think about why I'm here, it's the closest thing to a vacation I've had in years."

"I have to say your ability to adapt is impressive. I don't know anyone who would think being stuck in this house with a bunch of intense-looking watchmen is a vacation."

"Actually, these guys are great and very doting. I can't tell you how many times a day they ask if I need anything or if they can do something for me."

"Well, the feeling is definitely mutual. I think these guys are used to protecting old, rich, fat, extremely paranoid, and demanding businessmen. All things which you're not."

"Thank you, I think?"

"I'm sorry," said Ryan. "It's been a long couple of days. I think a few hours of sleep would do me good."

She paused for a moment, looking down at the floor. "Was it suicide?"

He didn't hesitate with his answer. "No, he was killed and then the scene was staged to look like he did it himself. I'm not sure who did it, but I am sure it happened fast."

"Did anybody care?" asked Kristina, raising her head to look at Ryan. "Or was everyone glad the monster was dead?"

She was trying to be strong, but was losing her battle to hold back tears. He never wanted to see her cry again.

"Me," said Ryan. "I care. And so does my team."

"I know you do," said Kristina, wiping her cheeks. "I'm sorry."

"Listen, I don't think I've ever thanked you for what you're doing. We've taken your life and turned it upside down, and all I've done is ask you to trust me. I want to thank you for doing just that."

"You're very welcome," she said, regaining her composure. "But you haven't turned my life upside down. It's more like you saved it."

Ryan fought off the usual protocol of remaining professionally, and physically, distant from civilians involved in a case. He sat next to her on the bed.

"I think the reason why it seems I've adapted so well is because I'm not surprised this is happening," she said. "I left the project over six months ago, but I was constantly looking over my shoulder. I knew they were about to cross the line, and it was only a matter of time before the technology superseded their humanity. I should've seen it coming. I should've left years ago, but the work we were doing was groundbreaking. It was incredible. I also felt like somebody needed to be there who actually cared about the test subjects. Someone that didn't look at them as guinea pigs the way the Colonel did. Someone that would make sure they knew exactly what was being done to them."

"Someone like you," said Ryan. "The funny thing is, they probably thought they were looking out for you, but the reality is that you were looking out for them. And what makes you more impressive is that you still are."

"I left them behind, Ryan," said Kristina with a slight quiver in her voice. "In my useless protest of quitting, I let the Colonel win. I let the Colonel take them and turn them into murderers."

"You couldn't have possibly known this was going to happen," said Ryan, reassuring her. "If you did, you never would've left them. I know that. The Colonel would've found a way around you, regardless of your attempts to keep them safe. I believe he sent those men in Baltimore to keep you quiet."

"You know, it really is true about having the feeling of being watched," said Kristina. "I've had it every day since I quit the lab until you showed up at the bookstore. I told you before, most of the men in my life feel like they need to protect me. The difference is, I believe you actually can."

"Take advantage of the next few days and get some rest," said Ryan, becoming uncomfortable being so close. "You may not have much time for that when you join us in Atlanta."

"Okay. Take care of yourself, Ryan."

"I'll see you soon."

Ryan walked downstairs to find Steve putting on his jacket and grabbing his keys. He said good-bye to his old friend and made it to the backdoor before he stopped and turned around.

"Steve."

"Yeah, buddy."

"Nothing bad happens to her. Do you understand?"

"Not on my watch, shipmate. And yeah, I do understand," said Steve with a grin.

13

BROKEN PROMISES

DEREK AND JOSHUA ARRIVED IN Atlanta several hours after Ryan's team landed. Joshua dropped Derek off at one of the three locations they used as hideouts. They spent a week at one and then moved to another, but never with each other. They only met when plans needed to be discussed. Joshua continued to the hideout located in the North Georgia Mountains a little over an hour outside of the city. Derek occupied the house on the south side of town.

When Joshua arrived, he only spent a few minutes in the house before he left again. A quick shower and change of clothes was all he needed to feel re-energized after the long drive. He was overcome with a familiar urge that wasn't genetically introduced by the scientists at the lab. It hit him when he drove through a small college town less than twenty minutes from his lair.

He was stopped at one of the two traffic lights when a young woman from the college was walking toward a local music venue. The twenty-something-year-old blonde wearing a short skirt and small tank top caught his eye. She crossed in front of him, not noticing his stare. The light turned green, but Joshua didn't accelerate through the intersection until he was sure she went inside the popular bar. He didn't want to draw attention from local law enforcement, so he resisted the urge to speed home. But he wasted no time returning to town.

He parked across the street from Danny's Pub with an unobstructed view of the front entrance. He barely moved in his seat for over three hours waiting for her to leave the bar. He only broke his patient stare for a few seconds when a group of drunken frat boys walked past his window. None of them noticed the danger.

His prize stumbled out of the doorway being helped by a young man. Joshua could feel the boy's perverted thoughts as she giggled, missing the last step down to the sidewalk and falling into Romeo's arms. She only slightly regained her composure as they walked together toward the campus.

A few hundred yards from the false safety of the dorm, the two preoccupied students had to pass by an unlit alley between two old brick buildings. Joshua easily covered the distance running silently at thirty miles an hour from where he parked the car at the end of the alley. He made little attempt to conceal himself in the shadows of the deserted town square. As he lay in wait, he thought about what was going through the young escort's mind as the dorm rooms came into his view. He chuckled to himself, knowing there was nothing the couple could do to change its destiny. He became lightheaded swimming in his own hyper-inflated sense of his new undeniable powers.

The furthest thing from his mind was being stopped. He knew his fingerprints and DNA wouldn't be in any law enforcement forensic databases. The Colonel literally erased the identity and history of all the Marines who volunteered for Didache. When the Colonel dug deep into Joshua's past, he discovered a juvenile arrest record sealed by the courts. The discovery was made several weeks after the first round of gene therapy was introduced to the volunteers. Pulling Joshua from the program would set them back nearly two months. It was critical that all the test subjects maintain the same therapy schedule. Removing one would necessitate starting over. Starting over at that point would have cost the program millions. Colonel Brown not only resealed Joshua's records, he had them destroyed.

The child psychologist assigned to Joshua's case wrote nearly fifty pages of notes about the offender's violent and sexually deviant behavior. The first occurrence dated back to a week after Joshua's tenth birthday. He forced two of the neighborhood children to undress and perform sexual acts on each other while he watched. When the seven-year-old girl refused to let the eight- year-old boy insert a toy inside her, Joshua choked her until she fell unconscious on the floor. The boy did nothing to stop him out of fear of the same punishment. Joshua then finished the game.

The girl never told her parents about the assault. He was caught after the eight-year-old boy tried to play the same game at school during recess. The new offender told the teacher where he learned the rules. After Joshua successfully completed his mandatory therapy, his family moved out of the county.

At an early age, Joshua had an advanced understanding of how to manipulate others into following his orders. He excelled at instilling fear in the young impressionable minds to avoid further interruption from meddling adults. For years after his first exposure to the thrill of controlling others, his games accelerated and evolved into sadistic rituals. Each successful engagement propelled him deeper into the darkness of a young sociopath. He became a master at using manipulation, fear, and punishment as tools to convince others to participate as his pawns. He rarely incriminated himself by being an active player in the games. He preferred to direct the action.

Three weeks before his fourteenth birthday, he was temporarily out of the game. He convinced three classmates to sneak out after dark and meet him in an abandoned cabin in the state park near his home. The two boys and sole girl showed up as ordered. Joshua drugged the girl with over-the-counter sleeping pills his mother kept in ample supply. He stripped and bound her face down on a mattress he had brought the day before in preparation for the event. He directed one of the boys to place a dog choker around her neck. He was told to pull back hard on the leash while he raped her. When the second boy was ready for his turn, the young girl started to regain consciousness. Joshua instructed him to pull even harder until she stopped fighting. He followed each command without question.

Two hours into the assault, a park ranger on patrol noticed a light coming from the old deserted cabin. When he entered, he saw the second boy on top of the motionless girl yanking hard on the leash. The ranger was so fixated on the assault he didn't notice Joshua quickly swallow several of the sleeping pills and fake being unconscious in a chair. The girl had been dead for nearly an hour.

All three were arrested for the murder of the fourteen-year-old girl, but Joshua was able to convince authorities he was a victim as well. There was no physical evidence he participated in the rape and murder. Test results showed he was drugged with the same substance as the victim, leaving reasonable doubt he had anything to do with the crime. The prosecution couldn't legally introduce any of the evidence from the prior offense when Joshua was ten. The community wasn't as easily convinced of his innocence, and the family was once again forced to move. Leaving the county didn't satisfy the locals. Joshua's parents didn't resist the pressure and quickly moved out of the state.

Joshua looked at the move as a fresh start and immediately began the recruitment of players shortly after the family settled in their new home. He learned a great deal from his previous brushes with the law and honed his skills of deception and discretion. His juvenile records were sealed when he turned eighteen.

On his birthday, his parents gave him a gift of a two-week vacation to Miami with several of his friends. He returned home to discover his key no longer fit the lock on the front door. When he peered inside a window, all of the furniture was gone. Joshua may have deceived the authorities, but his parents weren't as easily fooled. As soon as their legal obligation to allow him to live in their home was satisfied, they did their best to forget the pure evil they created.

With little money and no home, Joshua had very few options for survival in his new world. A few of his friends were looking forward to careers in the military and encouraged him to join. When his pockets were empty, he decided to join the Marines.

He soon discovered the military embraced his naturally aggressive behavior. For the first year, the lack of boredom removed the threat of pent up aggression turning into criminal violence. He easily displayed a deceptive respect for authority and excelled in the Corps. He scored high on both physical and mental aptitude tests and earned a position with the 2nd Special Operations Battalion.

Early into his second year, he was unable to suppress his sexually deviant behavior, but the Corps unknowingly had an answer for that problem as well. With extensive travel to underdeveloped countries, Joshua found an almost limitless supply of local women to assault with little worry of being caught by equally underdeveloped law enforcement. He no longer needed to live out his fantasies through manipulation of others. He'd wait patiently until the unit was scheduled to leave a foreign country before taking his victims. By the time the bodies were discovered, if they were discovered, he'd be safe back on American soil.

The new environment and rules to his games allowed for the rapid escalation of violence and brutality. Being left unchecked, the first murder was easy. Once he tasted the sweet completion of the game by taking a life, the result had to be achieved every time before he could feel satisfied.

The Marine Corps became the perfect incubator to cultivate his antisocial personality disorder. When Colonel Brown approached his unit with the promise of greatly enhancing their ability to hunt and kill the enemy, Joshua jumped at the opportunity. He thought about his great fortune handed to him courtesy of the U.S. Government as the young couple stepped closer to its doom.

Their senses and reaction time, slowed considerably by the booze, made it easy for Joshua to step out of the shadows directly in front of them. Before they could adjust their stride, he simultaneously punched both in the stomach using only a fraction of his strength. They crumpled to the ground, unable to catch their breath, and unable to scream for help. Joshua calmly picked up the petite girl under his arm and carried the six-foot-two athlete by the back of his belt. When he returned to the car, he bound their hands and feet with plastic zip ties and duct taped their mouths. The boy made the mistake of trying to fight off the predator and was easily knocked unconscious. Joshua whistled during the drive to his hideout, occasionally looking in the rear view mirror at his prize. He whistled louder as each mile passed, bringing him closer to the playground.

Anne was a senior at the college and Brad was two years behind her. He'd been waiting anxiously for the moment he could possibly hook up with the gorgeous blonde. He regained consciousness as the car turned off the country asphalt onto dirt. A few minutes later, the car stopped in front of a large plantation style home. It had been on the market for nearly three years, but the last prospective buyer drove away six months earlier. The next closest occupied house was nearly a mile away on the other side of a small mountain. They were completely isolated.

Joshua grabbed them both by the hair and dragged them from the car into the house. He wasted no time throwing Brad down a set of stairs leading to the basement with no windows and thick boards covering the only door to freedom. He held on to Anne as he lit a lantern to guide him down the stairs. He didn't want to toss her on top of Brad and run the risk of damaging her before he was ready. The lantern cast disorienting shadows along the stairwell wall as he carried her down to her fate. He dropped her on the hard ground and set the lantern on a long workbench. He turned up the flame to illuminate the rest of the cavernous room. Her red swollen eyes turned upward when she saw the medieval torture chamber he had created in the bowels of the house. She was silently begging God to save her life.

Joshua shackled Brad to a yoke he suspended with ropes from the ceiling. Two more shackles were anchored to the ground at his feet. With a tug on a chain, the yoke jerked violently upward, nearly dislocating both his arms. His muffled scream under the duct tape signaled to Joshua that he had achieved adequate tension on the rig. He didn't bother to tie Anne to the metal table he set up in the center of the room. He cut through her restraints, releasing her arms and legs. He held on to the back of her neck and forced her on her knees in front of Brad. He ripped the tape off both their mouths.

"What do you want with us!" yelled Brad, terrified.

"I want you to listen to me," said Joshua calmly. "If you speak again without my permission, I'll cut off one of your fingers for every word." He held up a pair of heavy-duty shears. "If you use more than ten, I'll start working on your toes. If you use more than twenty, I'll take your ears, nose, and lips. Twenty-four words and your tongue comes out. Most lose a few fingers. A few got all the way to the tongue. Of course, they didn't speak English, so they were at a slight disadvantage learning the rules. But they all eventually figured it out. How many cuts until you learn the rules?"

Silence was held in the basement as Joshua stared into Brad's eyes. "Good boy. Now, what's your name?"

"Brad, sir."

"Sir. Oh, yes, I forgot it's a military college," said Joshua with a sideways smile. "Would you believe I'm a Marine, Brad?"

"No, sir," said Brad, shaking. "I mean, yes, sir. Fuck, I don't know who you are and I don't care. I won't tell anyone about this place. I swear to God! Please, just let me go!"

"That's a bunch of unauthorized words, Brad," said Joshua, reaching up to his thumb with the shears.

"I'm sorry, I'm sorry!"

"You're lucky I'm in a good mood. Do you understand the game better now?"

"Yes, sir, absolutely."

He looked down at Anne who was trembling, but still trying to hold back her hysteria. "And who do we have here? Such a beautiful girl. I bet you have a beautiful name."

"Anne," she said, crying.

"Oh, that is a beautiful name," said Joshua, pulling her to her feet. "Is it okay if I call you Princess Anne?"

"Yes, sir," she said, quickly grasping the rules.

"Brad, did you think you were going to fuck Princess Anne tonight?"

"No, no, sir. She's just a friend."

"Oh, come on now, Brad. Look at her. You wouldn't fuck her? Are you gay? Are you a fag?"

No, sir, I'm not gay. It's just that I didn't expect anything from her tonight. I was only going to walk her to her dorm room and that's it, I swear!"

"I'm not her goddamned father, Brad. But the same rules apply when you lie to me. For every word of the lie, I'll take a piece of you. Now, were you going to try and fuck Princess Anne tonight?" asked Joshua brandishing the shears and stepping closer to him.

"Yes, sir. I was going to try. I've been trying for over a year. I'm sorry, Anne."

"That's better, Brad. But you don't need to apologize to her. She's known you've been trying since the first day you met her. That's how whores operate. They know, but they keep you dangling on the line while they suck every other dick on campus. When they finally drain every other guy dry and get bored, they might consider giving it up to you. Does that piss you off, Brad? Remember, only honest answers."

"It does, sir. I know she's been with two other guys in my frat. They could give a shit about her. She was just a piece of ass to them. I actually care about her. I really wanted to date her, but she kept blowing me off."

"Oh, no, Brad. She was blowing them, not you. She knew you cared, but that's when they put you in their pocket. They know you'd do anything for them, and they'll wait until they need something from you. They'll let you stare at their tits through a small tank top or let you buy their drinks all night long, but they'll never date you. She'll just bleed you dry and fuck your entire frat house before she lets a guy like you even touch her."

"Princess Anne, were you going to give it up to Brad tonight?"

"No, sir. I like him as a friend, but I wouldn't date him."

"Good, Princess. Good, honest answer," said Joshua. "Obviously, you want to keep your fingers and toes."

"Yes, sir, I do."

"Did he pay for your drinks tonight?"

"Yes, sir, he did."

"Brad, do you understand now that she was never going to date or fuck you? Do you understand she was going to use you and bleed you dry?"

"Yes, sir," said Brad, with a hint of anger. "I understand now. She was just using me."

"Good, Brad. You're doing so well. Here's where we start having some fun," said Joshua, putting Anne back on her knees and walking up close to Brad.

"Just follow my lead," he whispered in Brad's ear. "You and I are a team now. We're going to make it through this together. You and I are going to change everything. You're going to take from her what she would never give you. You're going to take what you deserve. Are you with me, Brad? Do you understand?"

"I do," he whispered.

He stepped back to Anne and pulled her up again. He started cutting her skirt with the shears and continued up through her tank top until she stood shaking in her bra and panties. He stood behind her for a moment, staring at Brad as tears were streaming down her face. Brad's eyes were fixated on her body. In that moment, he knew Brad would do anything he told him to do to her. He cut through the back of her bra and tore off her panties. He began to whisper in her ear.

"Fight him. He's going to try and rape you, but fight him off. He'll pay for it, I promise. Do you understand, Anne? You'll live if you fight him off."

"I understand," said Anne. "I want to live. I'll do whatever you want me to do."

Joshua left her standing naked in front of Brad. He unshackled his feet and grabbed the shackles on his wrists.

"Look at her," he whispered. "She has an amazing body, doesn't she?"

"Yes, sir, she does," he whispered back.

"You can do anything you want to that body. She won't be able to stop you, Brad. Pay her back for using you. Pay her back for teasing you then fucking all your friends. It's your turn now. I want you to fuck her."

"I can't –"

Before he could finish his sentence, Joshua grabbed two of Brad's fingers on his left hand and easily severed them with the shears. Brad tensed as soon as he heard the snapping of his bones, but didn't scream until Joshua threw them on the floor in front of him. Anne didn't make a sound or try to run. She was paralyzed with fear. Joshua let Brad scream for a moment, but ended the noise with a punch to his stomach.

"Enough, Brad," said Joshua. "The Princess here is going to think you're a pussy."

"Now, where were we?" asked Joshua. "Oh, yes, I was telling you to fuck her. And then you said –?"

"I will, I will," coughed Brad.

"That's my boy," said Joshua, wrapping his bleeding fingers in gauze. "When I release you, take off your clothes and get to work. Bend her over the table and show her no mercy. If she fights you, fight her back. If you make it hurt, you'll live, I promise. Do you understand? If you hurt her, you'll live."

"I understand," exhaled Brad. "I'll hurt her."

He released Brad from the shackles. For a brief moment, Joshua didn't know what Brad would do. He was free to run up the stairs, but he didn't. Joshua smiled when he ran straight at Anne who immediately attempted to kick him, but missed. Brad didn't hesitate to punch her hard in the face. She stumbled back against the metal table, dazed and bleeding from her nose. She swung her arms wildly, but her watering eyes made it difficult to focus on the blurry attacker. He grabbed her under her arms and turned her over onto the table. In spite of the pain of losing two fingers, Brad quickly became erect. He knew his life depended on it.

"Fight him, Princess! Fight him off of you!" yelled Joshua, ringside. "Come on, Brad, don't let that little whore kick your ass!"

She pounded her fist on the metal table and screamed as Brad penetrated her. She struggled and kicked, but couldn't get him off of her. He yanked her hair, causing her to scream louder. They were both fighting for their lives as Joshua stood behind them laughing at the show.

He could no longer restrain himself and began to hyperventilate. He welcomed the pain of the transformation as his hands started to mutate. The blood drained from his face, unveiling the pale, almost translucent skin covering the swelling blue veins. He pulled out his front teeth and opened his mouth wide as fangs pushed through his gums.

He lunged at Brad, sinking his teeth into the soft flesh of his neck while forcing his clawed hands deep into his back. His fangs hooked and ripped through both his jugular vein and carotid artery. Blood erupted from the large wound and sprayed several feet across the room. Death was almost instantaneous. The last vision of Brad's young life was the grotesque silhouette of the monster Joshua had become as he was tossed aside like human garbage.

Anne attempted to turn and look at Joshua, but he slammed her head into the table. It was his turn. He buried his claws into her ribcage while he brutally raped her. He leaned down and tore into her spine at the base of her neck with his powerful jaws. She stopped screaming and went limp when her cord was severed from his bite. He continued to force himself inside her until he was satisfied, several minutes after her heart stopped beating.

14

THE VIGILANT

DEREK PARKED NEARLY A MILE away from her house. He planned out his route days in advance. He walked along the most dimly lit roads leading to the woods near the house. When there was an absence of vehicles on the road, he would run. Derek wouldn't hit his top speed of forty miles an hour, but he would sprint fast enough to close the distance without drawing attention from any possible witnesses. It was one o'clock in the morning and a bad time to call attention. When he approached an occupied home or a car, he would slow to a casual walk.

It only took him a few minutes to reach the woods leading him to her back door. With only a quarter mile left and clear trails lit by a full moon, his twenty-mile-an-hour pace quickly brought him to the creek bordering the back of her property. He concealed himself in the creek bed and waited.

The hour was late, but he could see the back deck was lit with Tiki torches and candles. He heard soft music coming from the house. She usually went out with friends on Friday nights and afterwards would sit alone for a few cocktails in the peaceful setting. Two thickets of woods isolated her backyard from each neighbor. Derek thought about how dangerous it was for such an attractive woman to be cut off from help if a stalker were to make her his target. He chuckled at the irony as he crouched along the bank. Only a few minutes passed before she appeared.

She walked by the large French doors while moving towards the kitchen. In the summer heat of Atlanta, she only wore a thin robe barely reaching the top of her thigh. Standing in front of the kitchen window, he watched her pour a drink and heard her turn up the music. He knew she'd be going outside to the unprotected deck in a matter of seconds.

Derek scanned the area, trying not to let his excitement bring down his guard. No movement or sound came from any direction. The still air assisted his ability to hear a twig snap underneath a human foot for hundreds of yards in any direction. Like Joshua, nothing would stop him from taking his prize.

She walked out onto the deck and danced over to a chair. She held her drink in the air as she continued the dance while sitting. She swayed back and forth as her strawberry blonde hair brushed her shoulders. She was oblivious to the monster crouched at the creek less than fifty feet away.

He could've easily shot out from the darkness to take her while she was distracted by the music, but instead he waited. His incredible speed and agility would have made even a short scream impossible. Derek watched her swim in the moment, content and unaware of the danger. He took pleasure watching her and didn't want the serenity to end. But after a few moments, the urge became too powerful to ignore.

He didn't uncoil and strike towards her in a burst of inhuman speed. He simply climbed up the bank and slowly walked across the backyard. Her swaying stopped as she noticed the shadowy figure rise out of the ground and move toward her. She didn't scream or run into the house. She strolled to the first step leading down from the deck and stood beautifully defiant. Derek's heart began to race as he stared at the breathtaking warrior. He stopped his advance at the first step leading up to her.

"Do you have any idea how beautiful you are?" asked Derek in a slightly quivering voice.

"Do you have any idea how late you are?" returned the warrior.

"I'm sorry, sweetheart. Things are beginning to heat up in Dixie. All the players have arrived in town. It was killing me, but I had to wait."

"Well, you can stop being patient now. I kind of missed you," said Jennifer.

"I kind of missed you, too, baby," said Derek, moving up the last stair.

Jennifer Marlow wrapped her arms around Derek's neck and squeezed with all her strength. She knew she couldn't hurt him. He wrapped his arms around her and squeezed like he was holding a woman made of glass. He knew how easily he could hurt her.

"Where's Joshua?" she asked in a less inviting tone.

"Up north. I dropped him off day before yesterday."

"Up north? Where exactly up north, Derek?"

"You know it's not a good idea to tell you –"

"Derek," she said, firing a warning shot by narrowing her green eyes. "Where?"

"At one of our hideouts near Dahlonega."

She turned around and walked back to her chair. Lifting her glass, she motioned for him to sit beside her. He was very familiar with the posture and tone as he stood motionless.

"We're going to do this already?" asked Derek. "I was hoping for a kiss or maybe a few more sweet things to be said."

"How about this for sweet? I love you and I'm scared to death the next time we're supposed to meet you won't come back to me out of those woods. I'll just sit here waiting for the news that the FBI, Colonel Brown, the Marines, Joshua or any of the other countless people who want you dead finally got their wish. So yes, we're going to do this already because I'm not going to let them get their wish over mine. Am I clear, Marine?"

"Crystal, ma'am," responded Derek, taking the seat next to her. "Seriously, do you have any idea how beautiful you are, especially when you're irritated with me?"

"I'm not sure how, but someday you and I may look back on this and laugh. That's not going to be tonight, so I want you to pay attention. I really am scared."

"Okay, baby," said Derek, focusing on her. "What's going on?"

"Two college kids went missing the night before last from the military school in Dahlonega. One was a petite blond with blue eyes. The other was a male friend of hers. They're still missing."

Derek leaned back in his chair and looked up into the clear night sky. He knew what she was going to say next. Unlike the many times before, he wasn't going to argue with her. He couldn't argue with her.

"The first time I agreed it could've been a coincidence," she continued. "The second time raised my suspicion. The third time confirmed it for me. And now the fourth, how could you possibly not see that it's him? All of them petite blonds with blue eyes and all close to where he's been hiding out."

"I do see, Jenny," said Derek, leaning closer to her. "The things he's been saying to me. The two days he disappeared in Syracuse. I know it's him," he said, standing up and walking to the rail. "Fuck!"

Jennifer quickly went to his side and grabbed his hand. "Look at me." Her touch and voice immediately calmed him. "I know you didn't want to believe. I know you thought he wanted to help you end this, but he's not the one that's going to help you. Joshua has an agenda for Joshua and no one else. He needs you to achieve his goals, not ours."

"His goal is my goal, his agenda is my agenda," said Derek angrily. "We both want to kill everyone that did this to us. We both want to kill the ones that tried, and are still trying, to kill us because of what *they* did."

"Derek, you're wrong," said Jennifer, holding her ground. "Joshua doesn't want to kill the people that made him that way. He wants to kill the people that are trying to stop him. You said it yourself a month ago. You knew back then that he truly wants to be what he is now. But all you could think about was getting your revenge. And I can't really argue with you. I'd want it, too. But your revenge is going to save him and end us."

"What choice do I have? If I go at it alone, I'm going to end up dead like Peter and Richard."

"They killed Richard?" asked Jennifer, causing Derek to pause.

"I'm sorry, baby. Yes, they did. But Alex pulled the trigger, not the Feds. That's why I told you it's going to start heating up around here. We're next on the list."

"Is the FBI here? Is Ryan here?"

"Yes, he is. The same Ryan that put a bullet in Peter's head, hunted Richard in New Orleans, and is here to kill me. Yeah, that guy's here."

"Derek, you know he has no idea what happened to you. If he did, he wouldn't be coming after you."

"How can you say that about him? You haven't spoken to him in years. It's not like you two are close friends."

"Oh, okay. I forgot you were the one with the flawless perception about people," she said, firing another warning shot. "No, we're not close friends now, but we were good friends in school and several years after we graduated. We're good enough friends for me to know he has a good heart. We lost touch after he went to work for the FBI, but before that I'd see him several times a year when he'd visit on leave. And you know him well enough, too. Isn't he the reason you decided to join the Marines?"

"There were other reasons, but yes. Everyone looked up to him as a leader in school. We'd hear the stories all the time about where he was and what he was doing. He inspired more than a few guys to join, but I can't say I trust him. Can you?"

"I can't overlook the fact he's the one assigned to your case," said

Jennifer. "You look at it as a curse and want to kill him, I look at it as a blessing of someone who can help us. Do you trust me?"

"Of course, I do. You're the only one I do trust."

"Then trust me now," she said, reaching up and pulling his face close to hers. "Unhitch your wagon from Joshua and hitch it to me. Stop trying to protect me from what's happening and let me help you. Stop thinking about your revenge and start thinking about our future."

"Our future? What future? A future on the run? A future of always looking over our shoulders? That's not what I want for you."

"Our future is one day soon you and I sitting in our beach chairs on Bora Bora trying very hard every day to forget this nightmare. Do you remember that future?"

"It's what keeps me going, baby. But I just don't see how it can ever happen. I thought Joshua was the only way I could end this. I thought if we took them out before they got to us, we might have a chance."

"Listen to me," said Jennifer, putting her arms around him. "If you kill FBI agents, they'll never stop hunting you. Up until now, it's not your fault you killed those women."

"Don't talk about that, please," begged Derek. "I can't take hearing you say that. I can barely take thinking you know what I've done."

"It's not your fault, but murdering outside of what they're responsible for planting in your head will be. Killing federal agents or anyone associated with the lab *will* be your fault. That's what Joshua wants you to do. He wants you to get in so deep that you'll never find your way out. And when it happens, he'll own you. And I'm the only one that owns you, sweetie," she said with a smile.

"You really are an amazing woman," said Derek. "You know everything I've done, but you still stand beside me. You still love me. I don't know how that's possible, but you do."

"Because you always tell me the truth in spite of the consequences. Because I understand, Derek," said Jennifer, quickly. "And others will, too. We just have to push them in the right direction. And that pushing starts with Ryan. I believe he's the only one out there who'll at least listen. And if we can get him to listen, then there's hope we can get you help."

"Okay, sweetheart," exhaled Derek. "What's the plan?"

"It's simple, really. You follow Ryan until he's alone and then you call me. I'll take care of the rest."

"That's it? That's the plan you've been working on for months?"

"Brilliant, isn't it?"

"You want me to hunt the guys that are trying to hunt me? And you're asking me if that's brilliant?"

"A man as smart as you, I wonder sometimes why you can't see the elegance of finding simplicity in chaos."

"Well, your simple plan needs to happen fairly quickly," said Derek. "I'm supposed to meet Joshua at the mountain hideout to go over our not-so-simple plan to lure them into our trap. If I don't show, he's going to know something is wrong. We both know what he's capable of doing. It won't be safe for you here anymore."

"It's not safe for anyone as long as he's out there, Derek. How long can you stay with me?"

"Just a few hours, sweetheart."

"Then let's make them count."

Derek and Jennifer sat on the deck talking about subjects any couple in love would find familiar. For Derek, they were absolutely necessary to fill his mind with thoughts other than revenge. They talked about the house they would buy and the make of cars in their garage. Jennifer poured ideas about decorating and furnishing the home that would always be open for friends and family. They dwelled on the magical vacation Derek promised to the Southern Pacific. They'd lounge in their chairs in a cove cut off from the world which had recently turned upside down on top of them. Derek held back the anger and rage he felt for the ones responsible for crushing those dreams and giving him a reality he never wanted.

He was angrier when Jennifer's eyes became heavy after a few hours and she needed to sleep. He wasn't upset she was tired. He was upset he couldn't enjoy the simple peace of drifting away lying beside her. Instead, he carried her inside and placed her gently in the soft inviting bed. He stroked her hair and rubbed her back until he was sure she was a million miles away. Derek kissed her cheek and whispered that he loved her.

He double-checked every lock in the house and set the alarm behind him. He walked down the stairs from the deck and into the backyard. He stopped on the edge of the creek bank and turned around to look at the house. There was a slight unseasonable chill in the air as dew started to form on the leaves and grass. He closed his eyes and imagined himself curled up beside Jennifer's warm body in those soft sheets. With a smile, he crossed the creek and reentered the shadows of the woods behind her house.

Twenty yards into the darkness, he found his foxhole. He pulled back the camouflaged tarp and crawled into the dampness. He covered himself, trying to get as comfortable as possible. He had a clear view of her bedroom window and the entire backyard. He would sit motionless constantly scanning back and forth for any signs of danger. Derek would stay hidden until Jennifer safely left for work in the morning. He'd only leave his post to eat and grab a few hours of sleep at his hideout. He'd return as soon as the sun went down the next night.

Jennifer didn't know it was a routine he had repeated almost every evening since arriving in Georgia four months earlier. The less time he spent with her, the less chance someone would discover their relationship. For the time being, he had to limit his visits to a couple of short hours a few times a month.

———

As Derek settled into position, several miles away Ryan's untraceable phone woke the agent at four-thirty in the morning. He quickly sat up and answered it on the first ring. He had only been asleep a little over an hour.

"Is everything okay, Steve?" asked Ryan.

"*Sorry to wake you so early, buddy, but I knew you'd want to know as soon as Kristina arrived in Georgia. Only two kinds of people are out at this hour. Bad guys and cops. We didn't run into either.*"

"So everything is okay."

"*Roger that. I'm sending you a text message now with the address. I posted two of my best inside and four out. They know you'll be coming by.*"

"Thank you again, Steve. Really, I can't tell you how much I appreciate your help."

"*Save it, Ryan. If you need anything else, anything, don't hesitate to reach out.*"

"I won't. Good-night, Steve," said Ryan, ending the call.

It had been four days since Ryan and the team left Kristina in New Orleans. And each night Ryan found it difficult to fall asleep. He was worried about a number of things, but none as much as her safety. He took a deep breath and returned to his pillow. Ryan wasn't lying in a dirty hole outside Kristina's safe house, but he was close enough to her to find a few hours of elusive sleep.

15

LITTLE MISS SUNSHINE

IT WAS A VERY RARE occasion for another member of the team to be awake in the morning before Ryan. But when he made it downstairs, all three were in the kitchen of the small house used by the Atlanta FBI field office for visitors. Dallas had completed his sweep for listening devices and found nothing.

"Good morning, Boss," greeted Dallas, offering a cup of coffee. "It's about time you caught up on some sleep."

"Yeah, a little surprised I slept so late," said Ryan, taking the cup. "I guess my mind stopped racing long enough for me to doze off."

"You needed it," said Michelle. "Tom and I are heading out shortly to follow up on a missing persons report on the east side of town. The girl fits the profile of being a victim of one of our guys. We should be finished by early afternoon."

"Sounds good," said Ryan. "Oh, by the way, Kristina arrived in town last night. Could you stop in and see if she needs anything?" he asked, tearing off a piece of paper from his pad with the address to her safe house.

"Ah, the reason for the good night's sleep," said Dallas, knowing he screwed up the moment the words left his mouth.

"What's that?" asked Ryan.

"I mean knowing she made it to Atlanta safe," said Dallas, backpedaling. "I didn't mean that you're glad she's here or anything. I mean, I'm sure you're glad. We're all glad she's here, right, guys?" he asked, as both Tom and Michelle stared at the floor. "But I'm not saying glad for you per se. I mean…shit."

"No, Dallas," said Ryan, throwing him a rope. "I am glad she's safe. I know what you meant."

"Exactly," said Dallas.

"Okay, now that we've worked that out, I'm going to grab a shower. Dallas, you and I are going to canvas the neighborhood where Derek grew up. Maybe we'll get lucky and find a friend or family member he's reached out to recently," said Ryan, leaving the kitchen.

Dallas looked over at Tom and Michelle who were staring at him. "What are you two looking at? He knew what I meant."

"Then he's the only one," said Michelle. "Are you really that dense?"

"Come on, you two," said Dallas, defending his suspicion. "You're trying to tell me you don't see something going on there? A little spark maybe?"

"A little spark?" asked Tom. "Between Ryan and Kristina?"

"Yeah."

"Even if there was, which I seriously doubt Ryan would let happen, do you think he'd want you to know?" asked Michelle.

"Why not? What's the big deal? They're two consenting adults, right?"

"That's the major difference between you and him," said Michelle. "He's actually an adult."

"Poke your fun," said Dallas, "But I've known him for a long time and something is going on there. I'm just not exactly sure what it is."

"Well, good luck, detective," said Michelle. "And when he puts a boot up your ass, maybe you can detect which foot he used."

"You're a lucky man, Tom," said Dallas. "You get to hang out with this ray of sunshine all day."

———

Alex Tifton entered the secure section of the Michaels Laboratory, escorting two men with bruised faces. He knocked on Colonel Brown's open office door. "Sir, these gentlemen have something you're going to want to see immediately."

"What is it?" asked the Colonel, turning around in his chair. "Ah, the two morons that lost Dr. Anderson in Baltimore."

"They have a video from a jewelry store security camera covering part of the alley where they were jumped. It only caught a few seconds, but you may recognize one of the faces."

Alex placed a laptop on the Colonel's desk and started the video. He stopped it right after Paul from Red Team went airborne after getting his face smashed. The Colonel leaned in close to make the positive identification.

"Fucking Ryan," growled Colonel Brown.

"I don't know how he did it, but he got to Baltimore and back to New Orleans like he was riding a magic carpet," said Alex. "Do you think the Deputy Director knows he has her? I thought he was in our pocket."

"He is, and I don't think he knows," said Colonel Brown. "Right now, this might actually be a good thing for us."

"How?"

"Ryan must smell a rat. If he thinks his own boss is on the take, he won't let him or anyone else know he has her. He's trying to figure out what's going on, but he doesn't have all the pieces. The problem is, he *will* figure it out if he gets to the other Didache scientists. We can't let him do that."

"Those guys are scared shitless that Derek and Joshua are coming after them," said Alex. "I don't see them leaving the safety of this lab until those two are dead. How did Ryan know Dr. Anderson was even involved?"

"I think we have our own little rat problem."

"Do you know who it is?"

"I believe so, but don't worry about him," said Colonel Brown. "I can take care of it from here. I need you in Atlanta today. It's time for us to start tying up these loose ends. I need Dr. Kristina Anderson removed from the equation. Do you understand?"

"I do," said Alex. "What about Ryan and his team? They're not going to be happy when she turns up missing."

"I don't think he's willing to implicate himself to his boss at this point. If he had all the information he needed, he wouldn't be hiding her. But just in case, make it look like Joshua took her. Before you dispose of her, find out exactly what she told Ryan. We'll make a determination then if we need to remove him and his team as well."

"Kill federal agents?" asked Alex.

"Yes. We'll kill federal agents to insure the survival of the Didache Project," said Colonel Brown, glaring at Alex. "Are you still committed to that goal?"

"Of course I am, sir. The last thing I want to do is jeopardize the Project, but killing agents is going to bring a ton of heat and put a huge spotlight on us."

"You know all of this is part of the plan," said Colonel Brown convincingly. "We knew the FBI would have to get dangerously close to exposing the flaws of the program. It's the only way they'll be convinced this is an isolated case in which we're *not* involved. But you also knew if they came too close, we'd have to make some tough decisions to keep this lab intact.

"If we fail to do that, this lab will be shut down tomorrow. Think about how many of our brothers are going to die on the battlefield because they weren't given the abilities you have. Abilities that came at a steep price. It took over twenty years of research to develop, billions of dollars to manufacture, and cost us the lives of good men who would want us to carry on the mission. The days of turning on the news and watching our troops come home in flag-draped coffins will be over because of what we've accomplished here. What you accomplished here. I won't let anyone shut us down because of one stupid mistake that had nothing to do with us. You're the future of modern warfare, Alex. You're the future of the Marine Corps. You have to be protected and preserved at all cost."

"Yes, sir," acknowledged Alex. "I understand the importance of completing the mission. I won't let you down, Colonel."

"No, Marine. I won't let *you* down."

———

The heat of Atlanta was reaching its summertime peak as Tom and Michelle left the Rockdale County Sheriff's Office on the east side of the city. They quickly determined the missing girl wasn't a victim of Derek or Joshua. The timeline of her disappearance didn't fit either profile. The girl was also too young. She was seventeen years old, which was six years younger than their usual twenty-three-year-old targets.

"This is going to sound crazy, but what if Dallas is right about Ryan and Kristina?" said Tom, out of the blue while driving back to Atlanta.

"Where did that come from?" asked Michelle.

"Left field, but what if?"

"First of all, you saying Dallas is right about something is mind blowing enough. Add Ryan becoming involved with a possible material witness in the most bizarre serial killer case we've ever worked, and you're standing on a different planet. He'd never jeopardize his objectivity because of a crush."

"You need to cut Dallas a little slack," said Tom, earning a glare from Michelle. "He's a very intuitive person, and he knows Ryan better than both of us. The fact that Dallas doesn't have a filter between what he thinks and what he says is actually an enviable characteristic. You always know where you stand with him."

"Okay, for the sake of the argument I'll agree with you about that, but not about Ryan falling for a woman under his protection."

"Her name is Kristina."

"I know her name, Tom."

"I think maybe you've become *too* objective about her. You see her as just another player in this very complicated game. Why would it be so hard for you to believe Ryan may look at her differently? Haven't you ever been attracted to someone involved in an active investigation?"

"No, of course not," answered Michelle quickly. "It would only make the game more complicated. And we definitely don't need this one to become more complicated. I would hope Ryan understands that. I find it hard to believe you're being so cavalier about it. When have you ever known him to let down his guard?"

"Never, but it really has little to do with letting down his guard and more to do with him being human," said Tom.

"You're losing me," said Michelle. "We should be talking about the case, not Ryan's love life."

"Okay, okay. Obviously, I struck some kind of chord with you."

"No, I just think it would be terribly irresponsible of Ryan to get involved with a woman he barely knows under these circumstances."

"Kristina."

"Good Lord, Tom. You actually just made me wish I was with Dallas right now."

"Aha! I knew there was something going on between you two," said Tom with a chuckle.

"Okay, now you're just trying to piss me off. I will shoot you in the face," she said with an unconvincing smile.

"Just jokes, Michelle. Lower your weapon."

"Seriously, Tom, what's come over you?"

"I don't know. Maybe I'm just getting a little older and thinking about my empty house and open date book that's been that way for years. We all become so involved with the job that we forget to think about what happens after."

"After?"

"Yeah, after we're done with the job. And I don't mean this one in particular, I mean when we hang up our guns and rejoin normal society. At this point in my life, I'd just go home to that empty house wondering what to do next."

"Well, any concept I had of 'normal society' was skewed years ago because of this job," said Michelle. "And the last thing I want to do is join a group I don't understand anymore. At least here we hold the line and know the bad guys are on the other side. For me, it's actually a little comforting not having to think about someone waiting for me to come home. It's just me looking out for me."

"Do you really believe that?" asked Tom with a slightly hurtful tone.

"You guys are on that line with me, Tom. I know you're looking out for me on the job. But when I go home, it really is just me. Just like it's only you when you go home. I believe it's what makes us better at our job than most. There's nothing tying us down, and we're able to trek across the country at a moment's notice. There's no one to check in with and make sure the kids are set for school and the grocery shopping is done. That has to make sense to you."

"Oh yes, it absolutely does, and I agree with you," said Tom. "But one of these days, perhaps sooner than later, the job will let us go long before we're ready to let it go. I wonder how we'll deal with waking up the next morning without those kids and no food in the fridge."

"I'll borrow my sister's monkeys for an evening and order pizza," said Michelle. "After a night with them, I'll look forward to an empty house."

"I can't argue with that logic. Do you want me to drop you off at Kristina's?" asked Tom as they approached the neighborhood where she was hidden.

"No, I need to take the car in case I have to run out and pick up something for her."

"Okay."

Michelle stayed with Tom for a few hours at the FBI house and waited for Ryan and Dallas to return. All four had unproductive trips, and the team briefed each other on their progress hunting Derek and Joshua. With almost no new information, the brief lasted only a few minutes. Michelle grabbed her gear and headed out the door.

When she arrived at Kristina's, a man in tattered white coveralls and a baseball cap was sitting on the front porch reading a magazine. She also observed a windowless utility van parked beside an open manhole near the curb at the edge of the front yard. When she reached the porch, she noticed the tiny clear spiral tube running from the sentry's ear disappearing down the back of his paint-splotched clothing. She also noticed the butt of his automatic rifle peeking out from a pile of newspapers at his feet. He reached up and tipped his hat.

"Good evenin', ma'am. May I offah you a tall cool drink of lemonade?" he asked in an embellished southern accent.

"You'd make a thousand dollas selling that from a stand on the cawnah," said Michelle in an equally embellished accent.

"I'd make a million if you sat beside me with your smile, pretty lady."

"Well, I do declayah. How many are posted?" asked Michelle, dropping the accent.

"One in the van with a much bigger gun than mine," said the man, losing his accent as well. "Two around back in a shed with a three-sixty of the yard. Two more inside. And then of course, yours truly sipping lemonade and enjoying this Africa hot weather in coveralls. My name is Patrick Webber," he said, offering his hand.

"Michelle Dobbs, but you should already know that," she said, giving him a firm handshake.

"Yes, ma'am. We've been expecting you. Dr. Anderson is up in her room reading. That's pretty much where she's been since she arrived. I'm sure she's looking forward to the company."

"Apparently not mine," said Michelle, confusing Patrick, who didn't pry.

"If you need anything, let me know. These are my guys."

"I appreciate it, Patrick. I have to say, if your guys are associated with the New Orleans team, she's in good hands."

"Thank you. I was CIA for three years before joining Steve's outfit. The pay is much better, and the lines are less blurry."

"I know the feeling," said Michelle, finding herself lingering too long with the attractive young team leader. "Maybe I'll send my application in when my tour is up."

"I'll put in a good word."

"Thank you," said Michelle, entering the house. She closed the door behind her and stood in the foyer shaking her head. "Maybe I'll send in my application? Damn you for getting in my head, Tom."

"Michelle," greeted Kristina, startling her from the top of the stairs. "I thought I heard someone come in. Who were you talking to?"

"The only person that ever really listens…me. How are you?"

"Oh, I'm fine. I have my books," said Kristina, making her way down the stairs. "Can I get you anything? Coffee? Something to eat?"

"No, thank you. I'm actually supposed to be asking you those questions," said Michelle, following her into the kitchen.

"Well, these gentlemen are as doting as the group in New Orleans," said Kristina, opening a bottle of water. "A girl could get used to this."

"It would drive me crazy, but if you're sure you don't need anything, I'll leave you to your reading."

"Oh, you have to leave so soon?" she replied quickly.

"I don't want to disturb you," said Michelle, trying to make a fast exit.

"Disturb me? I've been cooped up inside with a bunch of serious-looking guys carrying guns. They've been very accommodating, but I have to admit there's been a lack of conversation other than asking if I need anything. Would you mind staying just a little while longer?"

"I guess it would be okay," said Michelle, reluctantly taking a seat at the table. "I can catch you up on the case."

"Actually, I'd rather talk about anything else. It's the reason why I've been doing so much reading, you know, so I don't have to think about what's going on out there. I guess I just tend to worry about everyone involved. This may be hard for you to understand, but Peter and Richard were good guys. Derek as well."

"It is difficult to understand after witnessing what they've done," said Michelle. "They may have been good guys at some point, but they're not anymore."

"So, how are the guys?" asked Kristina, changing the subject. "How's Ryan?"

"Dallas and Tom are good. Ryan hasn't been sleeping very much, but he seems to be okay."

"He does seem like a very intense person," said Kristina. "I can't help but feel a little responsible for his lack of sleep."

"Why would you feel responsible?" asked Michelle.

"I mean having to worry about lugging me everywhere while trying to find Derek and Joshua."

"Oh, I don't think he's worried about that. In fact, he's probably more relieved you're here. If anything were to happen, I'm sure he'd rather be here. You're right, he is a fairly intense person, but that's what makes him effective."

"You seem like a pretty close group," said Kristina. "When I was working at the lab, or anywhere else as a matter of fact, people tended to shy away from me. I never really became close to anyone. I had friends, but they always kept their distance. I'm sure I was partly to blame since I was always so involved in my work, but there were many times I wish I could've just hung out with them, you know, let our hair down and relax."

"I think they might have been intimidated by you," said Michelle, defrosting a few degrees. "Being an attractive, driven woman with a big brain tends to humble folks. They don't know what to do with you, so they keep you at arm's length. Speaking of people keeping their distance, imagine carrying a gun and a badge. It's crickets and tumbleweed whenever I walk into a room at a social gathering."

"Well, at least it's nice to know there are other women out there like me."

"Kristina, there are very few women out there like us. No offense, but we both walked into the men's club without a club. Most of them don't know what to do with us, so they try to ignore the fact we're even there. We have to be more creative about how to make enough noise to get noticed without getting kicked out."

"Very true," said Kristina with a smile.

Michelle and Kristina sat at the table talking for over an hour. They discovered they had more in common than either thought. In a predominantly male working environment, they both enjoyed the rare opportunity of not having one in the same room.

———

The chartered aircraft landed at Hartsfield International Airport in Atlanta late in the evening. Two vehicles were waiting for the six men which included Alex and the banged up Red Team. They were looking forward to paying back Ryan and Dallas for the painful gifts they received in Baltimore.

"I want the other guys to wait at the hotel," said Alex to Paul of Red Team. "I want you to follow Michelle and Tom. According to the GPS data, they're usually together. Right now, it's showing everyone at the FBI house. I'll be tailing Ryan and Dallas. One of them will eventually lead us to Dr. Anderson. When they do, I'll be the one taking her this time. Ryan will find it difficult putting me in a dumpster."

—

Scott Wilson stood in front of Colonel Brown's office door and took several deep breaths. His instincts told him to turn and run, but he knew Ryan wouldn't have a chance if he lost his only inside source to the lab. But more importantly, he knew Ryan had Kristina. If he left, they'd be on their own. She'd be on her own. He knocked on the door and entered the office.

"You wanted to see me, sir?" asked Scott nervously.

"Yes, I did," said the Colonel with a rare friendly greeting. "Please, sit down."

Scott had been wary of the Colonel since he started working at the lab years ago, but was on high alert sitting in front of the man running the show. The Colonel wasted no time showing his cards.

"I understand you've been talking to Agent Ryan Pearson."

"Yes, sir. We've had contact at each of the crime scenes. I only relayed the information you instructed me to divulge."

Two security personnel entered the office and stood behind Scott. His pulse skyrocketed as the Colonel watched the scientist turn pale.

"No, Scott. You told him much more than that. In fact, you told him exactly where to find Dr. Anderson. We know he has her, but not for long. Alex and a team are in Atlanta getting ready to separate the two."

"That's crazy. Why would I –"

The Colonel put his hand up for Scott to stop talking. It worked.

"The next words that come out of your mouth are going to be critical to your survival and hers. You have no idea how bad you fucked up, son. You need to start unfucking yourself right now. The only way that's going to happen is if you tell me everything you told him and everything you gave him. And yes, I know about the autopsy reports. If you even think about tap dancing around what I want, I'll end your life right after I show you photos of how I ended hers. The only chance you and Dr. Anderson have to walk away from this is for you to come clean."

16

RED TEAM REUNION

IT HAD BEEN TWO DAYS since Alex started shadowing Ryan and Dallas. He still had no idea where they were hiding Kristina. The GPS embedded in the agent's phones made it easy for him to keep his distance and stay concealed. Late in the evening on the second day, the locator map in Alex's laptop showed all four agents in the FBI house. His senses were alerted when he observed Ryan leaving the house alone, but the GPS signal indicated no movement. Alex called his team and told them to prepare to move as Ryan's car left the driveway.

Twenty minutes later, Alex contacted Colonel Brown to inform him that he had Kristina's location. Red Team mobilized from the hotel and set up positions around the house as Alex waited for Ryan to leave. They noticed one unidentified sentry in the backyard and another in a van parked by the curb. He estimated there would be at least two more inside.

Ryan was in the house for thirty minutes before reappearing on the front porch. He drove away, leaving the perimeter protected by only two of Steve's men. Red Team had four men ready to assault the house from the back as Alex and three others were poised to take the sentry in the van. All had orders that nobody inside was to be left alive. Alex would take out Dr. Anderson himself.

A few moments before Alex gave the order to advance, Steve's men made it easier for the assault team. Both the front and back sentries abandoned their posts and entered the house. They would have had a slightly better chance of survival if they had skipped dinner and stayed outside. Their absence allowed Alex's assault team to creep up to the doors undetected and seal everyone's fate inside.

Alex keyed his radio three times, signaling both teams to breach the doors. It was unnecessary to use the battering rams to knock them off the hinges. Steve's men didn't lock them when they entered. Nearly every light was on as they silently crept into the house. When the two teams met in the middle after quickly clearing several rooms downstairs, they were engulfed in darkness as the power was cut off from the street.

At the same time, a radio jamming device was activated, rendering their communication equipment useless. Red Team bolted for the back door when they realized they'd been set up, but they were met by a blinding floodlight and several orders to freeze. The first man out raised his weapon. He was cut down by automatic fire before he could squeeze the trigger. Each muzzle outside was suppressed with a silencer. The only sound heard were the metal clicks of the firing mechanisms.

Deciding where to set up the decoy house was as important as its function. It was adequately isolated from any potential collateral damage to bystanders or witnesses. The second man out took two rounds to the chest before he could react. The remaining weapons from Red Team quickly hit the ground as all hands went up in the air.

During the chaotic few seconds of discovering it was a trap, Alex quickly separated himself from the sitting ducks. In the blink of an eye, he jettisoned himself through the large living room window and accelerated to nearly forty miles an hour. He disappeared through the neighbor's backyard before the agents or Steve's men could put their gun sights on him.

Dallas was the first to approach the surrounded and stunned Red Team. He was also the first to spot the vehicle following Ryan when he had left an hour earlier. Whenever someone went to check on Kristina, another agent followed them as if they were the bad guys. When Ryan was alerted to the tail, he drove to the decoy house they had set up prior to Kristina's arrival. The two guards posted outside entered the house and donned their night vision goggles as they set up in their ambush positions upstairs. Tom and Michelle directed the eight-man strike team Steve stationed less than a mile from the FBI house. The hunters were being hunted as soon as they arrived at the decoy. Dallas was pleased to see the two men he and Ryan disabled in Baltimore.

"Hi, guys," greeted Dallas. "Fancy running into you again. No old ladies or pretty scientist here to beat up. Just us stupid feds. Man, that's gotta piss you off," he said as Ryan entered the house.

Without saying a word, Ryan walked up to Paul of the Colonel's Red Team who had chased Kristina down an alley less than two weeks earlier. He stared at him for a brief moment and then knocked him off his feet. He hit him square in his semi-healed nose. He leaned over the man writhing in pain.

"You rub a puppy's nose in its own shit a few times and it'll stop crapping on the carpet. How many times am I going to have to break yours before you stop crapping on mine?"

"Respectfully request permission to re-injure my guy, Boss," said Dallas.

"Granted," responded Ryan without turning around and still hovering over Paul.

Dallas's man left his feet as quickly as Ryan's, but he didn't wiggle when he hit the floor. He was out cold. Ryan grabbed Paul by the collar and dragged him into an adjacent room and threw him into a chair. He told Dallas to drag his in as well. The other members of Red Team were being disarmed by Steve's team while being held at gunpoint in the living room. In Ryan's mind, the situation had changed. He wouldn't be leaving them behind in a dumpster. He was taking them completely out of the game.

"I was pissed in Baltimore, asshole. Imagine what I'm feeling right now," said Ryan.

"I could give a shit about—" Before he could finish his sentence, Ryan pulled his gun and jammed it hard into Paul's mouth, breaking his front teeth. He pulled it out and rested it between Paul's eyes as parts of his teeth mixed with blood spilled down the front of his shirt.

"I'm assuming that was Alex that did a Batman out of the window?" asked Ryan. "Think about the pain in your face before you give me a smartass answer."

"Yes," mumbled Paul.

"Is he as strong as the others?"

"Yes."

"You obviously came here for Dr. Anderson," continued Ryan. "Did Colonel Brown send you? What were you going to do with her?"

"Yes, he sent us," answered Paul. "He also sent us to Baltimore to pick her up. I don't know what he was going to do –" Ryan cut him off by grabbing his throat.

"I swear to God I don't know," gurgled Paul. "We were supposed take out the guards, and Alex told us he was going to take Dr. Anderson. Yes, I think they were going to kill her."

Ryan released his grip. "How did Colonel Brown know I had her?"

"We got a hold of a videotape showing you in the alley. As soon as he saw it was you, he sent us down here."

"How many?"

"Everyone you have here plus Alex. But the Colonel has close to twenty other guys he can send."

"Are they all as good as you?" There was no answer. "Is Alex the one that shot Peter Arrington and made Richard Elliot look like a suicide?"

"I know he shot Arrington because I was there. I don't know about Elliot, but I'm pretty sure he was in New Orleans at the time."

"Why does the Colonel want to kill them? Isn't he the one who created them?"

"No, I don't think he did," said Paul. "Or at least he acted like he had no idea when they started changing. He seemed just as surprised as we were. I remember him yelling at the other lab geeks, telling them to reverse the effects. They were scared shitless, but they told him it wasn't that easy and that the mutations may be permanent. He didn't want to kill the Marines at first, but I guess he changed his mind. That's when the Colonel ordered us to lock down the entire lab. All four busted out a few weeks later. We've been chasing them down ever since. That's everything I know, I swear to God!"

"Agent Pearson, can you take this call from our boss?" asked one of Steve's men, handing him a cell phone.

"Absolutely."

"Ryan, you okay, buddy?"

"Not a scratch, but I can't say the same for a couple of the goons. One's dead, one's close, and I may add a few more to the list before I'm done," said Ryan, glaring at Paul. "But all your men are fine. They were fantastic, Steve. Real professionals."

"I appreciate that. I also have a few that are experienced at making things disappear. They'll start with that body. We'll take the injured man to the physician on our payroll. We have a triage center as good as any E.R. that doesn't report gunshot wounds to the cops. Once they're patched up, I have a special place where we can keep them on ice until you decide what to do with them."

"Thank you, again. My tab with you is getting bigger every day."

"When you come back to visit after we're through with this little project, bring me a bottle of Jameson Reserve and we'll call it even."

"Your taste has changed slightly since your home brew days."

"Take care of yourself, Ryan. I'm here if you need me."

"Will do," replied Ryan, ending the call and turning his attention back to Paul.

He knelt down beside the chair and stared at him for a few moments. Whenever Ryan wanted someone to remember his words, he'd lean in close and speak in a whisper.

"You're done. If you survive where I'm sending you, take your guys and find different jobs. You suck at this one, but you did manage to start getting on my nerves. If you and I cross paths one more time, I'm not going to break your face again; I'm going to put one in your ear. Do you believe me?"

"I do," said Paul. "But it doesn't matter. I'm a dead man either way. The Colonel won't let anyone jeopardize his pet project. He's already tying up loose ends, which now includes me. You, your team, and Dr. Anderson are on that list, too. "

"Did you hear that, Dallas? We made the list."

"Yippee. If the Colonel keeps sending bozos like these to scratch off names, I don't think I'll be losing any sleep."

"That's funny," said Paul. "But you haven't had the pleasure of meeting Alex up close and personal. That freak of nature will change your mind pretty quick, tough guy."

"He's a bit of a freak of nature himself," said Ryan. "If Alex has a heartbeat, Dallas will find a way to make it stop."

"Thanks, Boss. I think. Are we through with these guys?" asked Dallas.

"Yeah," said Ryan. "Send Tom with Steve's team and make sure they don't run into any problems moving these guys. You, Michelle, and I need to make a stop before we head back to the house."

Tom and Steve's men cleaned up the scene and loaded Red Team into vans for transport. Ryan drove away from the decoy house, followed by Dallas and Michelle. They didn't have a second decoy set up, so Ryan needed to make sure he didn't pick up another tail. The team arrived unchallenged at Kristina's safe house after a few trips circling the block. They were met at the end of the walkway by the leader of Kristina's security detail, Patrick Webber.

"Agent Pearson," greeted Patrick. "Glad to hear everything went well. Dr. Anderson doesn't know what happened. I'll give you one guess where she is and what she's doing."

"In her room reading?" said Ryan.

"We have a winner. Are we going to be moving her tonight?"

"I don't think that'll be necessary. We believe we wrangled all but one of the bad guys, but I doubt he'll try to take her alone. I think we're good for tonight, but be ready to move at any time."

"Understood, sir. Agent Dobbs, good to see you again," said Patrick, ignoring Dallas as Ryan walked inside. "I'm sorry I don't have any lemonade to offer. I sold out at my stand on the corner."

"Told you," replied Michelle with a handshake lasting long enough to get Dallas's attention. "I get half the profits for finding the location."

"Seventy-thirty since I did all the sweating."

"Okay, I'll take the seventy," replied Michelle with a smile.

"Ehem," coughed Dallas, clearing his throat.

"Oh, I'm sorry," said Michelle. "This is my driver, Dallas."

"Lucky man," said the young team leader. "My name is Patrick. Good to meet you," he said, quickly turning his attention back to Michelle.

"Any problem with the thugs tonight?"

"No, they didn't know what hit them," said Michelle. "They were like deer caught in the headlights. One moron raised his weapon, but your guys let him know it was a very bad idea."

"Yeah, most of us have extensive backgrounds in tactical assault—"

"I'm sorry, this is riveting stuff," interrupted Dallas. "But we need to get inside."

"Um, not really," said Michelle. "But you go ahead."

Dallas stood there for a moment like a dismissed child, staring at her with a half-open mouth, but unable to put two words together. He had no idea what to say. Michelle and Patrick stared back, waiting for him to speak. He closed his mouth, turned to look at the parked car for no reason, and then walked purposefully into the house. Ryan had already made his way upstairs. Dallas took a seat at the kitchen table and watched Michelle and Patrick out of the corner of his eye.

"That was a little strange," said Patrick. "Are you two –?"

"Baha!" exploded Michelle in an uncontrollable response. "Oh, dear Lord, no."

"He seemed a little displaced," continued Patrick. "Of course, I couldn't blame him for being thrown off. You're a very captivating woman."

"Now I feel a little displaced after that line," said Michelle. "Are you flirting with me, Mr. Webber?"

"Would that be a bad idea?"

"Probably."

"Then, no, I'm not. Would asking you out for drinks be considered flirting?"

"More like dangerous. You do know I carry a gun, right?"

"So do I, but I also have one in my holster," he said, pushing his jacket aside.

"Ouch," said Michelle with a grimace. "You almost had me at captivating, but blew it with the phallic pistol reference." As she walked past him, she added, "Thank you for reminding me why I'm better off single."

"Wait, I'm sorry. That's not what I –" he stopped, knowing there was no recovery.

She entered the kitchen and noticed Dallas engrossed in a magazine. She walked over and turned it right side up. "What was that all about?" she asked.

"You were embarrassing yourself hitting on that kid. I was just trying to help you out."

"I was hitting on him?"

"It was very obvious, Michelle."

"So is your second-grade reading level, but you don't see me trying to help you out, so you can stop trying to help me," she said, turning around and heading upstairs to find the boss.

Ryan knocked on Kristina's bedroom door. She opened it, expecting one of Steve's men, but was surprised to see him standing in the hall. It surprised Ryan more when she took a step toward him and threw her arms around his neck. She squeezed him tight for a moment, but quickly released him and took a step back.

"I...shouldn't have done that," exhaled Kristina. "I'm sorry."

"Nothing to be sorry about, Kristina. It's good to see you, too. But something happened tonight you need to know about."

"Should I sit down?"

"Please," replied Ryan as they both took a seat. "We have a security measure where we set up a decoy house if someone tries to follow us here. And tonight I was followed. Eight men from the lab including Alex Tifton were planning on taking you. But instead, they walked into our ambush. One of them was killed when he raised his weapon at my team. Unfortunately, Alex escaped."

"Oh, my God," whispered Kristina. "Were any of your people hurt?"

"No, they're all fine. Michelle's with me and she'll be staying here tonight. I'll decide tomorrow if we need to move you to a different location. I don't think they'll try again so soon, but I do think they will try again."

"I just wish I knew what they want with me. I don't know what happened to them. I don't have any of the files, DNA samples or access to a lab to even begin to figure out what actually did go wrong."

"What?"

"I said I don't know what they want with me."

"No, no," said Ryan, standing. "You could figure out what went wrong if you had DNA samples?"

"Well, yes," replied Kristina. "And a lab, but I'm not talking about a high school chemistry lab. I'd need access to equipment that's pretty hard to find. I'd also need several recent DNA samples and at least one old one from their medical records for comparison."

"I think you just found the reason why they want you," said Ryan. "It's not because of what you know, but what you could figure out.

"That's why Colonel Brown is trying to get rid of them, you, and anyone else that could possibly find out and shut down the Didache Project. He wants to bury everything, and he's covering all his bases to do it. If he buries the four Marines, we'll lose any chance of recovering their DNA. If he buries you and the other scientists involved, we'll lose any chance of figuring out what happened to them. And if he buries everyone, he'll be home free with no evidence to link him to the murders or any wrongdoing at the lab. And thanks to me and the federal government, he has the bodies and physical evidence of every woman they killed since this started. I'm pushing forward, doing exactly what he wants me to do, and he's behind me erasing everything implicating him or the lab."

"It doesn't sound like it's going to get any easier for you," said Kristina sympathetically.

"No, it doesn't. But at least now I'll be able to throw a bigger monkey wrench into the Colonel's plan."

"How are you going to do that?" she asked.

"I don't have the slightest idea."

"Knock, knock," said Michelle, entering the room. "Looks like we're having a girl's night," she said to Kristina.

"Did you bring any wine coolers?" asked Kristina with a smile.

"Michelle, can I talk to you in the hall for a moment?" asked Ryan, stepping out of the room.

"What's up?" she asked as she joined him.

"I don't want you to think I'm turning you into a babysitter, but I'd like for you to stick close to her tomorrow as well. You won't be missing much. I plan on using the guys to interview Derek's family and friends for the next few days."

"No problem," said Michelle. "She's kind of growing on me, too."

"On you, too?" asked Ryan.

"Is there something in the water around here?" she asked. "I didn't mean anything by that. I'm just pointing out she's an interesting person."

"Okay, sorry," said Ryan, slightly confused. He poked his head back in the room and said good-bye to Kristina. Michelle rejoined her as Ryan and Dallas left the house.

"What is with the guys turning into hypersensitive meatheads all of the sudden?" asked Michelle, not expecting an answer.

"I knew I shouldn't have done that," said Kristina, surprising her.

"Done what?"

"He didn't say anything to you?"

"Who?"

"Ryan."

"Oh, my God, it's happening to you, too," said Michelle.

"I'm not being hypersensitive," clarified Kristina. "I apparently lost impulse control and hugged Ryan when he showed up tonight. He didn't seem very happy about it. I thought maybe he said something to you in the hall."

"It's like I've traveled back in time to high school," said Michelle. "Dallas getting creepy jealous I was talking to another guy. That guy wanting to show me his 'gun.' You telling me you have a crush on my boss, and Tom getting all mushy on me in the car. In the last forty-eight hours, my life has turned into a soap opera."

"I don't have a crush on Ryan," said Kristina. "Well, maybe a little. Oh, hell, I don't know. It's ridiculous. I hardly even know the man."

"I'll be right back," said Michelle.

"You're going to get wine coolers, aren't you?" asked Kristina.

"Oh, no, sister. I'm getting us something much stronger."

17

DANCING IN THE KITCHEN

RYAN TURNED DOWN THE LONG gravel driveway of Stacy Jorgensen's country home located an hour east of Atlanta. The sprawling front yard was manicured, and flower beds flanking the long walkway to the front porch were in full bloom. When he stepped out of the car, he was hit with a subtle sweet smell from the confederate jasmine growing up a large arbor at the end of a stone walkway leading to the house. A woman was watering brightly colored perennials in ornate flower boxes that were under every window on the first floor. The entire property reeked of southern hospitality. Stacy put down her watering can and took off her gardening gloves as the expected visitor arrived. In a wide brim hat, the older sister of Derek Mathews walked up and greeted the federal agent hunting her brother.

"Agent Pearson, I presume?" asked Stacy.

"Yes, ma'am," said Ryan, shaking her hand. "You have an absolutely gorgeous home. I've seen less beautiful houses on the cover of Southern Living."

"How sweet, thank you. It's my little sanctuary away from the city. The commute is murder, but it's worth every mile when I get home. Can I offer you something cool to drink? Sweet tea maybe?"

"It would be a crime to not have a glass while sitting on your front porch, Mrs. Jorgensen."

"Please, call me Stacy. Make yourself comfortable. I'll be right back."

Ryan selected one of the four large white rocking chairs on the wraparound porch. The lazy ceiling fans pushed just enough air down to stop the sweat and keep the irritating gnats at bay. Even the birds seemed more polite in her yard as they patiently waited their turn at the feeders. Stacy handed Ryan a tall glass and sat in the rocker next to him.

"Thank you," said Ryan, taking a long drink. "Oh, that's magical."

"There really is an art to making good sweet tea," she said. "Most people just boil the flavor right out of it. I use nothing but the sun when I make mine. Quite a difference, don't you think?"

"It really might be the best I've ever had. Stacy, I'm sorry I couldn't be more specific on the phone about why I wanted to speak with you about Derek. To be honest, there are specifics about his case that I simply can't discuss. Primarily because it's still an ongoing investigation. When was the last time you saw or spoke with Derek?"

"Oh, it would have to be several months ago around the holidays. He was here for Thanksgiving with the family and then spent Christmas in the city with his friends. I think he might have been seeing a young lady at the time, but I don't know for sure. What I do know is that he seemed a little distant."

"How so, if you don't mind me asking?"

"The entire family always looked forward to Derek's visits. He's one of the funniest people I know. We'd all sit around the table or outside on the deck and just laugh and laugh. But when the holidays come around, it's even more special. He really does love being home during the season. He's always been very sweet, but he'll smother you in it from Thanksgiving to New Year's Eve. But this year, he seemed so quiet. He doted on our parents and played with his nieces as usual, but he didn't talk very much at all to me or Elizabeth. That's our little sister. And we're very, very close siblings. We're more like best friends."

"And she lives a few hours away, correct?"

"Not quite, but far enough to where we don't see her as much anymore."

"Is that the last time you spoke with him as well?"

"No, I believe the last time we talked on the phone was about three months ago. But we only talked for a few minutes. He seemed fine then. More like himself."

"Three months ago," said Ryan. "I'm sorry, Stacy, but we checked all his phone records, and there were no calls to your home or cell phones."

"Oh, he didn't call me here. I was at a birthday party at a friend's house."

"Did it seem a little strange he called you there?"

"A little, but I didn't think anything of it at the time."

"Could I have that number, please? And any numbers you may have of his friends?"

"Sure, I'll write them down for you," she said and then paused for a moment before speaking again. "Is he in trouble, Agent Pearson?"

"That's why it's very important I speak with him. He may be in trouble, yes."

"Is he in any danger?"

"I'm afraid so," said Ryan, wanting to be honest to his host. "If he tries to contact you or if you see him, would you please let me know? I hope you believe me when I say all I want to do is help him. I was a Marine myself for many years. We tend to look out for each other."

Ryan stood and thanked her for her hospitality and the phone numbers. He returned to his car and immediately relayed the new information to Michelle. She was still with Kristina but could access databases discreetly from the safe house. He left the peaceful scene of Stacy's home and headed back to Atlanta.

When the dust settled on the gravel road, the doors to the barn behind Stacy's house opened and a small SUV pulled up to the flowered walkway. Derek stepped out of the vehicle and trotted to his sister still sitting in the rocking chair.

"He seemed like a nice guy," said Stacy.

"They're trained to be nice when they need something from you," said Derek.

"I told him everything you wanted me to say. Were you able to put that gizmo under his car?" she asked.

"The GPS tracker, yes. You did perfect. Thank you, sis."

"Well, I just lied to a federal officer. I hope you know what you're doing, Derek. He said you might be in danger. What did he mean?"

"If I was in any danger, which I'm not, it would be from them. But thanks to you, I'll know exactly where they are. I knew one of them would eventually show up here. I need to go. And thank you again for letting me use your car. I'll get it back to you as soon as possible."

"Don't worry about it. We just kept it to give to your niece when she's old enough to drive. So just have it back in a few years and we'll be good. But don't bring it back on empty."

"Yes, ma'am," said Derek, giving his sister a hug. "I love you."

"I love you, too. Please be careful. I know you know what you're doing, but I still can't help worrying."

"Everything will be fine. It'll be over soon, I promise."

He hugged his sister again and sped off after Ryan. He called Jennifer to let her know the agent in charge was alone. With the GPS tracker attached to Ryan's car, Derek could easily stay concealed while keeping the man hunting him within his reach.

———

Dallas and Tom were still investigating missing persons cases that might be connected to Derek or Joshua. They were on the north side of town and a few hours from finishing their interviews. Ryan decided to stop and have dinner at one of his favorite pubs not far from the FBI house. He was looking forward to having a few cocktails with his meal and maybe even run into some old friends who used to frequent the Village Tavern. It had been nearly ten years since his last visit, but he immediately recognized the bartender who smiled and shook his head when Ryan walked inside.

"You have got to be kidding me," said Jack, frozen in place. "Did they finally pull your clearance?"

"I've seen too many skeletons for them to let me go alive," said Ryan, shaking Jack's hand. "You haven't changed a bit. You look good, buddy."

"I'm basically falling apart on the inside, but I'll take the compliment. Did you take some time off?"

"No," said Ryan, taking a seat at the bar. "But I'm taking a little time off tonight. I'm here working on a case for Uncle Sam. I figured I could finish up a little paperwork over a cold one."

"How long do you think you'll be in town?" asked Jack, handing Ryan a beer.

"No telling at this point."

"You working on anything you can talk about?"

"Trust me when I say you don't want to know," said Ryan. "Any of the old group still come around?"

"Oh, yeah," said Jack. "You'll probably see a few familiar faces in a bit. It's still kind of early for most of them. Hey, would you mind if I made a few phone calls? If a couple of them found out you were here and I didn't call them, they'd kill me."

"No, go ahead. I can stick around for a couple hours. Speaking of the old group, do you remember a jarhead named Derek Mathews?"

"Derek, sure," said Jack. "Great guy, but I probably haven't seen him in almost a year. He'd pop in every once in a while when he was on leave. Why?"

"Turns out he was assigned to my old unit at Camp Lejune. Just figured I'd look him up while I was here. If you get an ear on where he might be, would you let me know?" asked Ryan, giving Jack one of his cards.

"No problem."

Derek parked in front of a retail store attached to the same shopping center where the Village Tavern was located. Less than thirty minutes later, Jennifer pulled up in front of the pub. She stood motionless by her car for a moment, knowing Derek was somewhere close watching her. She ran her fingers through her hair. It was the signal for him to leave the area. She'd take it from there.

"If I didn't know for a fact Mr. Ryan Pearson would never come to town without letting me know, I'd swear you were him," said Jennifer from across the bar.

"I don't know a Mr. Ryan Pearson, ma'am. But he'd be a lucky guy having you looking for him," said Ryan jokingly. "Do people not age around here? You look fantastic, Jennifer." He stood up to give her a hug.

"Did Jack call you?" asked Ryan.

"No, I was doing some shopping and decided to stop in," lied Jennifer. "I haven't been here in a while. The place hasn't changed much."

"I'm not quite sure how to take that," said Jack.

"Take it as you look good, Jack. There are some serious memories flooding my head right now."

"Same here. It's good to see you," said Ryan. "Please, have a seat."

"Oh, no, I don't want to bother you – of course you'd better offer me a seat!"

"What can I get you?" asked Jack.

"A beer would be great, thank you. So, Ryan, what brings the prodigal son back home? Or would you have to kill me after you told me?"

"No, you're safe. I do quite a bit of traveling for work these days, and the job brought me close. I figured I'd pop in and see how the old place was doing."

"Well, next time you decide to pop in, let us know, please. I'm sure there are a few folks that would love to see you. How long are you staying?"

"I'm not sure. Basically, until I catch the bad guys."

"They must be pretty bad to have Super Fed on their tail. I'm sure you'll get your guy soon."

"That's the plan. Listen, while I was here, I was going to try and catch up with a couple guys from my old Marine unit. Do you know Derek Mathews or Joshua Bell?"

"Of course I know Derek. He comes around every now and then. He has family around here. I think his sisters live pretty close. The last time I saw him was around the holidays, though. He mentioned something about receiving orders to a training facility in New York or something."

"Maine, actually," said Ryan. "What about Joshua? Have you heard anything about him?"

"I don't know Joshua. At least, Derek never mentioned a friend by that name. But again, it's been a while since I've spoken with him."

"If you do, would you let me know?" asked Ryan, handing out more cards.

"Sure. Is he the guy you're looking for?"

"Oh, no, I just thought since I was in town I'd look him up. No telling when I'll get back to visit."

"Are you going to have dinner here?" asked Jennifer as Jack laid a menu in front of them.

"I am. I'd love for you to join me. Do you want to get a table or eat at the bar?"

"Let's eat at the bar with Jack," she said. "It'll be like old times."

Ryan and Jennifer sat and talked for nearly two hours while they ate and enjoyed a few cocktails. Several more of Ryan's old friends and acquaintances arrived, extending his initial timeframe of a few hours for dinner closer to four. He didn't mind the pleasant distraction from the serious business he was in town to conduct. For a short period of time, Ryan remembered what it felt like to have very few cares in the world.

Jennifer noticed him looking at his watch with more frequency as the midnight hour started to creep up on them. It was time to put her plan into action. She took her phone out of her purse as if she were receiving a call. She spoke loud enough to make sure Ryan heard her fake conversation.

"Hello? Yes, I am," she said and paused briefly. "No, no, that's fine. If the doors and windows are locked, I'm sure it was a false alarm. Sometimes when the air conditioner kicks in it blows the curtains and sets off the motion detector." Jennifer paused again and noticed Ryan listening to her call. "Okay. Thank you very much. I appreciate the fast response. Good-bye."

"Is everything okay?" asked Ryan.

"Yeah," said Jennifer, exhaling. "My house was broken into a few months ago while I was at work. It freaked me out a little, so my dad installed a security system. Actually, he had no choice. Either he installed the system or I was going to become a permanent resident in his basement man cave."

"Was that the monitoring service that called?" asked Ryan.

"Yeah. They said a motion detector went off inside, but when they sent a patrol car to check it out, all the windows and doors were locked. I guess maybe it was the air conditioner blowing the curtains."

"I need to call it a night," said Ryan. "Why don't you let me make sure your house is clear. I am Super Fed, remember?"

"Why Mr. Pearson, are you asking to come home with me? That's a little forward after all these years."

"Funny girl. But, yes, I'm asking to go home with you."

"Seriously, Ryan," said Jennifer, playing him like a fiddle. "I'll be fine. I'll have my mace and cell phone at the ready."

"I won't go into gory detail, but it would make me feel much better knowing nobody was in a closet waiting for you to lock up, thinking you're safe, and climb into bed with you."

"You sound like you're talking from experience," said Jennifer, showing genuine concern.

"Too much experience," said Ryan, standing from the table. "Shall we?"

Ryan and Jennifer said their good-byes and left the Village Tavern. He followed her the short distance to her home. They pulled into her driveway and Ryan did a quick perimeter walk while Jennifer waited in her car. When he finished, he told her to unlock the door, disarm the security system, and then return to her vehicle and wait for him to clear the rooms inside.

He walked inside the small one-story ranch home, drew his weapon, and turned on his high-powered flashlight. From her vantage point outside, she could see the beam of light enter and then exit each room. When he entered the furthest room from the carport door, Derek Mathews quickly and silently entered the house. Jennifer exited her car and positioned herself in the doorway. She could see Derek crouched behind the breakfast bar in the kitchen ready to ambush Ryan when he reappeared from the back of the house. The agent turned off his flashlight and holstered his gun as he walked through the hallway toward Jennifer.

"All clear," said Ryan, approaching the kitchen. "I found a lightning bug, but he evaded me and went into the air-conditioning vent in the spare room. If he gives you any trouble –"

As Ryan passed the breakfast bar, he instinctively went for his gun when he felt a presence followed by movement out of the corner of his eye. Before he could aim, Derek uncoiled into him, sending them both crashing into the dining room table. His gun hovered in the air for a moment then fell to the kitchen floor as the impact jarred it from his grasp. The genetically enhanced soldier with adrenaline firing through his veins continued through the table, overshot Ryan, and buried himself into the far wall.

The FBI agent quickly recovered to his knees. "Run!" yelled Ryan. "Get out of here! Run!" His eyes stayed focused on the intruder as he attempted to keep himself between Derek and Jennifer's escape. As both men scrambled to get back on their feet, Ryan saw Jennifer still standing in the doorway. He yelled for her to run again as he reached down to his ankle to draw his backup pistol. In the blink of an eye, Derek launched again from across the room, sending them tumbling back into the kitchen. Adjusting his trajectory, the Marine easily pinned the FBI agent's arms while driving his head down to the tile floor. Ryan was immobilized.

He turned his head to the side writhing in pain to see Jennifer still standing in the doorway. "He's going to kill you. Run," gasped Ryan, unable to catch his breath in his contorted position.

"He's not going to kill me, Ryan," said Jennifer calmly. "And he's not going to kill you either."

She walked over to a corner in the kitchen and recovered Ryan's gun. She held it in one hand while putting the other on Derek's shoulder.

"He's not going to kill you," said Jennifer, looking directly at Derek.

18

LEVERAGE

JOSHUA SMILED AS THE YOUNG woman returned to the backcountry shelter carrying a plastic container full of clean water. Her hiking partner gathered up the rest of the dishes they had used for dinner on the second night of their ten-day sabbatical. They started their scenic vacation journey on the Appalachian Trail at Amicalola Falls State Park in North Georgia.

The couple boasted how they left their cell phones and any other modern conveniences behind to put as much distance as possible between them and the hectic pace of their normal lives. The boyfriend of the young woman was an Army Ranger and instantly felt at ease with the special forces Marine who claimed to be looking for a little distance himself.

As the isolated hikers were cleaning up after their meal, Joshua startled his new friends when he jumped to his feet and walked out of the shelter. He jogged over to an open field illuminated by the bright full moon. He closed his eyes and concentrated on the sense of anxiety which overwhelmed him seconds before. Less than a minute later, he felt an unprovoked rush of adrenaline pump through his veins. He instantly knew the feeling was originating from Derek, but he couldn't pinpoint the reason. If Derek had been killed, he would have experienced the debilitating pain similar to what he felt the exact moments Arrington and Elliot died. What Joshua sensed was something different, but significant enough to evoke the intuitive reaction experienced by some identical twins.

The feeling left as abruptly as it arrived. Whatever Derek experienced, it only lasted a minute before his excited state returned to a manageable level. Joshua and Derek spent weeks learning how to control the intuitive response. If they didn't, Alex would be able to intercept the non-verbal communication and be more effective at hunting them down. Because Arrington and Elliot were emotionally weak, Joshua knew they'd be easy prey for the only uninfected Marine from Didache. Joshua mastered the skill while intentionally leaving Derek less capable in order to remain the most powerful of the five super soldiers.

Joshua sensed something was wrong with Derek and felt a sense of urgency to find him before the next designated rendezvous date in one week. But he had unfinished business deep in the woods with his two new friends. He heard the Army Ranger walk up behind him in the field.

"Are you okay, pal?" asked the young soldier.

"Yeah," said Joshua. "I think the trail food was just trying to come out of me before I was ready," he laughed, putting his arm around the soldier's neck. "But there's no way I'd let you think an Army stomach is stronger than a Marine's."

"There's no way a –"

While he laughed, Joshua snapped his neck. The sound of the trauma which instantly killed the young man echoed in the still night and startled his girlfriend thirty yards away. She poked her head around the corner of the shelter, but didn't see either of the men. She called out their names with no response. She turned around to dig out the flashlight from her backpack, but instead found Joshua standing in a dark corner. She could see his shadow from the campfire near the opening of the three-wall shelter rise and fall from his heavy breathing.

"Shit!" she yelled. "You nearly scared me to death. I told you two no creepy crap or I'd walk back to the car." She paused, noticing something odd about Joshua in the dimly lit room. "Where's my boyfriend?" she asked in a demanding tone.

"He slipped and fell off the mountain," said Joshua, taking a step forward into the light. "I guess that means you're single now, sweetheart."

As the light revealed his mutated face, she screamed and fell back against the wall. Joshua calmly walked up to her and punched her in the stomach.

"That's enough of that," he said as the blow stole her breath and left her silent. "I'm sorry we can't play, but I have to make this quick."

Ryan sat on the kitchen floor with his back against a cabinet, trying to wiggle out of his own handcuffs. His ankles were bound together with a tightly wrapped extension cord. Derek hogtied him before stepping into the next room to talk to Jennifer. They spoke for a brief moment and then returned to the kitchen. Without saying a word, the Marine pulled Ryan up by his shirt collar until his feet were dangling off the ground. He stared into the FBI agent's eyes only a few inches away from his.

"If it were up to me, I'd tear you out of your skin for what you did to Peter," said Derek, gritting his teeth. "But for some unknown fucking reason, she thinks she can trust you. Me trusting you is going to be a different story."

"The real question is, can she trust you?" asked Ryan defiantly. "Does she have any idea what you are and what you've done?"

"I use more energy scratching my ass than it would take to kill you right now," said Derek, holding Ryan up with one hand while wrapping the fingers on the other around his throat. "So I suggest you stop pissing me off."

"Derek," said Jennifer in a disarming tone. "I know you're angry, but I need you to focus on what we talked about. You need to let this play out."

He released his grip from Ryan's throat and put him back on his feet. He stepped back as Jennifer stepped forward.

"We'll answer every question you have, Ryan, I promise," said Jennifer in the same disarming tone. "But if you push him, he'll push back much harder."

"You have no idea what you're dealing with, Jennifer. He's a monster. He's killed –"

"He's killed women," interrupted Jennifer. "I know. He's taken four and he'll kill again in a little over a week. And if the thought enters your brain I condone it or I'm some kind of accomplice, then you're only going to prove his point that this was a mistake. And when you do, you need to get far, far away. So clear your head and listen to what we have to say for just a few minutes."

"Looks like I don't have much of a choice," said Ryan, looking down at his restraints.

"Neither did Derek," replied Jennifer. "The difference being, he's not going to kill you. He's not going to hunt you down and shoot you like you did to his friend. This is a fucked up situation, Ryan, and I'm running out of options before he starts piling up bodies. Help me stop that from happening. Please."

Ryan could see the pained look on her face as well as hear the exhaustion in her voice. He always thought of Jennifer as a strong woman who didn't take shit from anyone. It baffled him how she could be involved at any level with a man wanted for rape and murder, but he was more intrigued at what they had to say.

"So you're just going to let me walk out of here?" asked Ryan.

"It's as simple as that," replied Jennifer. "All you have to do is listen. If you know anything about me, you know I keep my word. You should also know I consider you a good friend and wouldn't let anything happen to you."

Ryan looked down again at his bound feet. "It's a little late to put that out there."

"What choice did we have, Ryan, really? Would you have just walked in here with a smile, sat on the couch with a cup of coffee, and took notes? No, you would've done your job and called in the cavalry. But after what happened to Peter and Richard, can you really blame us for being cautious?"

"How do you know what happened to them?"

"Because Derek can feel it when the others are hurt or scared," said Jennifer. "I know it sounds crazy, but I was with him when Peter died. He doubled over in pain and told me you were killing him. He felt every bullet fired into Peter. But the worst part was Derek telling me he could also feel Peter's fear. I believe him, Ryan. If you had been here when it happened, you'd believe him, too."

"Jennifer, I can't just walk away from here," said Ryan, trying not to deceive them. "You said it yourself. He's going to kill another woman in a week. I can't let that happen. I'll protect him, but he needs to come in with me. I know people who may be able to help."

"That isn't part of the deal," injected Derek. "Are you that cocky, or stupid, to think I'm going to walk to my own execution? Christ, I thought you were smarter than that. This was a mistake." Derek, irritated, turned to Jennifer. "This isn't going to work."

"It's not about me being smart, Derek," continued Ryan. "It's about you being smart. It's about saving innocent lives."

"Shut the fuck up, Ryan," grunted Derek. "Jennifer thought you'd listen, but you've obviously already made up your mind about me."

"Derek, please," exclaimed Jennifer. "Getting angry isn't –"

"He's not going to listen, baby. He's going to leave here and call in his death squad to take me before he leaves the driveway. He's going to take you. I won't let that happen," said Derek, taking a step toward Ryan. "For the record, Fed, if one of you puts a finger on her, I'll end all of you."

Ryan narrowed his eyes as he noticed the color leaving Derek's face. Faint blue streaks started appearing across his forehead and down his cheeks to his neck. His captor began to breathe heavy through his nose, resembling an animal snorting a warning to its adversary. Derek raised his hand and pulled at his front teeth.

"Stop it!" yelled Jennifer, stepping in front of Derek. "Both of you. Derek, I want you to go into the living room. Give me one minute with him, please." She put her hands on his face as her eyes were welling with tears. "Please. Think about us on the beach in Bora Bora for just one minute. After, you can do whatever you want with him. I won't stop you, angel."

Derek reluctantly turned and walked away. Jennifer had won her minute. She opened the kitchen drawer and pulled out a pair of cooking shears. She cut the cord around Ryan's ankles and removed the cuffs from his wrists. With a puzzled look on his face, she handed him his gun.

"If you're not going to listen, put a bullet in us now," said Jennifer, defeated. "I'm so fucking tired of trying to convince him there's a way out of this. I'm so fucking tired of everyone hunting him like an animal and not giving a shit about what *they* did to him. Before this happened, he was the most gentle, sweetest man I'd ever met. They've made him hate himself so much he'll barely touch me. A man so full of love and kindness can't even hug me without feeling the pain of what he's done. We're on the edge here and one tiny step from going over. You're the only one that can give us hope."

Ryan watched the tears run down her desperate face and felt enough sympathy to holster his weapon. "I'll listen, Jennifer. I promise."

"Thank you," she said, as they both walked into the living room. Derek jumped to his feet, alarmed at seeing Ryan free from his restraints.

"Sit down," ordered Jennifer. She was through with the tears. Even Ryan was startled by the force of her command.

"Something tells me you should be more afraid of her than me," said Ryan.

"You have no idea," replied Derek, taking a seat.

———

A black Suburban pulled up to the curb at the arrival gate for the airport in Atlanta. Colonel Brown and four men mounted the vehicle being driven by Alex Tifton. They drove several miles before the Colonel spoke.

"No more mistakes, Alex," said Colonel Brown. "Not only did we miss the opportunity to end this, you managed to hand over the entire Red Team to Ryan. I still can't wrap my head around how badly you fucked up, Marine. But I can't dwell on that. I have to fix this myself. Right now, I'd rather have a troop of fucking Boy Scouts running this operation. Is your head on straight, son? Can I count on you to finish this mission?"

"Yes, sir," replied Alex. "You can. I won't fail again."

"You can't fail again. Do you understand me? You cannot fail again."

"What do you need me to do?" asked Alex obediently. "Do we take out Ryan and his team?"

"Luckily for you the Deputy Director of the FBI still has no idea he has Dr. Anderson or our men. Ryan doesn't know who to trust, so he's running the show under the radar. But that won't last long. We need to find Dr. Anderson, and we need to do it fast. If we take her out of the picture, Ryan won't have shit. He has absolutely no evidence against us. We can still point the finger at the scientists who are crying like babies for us to protect them. We'll simply hand them over when this thing is through and you and I will walk away."

"Ryan has help," said Alex. "The guys that set us up at the decoy house were pros. She may not even be in the state."

"They weren't FBI, and that's a good thing for us," said Colonel Brown. "We'll know who they are soon enough and we'll get our morons back. But first things first, we need to get our hands on Dr. Anderson."

"Do you think he'll lead us to her?"

"As long as I have his daughter, he'll do anything I fucking tell him to do."

Colonel Brown turned around in his seat and glared at Scott Wilson. As soon as he realized Scott was feeding Ryan information, he had Alex abduct his ten-year-old daughter from her bed. Scott sat motionless in the back seat, staring out the window thinking about his child being held at the lab. He'd do whatever it took to keep his little girl safe.

"Are the vehicles at the hotel?" asked Colonel Brown.

"Yes, sir," replied Alex. "Stocked with weapons and gear."

"Good. Are you listening, Scott?"

"Yes, I'm listening."

"You're taking this car after we reach the hotel and driving straight to Ryan's. I don't care how you do it, but get him to take you to Dr. Anderson tonight. The GPS transmitter will do the rest. Once we have the doc, I make the phone call that sends your little girl home. Are you clear?"

"I am," replied Scott. "What are you going to do with Kristina?"

"You should be more concerned about what you're going to tell your wife if you fuck this up."

Scott moved into the driver's seat after they arrived at the hotel. The Colonel gave him final instructions before they went inside. Thirty minutes later, Scott pulled up to the FBI house.

"Hey, little buddy," greeted Dallas at the door.

"I need to talk to Ryan."

"Good to see you, too," said Dallas. "But he's not here. Anything I can help you with?"

"Get him on the phone, Dallas. I need to talk to him right now."

"Okay, come on in," said Dallas, dialing Ryan's number.

"Hey, Scott," said Tom, shaking his hand. "What's going on?"

"I really need to talk to Ryan first."

"Sorry, Scott," said Dallas. "He's not answering."

"Where is he?"

"He went to talk to some of Derek's family out in the boonies. He's probably just out of cell range. I'm sure he'll call back soon. Take a load off. I've got some cold ones in the fridge. You look a little tense."

"Is Michelle with him?"

"No, she's with Kristina at the safe house. Why?"

"Michelle's the only one watching her? Are you people mental? Alex is out there looking for her and you have one fucking agent protecting her?"

"Whoa, chief," said Dallas, putting up his hand. "She's got a little army around her."

"A little army?"

"Yeah," said Dallas. "A buddy of Ryan's from his old unit owns a top-notch security group. Those guys are better than some of the FBI SWAT teams I've worked with. She's in good hands."

Scott immediately saw the opportunity to get his daughter back earlier than he'd hoped. He excused himself to the back deck of the house to make a phone call.

"He's not here, Colonel. He's going to be out of touch for a while."

"Finally, a fucking break. Good work, Scott. You make this happen tonight and you'll be having breakfast with your little girl in the morning. Listen, things are going to start jumping there in a few minutes. You're a smart guy. Use it to your advantage."

Scott ended the call and walked back inside. "On second thought, I'll take that beer."

19

WITHOUT REMORSE

U NDERNEATH A PILE OF SPLINTERED wood in Jennifer's dining room, Ryan's shattered cell phone couldn't alert him to the several messages in the queue. He leaned forward in his chair as Derek and Jennifer sat holding hands on the sofa.

"What do you know about the Didache Project?" asked Derek.

"In a nutshell, the military contracted civilian geneticists to build super soldiers," answered Ryan.

"Basically," agreed Derek. "But it's a little more complicated than that. Five of us were selected out of about a hundred volunteers. Every few weeks, we'd be injected with another round of gene therapy designed to make us stronger and faster." Anticipating his question he added, "It wasn't like steroids. We didn't have to exercise any harder to build muscle mass or keep what we developed. The way it was explained, our muscles and organs were being enhanced at the cellular level. They were being genetically mutated. It was important to them that we looked like typical Marines, but with atypical abilities.

"They developed those abilities in a somewhat natural progression. For example, one of the first rounds of therapy increased the density of our muscles, but not the size. When I weighed in the day we received the shots, I was 182 pounds. Two weeks later, I was 210 without any visible size increase. After that success, they had to increase the density of our bones as well to take the stresses of the stronger muscle tissue. After that, they had to increase the density of our heart muscle to pump our newly enhanced blood designed to carry more oxygen and fuel to support our stronger muscles. After that, they had to enhance our respiratory system to intake more oxygen to support our more demanding organs and systems. And that's how it went for years. They'd enhance one part of us and then have to adjust and tweak our other systems to support the original enhancements. Are you still with me?"

"That's actually a better explanation than the one I received from the scientists," said Ryan. "They just made what you already had in you stronger."

"Correct. And we were all fired up about it, too. There was virtually no pain involved and the discomfort was minimal. And if we did experience any discomfort, they'd stop everything and figure out the problem. Almost overnight, I remember hitting the track one morning and they clocked me running at nearly 30 miles per hour. I wasn't even trying. The same thing happened in the weight room. In a matter of weeks, I went from bench pressing 300 pounds to pressing over 800.

"I will say, the weirdest enhancement was my vision. It took a while to get used to the changes. Try walking around your house wearing binoculars and you'll have a good idea what it was like. It took our brains a little while to catch up with that one, but eventually it did. Everything they were doing to us we wanted. And after we started experiencing the results, we wanted more. We felt like superheroes."

"How did they make you guys sensitive to one another's pain or location?" asked Ryan.

"Nothing that we know of," replied Derek. "They just kept telling us it was an anomaly associated with the treatments. I mean, it didn't really concern us at the time. In fact, it made us feel more like brothers than volunteers for biomedical research. It was kind of cool."

"When did you start having the urge to kill?" asked Ryan, changing the mood from light to dark. He could see Jennifer's hand squeeze Derek's.

"About seven months ago," answered Derek. "It happened just like the other changes. There was a funny feeling almost immediately after the treatment, but it really started kicking in a few days later. That's when the pain started. It was mainly in our mouths and hands, but then it spread everywhere. About a week later, I woke up one morning with a toothache that was making my head spin. I looked in the mirror and my gums were bleeding and I could see bulges forming above my canine teeth. By late afternoon, the pain was fucking blinding. We had to beg the doctors to pull out our front teeth. I'm wearing dentures now."

"That's what made you want to murder women?"

"No, not the pain," Derek corrected him. "That was just an indicator that something went wrong with us. Well, all of us except Alex."

"What do you mean?"

"A week before that treatment, they discovered a hereditary disease in Alex's DNA. They actually removed it and replaced it with normal DNA, but they were going to wait a week or two to catch him up with our treatment schedule. When things started going bad for us, they opted not to give him the same juice. That's why he wasn't affected. He simply missed that day of class."

"As far as us killing, less than a week after they yanked my teeth, I started having very weird thoughts. We all did. But the craziest thing is, we were all having the exact same weird thoughts."

"What were they?"

"Actually, it was more like urges than thoughts. There was a twenty-three-year-old intern named Bethany. She was a medical student working through a semester at the lab. She was a very pretty girl with blonde hair and blue eyes. I think she dated one of the super geeks."

"Super geeks?"

"Yeah, he was one of the four young genius scientists running the show. Apparently, they were some of the smartest people on the planet. They looked like teenagers. Dr. Kristina Anderson was the only one that actually looked like an adult."

"Okay, what happened with Bethany?"

Derek hesitated and looked over at Jennifer with very heavy eyes. Ryan didn't miss the significance. If Derek confirmed his suspicion and talked about the details in front of Jennifer, it would change everything.

"Derek?"

"The urges, the thoughts I had were…" said Derek, hesitating again. "Sweetheart, I don't know if I can talk about this with you in the room. You shouldn't have to listen to this."

"Baby, I have no idea how horrible this must be, but I'm in this fight with you. It's not your fault. I know it's not your fault, but you have to tell him. You have to tell me, too."

Derek turned his eyes to the veteran FBI agent who had witnessed some of the worst things evil humans could possibly do to another. If

Derek was trying to pretend he was a man in unbearable anguish, Ryan thought he'd win an Oscar.

"I went to one of the therapists assigned to the Didache team and told him about the urges. I told him Bethany was in danger from all of us. At first, he dismissed it and tried talking me down with some psychobabble bullshit. I shut him up when I told him about the things I wanted to do to her. What we all wanted to do to her. I told him to think of Bethany as his own daughter. Her internship was cancelled the next day. She was told she wasn't allowed back on the property."

"Do you know where she was attending medical school?" asked Ryan, hoping for the answer he wanted.

"Syracuse University. Why?"

"Please continue, Derek. What happened next?"

"Even though she was gone, we all thought about her every second we were awake. We were beyond obsessed. The super geeks were scrambling to find out what was happening to us when Joshua approached the guy on staff who dated Bethany. He only talked to him for a few minutes, but he came back with an address. I remember looking over at the guy. He was visibly shaking. Whatever Joshua said, it terrified him.

"Later that night Joshua pulled us aside. He told us he knew where she was. I wish I could tell you we fought the urges and told him we didn't care, but that wouldn't be the truth. We listened and thought about the relief we would feel if we could just get to her. If we could do what we all wanted to do."

"What did you want to do?"

———

Dallas's phone rang as he was sitting with Scott and Tom at the kitchen table. It was Deputy Director Donaldson.

"Agent Chase, is Ryan with you? He's not answering me, and we can't locate him through the GPS in his phone."

"He's interviewing Derek's sister and probably out of cell range, sir."

"Shit. Agent Chase, we have good information on Derek and Joshua's location. I've mobilized the Atlanta SWAT team, and they're heading to the Paulding County Sheriff's Office now. You and your team need to get there as soon as possible for the assault briefing. We have a chance to end this tonight, so

stop talking to me and get everyone over there now. I'll send some other agents to go look for Ryan."

"Yes, sir," replied Dallas.

"Tom, call Michelle and let her know we're coming to get her. That was Donaldson. They have good intel on Derek and Joshua's location. It's not far from here."

"We need to wait for Ryan," said Tom immediately.

"The director doesn't want us to wait," said Dallas. "And I don't want to wait either. We have a chance to put them on ice tonight."

"You guys can't leave," said Scott, turning both their heads.

"What are you talking about?" asked Dallas.

"That's what I needed to talk to Ryan about," said Scott. "Colonel Brown, Alex, and another team are here to take Kristina tonight. They know where she is. You need to move her out of wherever she's being held."

"Fuck," said Dallas, frustrated. "We need to take those guys now, Tom."

"This is moving too fast, Dallas," replied Tom. "We need to slow down and wait for Ryan to call."

"Slow means a missed opportunity to take both of them now. Do you really think Ryan wants us to sit on our fucking hands while the SWAT team goes after them? They have no idea what they're dealing with and we do. We need to go."

"Dallas, did you hear what I said?" asked Scott, becoming agitated. "They're going to kill her. I can't let that happen. I won't let that happen," he said, drawing on the emotion of visualizing his daughter scared and alone in a cell.

"Ryan, answer you damned phone," said Dallas, looking out the window.

——

"I wanted to tear her apart limb from limb," exhaled Derek. "I wanted to make her feel unimaginable pain. And I..." He hesitated once again. "This is the craziest part, but along with the urge to hurt her, I also wanted to taste her blood."

"What?" asked Ryan. "You wanted to taste her blood? I'm assuming you're not speaking metaphorically?"

"No, I'm not," said Derek. "And yes, I wanted to actually taste her blood. It was a big part of the addiction. I wanted to tear into her neck, sever her arteries, and drain every drop in her. Listen to me, Ryan. I have no fucking idea why. I have no idea why I wanted to hurt her, let alone drink her blood, but the urge was there. It consumed me, and all of us, to the point that we didn't care how Joshua found out where she was. We just wanted to get to her. It seemed like the only way to end it. I had no idea why we felt that way. All I knew is, they must have put it in our heads. They must have done something to make us go from normal people to what we were."

"Was the urge to rape her as intense?" asked Ryan.

"No, it wasn't," answered Derek, looking down at the floor. "I didn't feel any urge to rape her or any of them. I don't think Peter or Richard felt it either."

"You answered as if you knew I was going to ask."

"Tell him, Derek," said Jennifer. "Tell him about Joshua."

———

Dallas paced back and forth across the kitchen. Tom sat quietly in his chair after calling Michelle to let her know they were coming to get her.

"Steve's men can handle the relocation," said Dallas. "We need to go now."

"Michelle agrees this is moving too fast," said Tom. "She has a feeling something is wrong."

"Ryan has been breaking his neck trying not to let the deputy director know we're on to him, but Donaldson has been right on the mark about finding Arrington and Elliot," said Dallas, pleading his case. "I believe Derek and Joshua are where he says they are. If we disobey Donaldson, he's going to know we doubt him. Do you think Ryan's ready to let that cat out of the bag?"

"I'm not saying they aren't there," said Tom. "But the fact that Colonel Brown plans on taking Kristina tonight makes me extremely uncomfortable leaving Steve's men to handle the relocation alone."

"I'll go," said Scott. "I'll make sure she's safe."

"No offense, Scott," said Tom. "But I don't think you're qualified to run the relocation."

"He won't be running it," injected Dallas quickly. "He'll be a familiar face to keep her calm. I'll give him my phone so Ryan can call him as soon as they arrive at the new location. I like the idea, Scott. Let's make it happen, Tom."

———

"I didn't want to believe it at first," said Derek. "But after Jennifer put it all together, I couldn't deny it anymore."

"Deny what?" asked Ryan.

"That Joshua was enjoying it. That he embraced being what he was and wanted more beyond the urges they put in our heads. You see, with Peter, Richard, and me, we'd fight the urge to stalk and kill as long as we could. But every six weeks, there are two or three days that we simply can't. I know that's impossible for you to believe, but it's the truth. It's an indescribably powerful addiction."

"Why do you think Joshua's urges are more intense?"

"I really don't know," said Derek. "We left the facility the night he found out where Bethany lived. It was easy to slip past the security detail. None of us hesitated or tried to talk each other out of it. Like I said, we just wanted to get to her."

"Wait," said Ryan. "Where did she live?"

"The lab had its own dorms set up a couple miles away for the staff and interns from all over the country. It only took us a few minutes to cover the distance."

"So she didn't make it back to the campus in New York?"

"No, but her room was full of boxes. The poor girl was probably leaving the next day. Why do you ask?"

"The file I received from my boss put the murder scene near the Syracuse campus. The file also failed to indicate any connection between her and the lab. Two very important pieces of information that would've had us looking hard at the facility six months ago."

"Are you saying the deputy director is in bed with Colonel Brown?"

"It's very much looking that way," said Ryan.

"Jesus," said Derek, "You're about as fucked as I am."

"Again, it's very much looking that way. Okay, what happened next?"

———

Tom, Dallas, and Scott left the FBI house and drove to Kristina's location. Michelle met them outside on the sidewalk. Patrick, the leader of Steve's security detail, was with her.

"Has anyone talked to Ryan?" was Michelle's first question.

"Not yet," said Tom. "We need to follow through with Donaldson's orders. I don't think Ryan is ready to tip our hand at this point. The fact that he can't get in touch with him is bad enough. If all of us don't show up, he'll know something is wrong."

"How do you know the Colonel is coming after her tonight?" asked Michelle, glaring at Scott.

"I was standing beside him and Alex when they were making the plans. Is that good enough for you?" asked Scott, glaring back at her.

"When will you be ready to move, Patrick?" asked Michelle.

"The plane will be at the airport in forty-five minutes. We'll leave here in twenty."

Michelle pulled Patrick away from the group. She put her face inches away from his.

"I'm not going to lecture you on how dangerous these people are," said Michelle. "But you need to be ready for anything. If things go bad, you grab her and run. Don't engage in the fight. You won't win. We had the element of surprise and two assault teams ready to ambush them at the decoy house. That won't be the case if you run into them again. You just grab her and run. Do you understand me, Patrick?"

"I understand, Michelle, I really do," said Patrick, convincingly. "As long as I'm alive, they won't get to her, I promise."

Michelle reached out and squeezed his arm. "Look, you get her out of here and safely tucked away, and I may forget that awful line you used on me. I hate to admit it, but I've grown a little fond of her. Do your job, and dinner's on me."

"I'm on it," smiled Patrick.

Michelle opened the car door but took one last long look around before climbing inside. She smiled at Patrick as he and Scott stood in the front yard. The vehicle lurched forward as the team headed for the briefing in the neighboring county.

"We arrived at her dorm just after three o'clock in the morning," continued Derek. "There really wasn't much of a plan. We were all shaking, thinking how close we were to having her. Sneaking past security at the dorm was easy. Only the front and back entrances had cameras on the doors. It was nothing for us to jump straight up and grab the rail on the balcony of her second-floor room. We slid the glass door open and walked right in.

"Joshua punched her in the face while she was sleeping to keep her unconscious. He picked her up, jumped off the balcony, and calmly walked into the woods with her over his shoulder. He was carrying a large duffel bag in his other hand. The three of us followed behind like ducklings to an abandoned steel mill less than half a mile from the dorm."

"And then you killed her," said Ryan.

"No. I wanted to and thought I would. I replayed the moment over and over in my head as soon as we grabbed her. But when we saw her lying on the dirty floor with a broken nose, we just couldn't do it. Whatever they pumped into our heads hadn't completely removed our impulse restraint. We lost all control a few weeks later; none of us could stop it then."

"Joshua killed her, didn't he?" asked Ryan.

"He became irritated, but he didn't seem pissed that we could fight off the urge. He told us he couldn't do it either and he was going to take her to the hospital. Peter, Richard, and I ended up going back to the lab. Joshua said he'd rather be the only one taking the risk trying to get her help for her injuries."

"She never made it to the hospital, Derek. You didn't see Joshua back at the lab for two days, right?"

"Yeah, the staff at the lab was asking us questions about him, but we told them we had no idea where he was. We thought maybe he was picked up by the cops once he tried to get her into an E.R. When he did come back, he told us he almost did get caught and had to hide out in the woods after he dropped her off."

"He killed her, Derek. He kept her alive for two days while he brutally raped and tortured her. The things he did to her were inhuman. You had no idea?"

"I don't think you fully appreciate how fucking confused, scared, and isolated we were. We were in constant pain, and the thoughts we could control were slowly losing the battle to the ones we couldn't. And nobody there seemed to know why."

"I'm sorry," said Ryan, "You're right. I have no idea what you went through."

"What he's still going through," added Jennifer.

"Did you tell anyone what happened?"

"No. We didn't even talk to each other very much after. When Joshua returned, we pretty much kept quiet. We all knew it was a terrible thing we did, kidnapping and hurting her, but we were still trying to wrap our heads around why we did it in the first place."

"If you thought the girl was still alive, why did all four of you run?"

"Joshua came to us a day later and said the girl identified him as the man that attacked her. That's when I told him I talked to the therapist about our urges. He said the therapist and the other scientists went to Colonel Brown to tell him we needed to be destroyed. Joshua overheard Colonel Brown telling the super geeks to inject us with potassium chloride instead of the painkillers."

"You thought they were going to kill you in order to preserve the Didache Project," said Ryan, putting more pieces of the puzzle together. "If it were leaked to the press that the government was responsible for manufacturing serial killers, they'd shut it down for good."

"Absolutely," said Derek. "There's no way the Colonel was or is going to let that happen. Colonel Brown *is* the Didache Project."

"Why did Peter and Richard separate from the group?" asked Ryan. "Seems to me you'd be more formidable together."

"Because they figured out what Joshua was before Derek did," answered Jennifer. "They figured out he was pure evil. I think he was a monster long before he volunteered for the project."

Jennifer told Ryan about how young women were reported missing, raped or killed wherever Joshua was hiding out. Derek gave Jennifer's theory more weight by describing how Joshua would disappear for days within the timeframes of many of the abductions and murders. For the first time since he accepted the mission from the deputy director, Ryan was finally getting his answers.

Colonel Brown stopped the vehicle less than a block from Kristina's safe house. Behind the dark tinted windows of the SUV, the men inside wearing black camouflage released the safeties on their weapons.

"You can bet they'll have at least three or four outside and two, maybe three, inside," briefed Colonel Brown. "There should be no FBI presence anywhere near the place."

"Do we bring Scott with us or leave him on his own?" asked Alex.

"Everyone at that house dies tonight, Alex. Are you clear? This is where you erase your fuckup. This is where we end this and save Didache."

"Yes, sir."

2Ø

KNUCKLES

DALLAS PARKED THE CAR IN the nearly empty lot of the Paulding County Sheriff's Department. He stepped out of the vehicle and looked at his watch. It was a little after 2 a.m. when the uneasy feeling hit his stomach.

"We're at the right place," said Tom, looking at the large departmental sign.

"Maybe we just beat the SWAT team here," said Dallas. His phone alerted him to an incoming call. He paused before he looked at the screen as he made a silent wish it would be Ryan.

"Agent Chase," greeted Deputy Director Donaldson. *"Sorry to send you out so late on a false alarm, but we just received word from the scout team that it was the wrong two bad guys. I've already notified Atlanta SWAT to stand down."*

"Sir, are you positive?" asked Dallas as the uneasy feeling turned to nausea.

"I'm quite sure, son. You guys can stand down as well. Have you heard from Ryan?"

"No, sir," said Dallas, turning pale.

"All right, just have him call me in the morning. I think we could all use a little rest."

"Goodnight, sir," said Dallas, ending the call.

"What?" asked Michelle, noticing his color.

"Director said it was a false alarm. He said it was the wrong guys and nobody's coming. I'm not exactly sure what –"

All three of their phones simultaneously chimed and vibrated. It was Kristina's panic button.

"Get in the fucking car, Dallas!" yelled Michelle, jumping behind the wheel. Dallas stood motionless near the front bumper. "Dallas!" screamed Michelle, snapping him back to reality.

——

"Do you know where Joshua is now?" asked Ryan.

"Yes," said Derek. "We have several hideouts around Atlanta. He's at a house near Dahlonega in the North Georgia Mountains. I'm supposed to meet him there in a few days. Our plan was to go to Maine while everyone was down here looking for us. He was certain Colonel Brown would send most of his guys, leaving him and the scientists relatively unprotected."

"What were you going to do with them?"

"We were going to kill them all. Everyone that had anything to do with destroying our lives, we were going to kill. Joshua and I both agreed that the only way they'd ever stop hunting us is if we were dead, or they were. I opted for them."

"I'm guessing I'm on that list," said Ryan.

"You were for what you did to Peter."

"He murdered a woman in cold blood in front of our eyes," explained Ryan. "And he did it after I identified myself and ordered him to freeze. He ripped her throat out, threw a bed at us, and killed two of my agents when he tried to flee. I didn't show up to kill him, Derek. All I knew was what they told me about him. The evidence was overwhelming."

"He doesn't feel that way anymore," said Jennifer. "He understands this was all part of Joshua's plan for revenge and freedom. He understands Joshua was using him like he uses everyone else, including you."

"Is that true?"

"It is, Ryan," said Derek, taking a deep breath. "I'll answer for what I've done to those women, but so will they. If I kill them, they'll just be replaced. If I show the world what they did to us, they'll be shut down forever. They'll never do this to anyone else again."

"But you're not turning yourself in, right?"

"I don't think you understand," said Derek. "You can't stop Joshua on your own. He's the one that handed over Peter and Richard to you and the Colonel. The only reason they're dead is because he wanted them that way. You have no idea the damage he's capable of doing. And if you lock me up, you're locking up the one man that can stop him. And when he's finished with all of you, I'll be a sitting duck in my cell."

"We're not all morons in the Bureau, Derek. If you expose what really happened at the lab, neither the Colonel nor my boss will be able to keep a lid on this any longer. We'll get the support we need to find and stop him."

"The same governmental support they used to find and stop Bin Laden?" asked Derek. "If the entire FBI can't catch one terrorist, what makes you believe you can catch Joshua? Be realistic, Ryan. You know I'm your best shot."

Ryan found it difficult to argue with his logic. Derek wasn't finished explaining why he wasn't turning himself in.

"See this woman sitting beside me?" asked Derek. "After everything that's happened, after everything I've told her, after everything she just heard, she still believes in me when nobody else on the planet would. She's also the one who convinced me to take a chance with you. And because of that, she's willing to put herself in harm's way. If the Colonel finds out about our relationship, he'll kill her. When Joshua finds out I betrayed him, she won't be safe anywhere until he's dead. There's no force on the planet that will prevent me from protecting her. I can't do that in jail. Do you understand?"

He immediately thought about Kristina and understood why Derek couldn't leave Jennifer. But the obvious issue needed to be discussed before Ryan could walk away from the killer.

"I'm sorry I have to ask this in front of you, Jennifer. But I have to know."

"You want to know when he's going to take another woman," said Jennifer. "He has about five days."

"That doesn't leave us much time to sort this out. Derek, I can't let you take—"

"We have an idea," said Derek. "We knew you'd ask. It may sound a little ridiculous, but it makes sense to us."

"It's not ridiculous, sweetie," said Jennifer, "It's simple. And simple seems to be working for us lately."

"What's the idea?" asked Ryan.

"The urges last about two days," explained Derek. "I can usually fight them off for the first day, but not the second. I'll go with you when I get close to losing my grip. You're going to take me somewhere very isolated, restrain me as best you can, and then knock me out for a day or two with a heavy sedative."

"You really think that's going to work?"

"We believe it's a chemical response in my brain set on some kind of biological timer. Whatever is released into my system kicks in and gets more intense as the day progresses. But on the third day, there's nothing. The urges are completely gone. We're thinking, if I'm basically paralyzed during that time, I won't be able to act on the urge."

"You're right," said Ryan, "That does sound too simple. You don't think the urge will linger until you satisfy it by killing? And how can I be sure you won't just tell me you're fine, I release you, and then you kill another woman, not to mention me?"

"Because I can't control the physical mutation during that time," said Derek. "I can concentrate and make it happen anytime I want, but during those two or three days, it's involuntary. I can't control it. I'm like a junkie looking for a fix. I'll start sweating, shaking, hyperventilating, and then I'll change. Believe me when I say you'll know if I'm going to kill. After the third day, if I look normal, I'm almost positive that'll be a good indication the urge is gone. I guess I'm asking you to trust me, Ryan. Do you have any other ideas?"

"Not off the top of my head."

———

The sedan screamed around the curve, sliding across two lanes of traffic as Michelle stood on the gas pedal. Tom was being slung around the back seat while he continued trying to reach Steve's men posted at Kristina's safe house. Between attempts he would dial both Ryan's company issued and untraceable cell phones. There were no responses on any of them as they approached the safe house.

The blue and red lights flashed chaotically around and inside the unmarked car. Each strobe illuminated the concern on their faces. They knew something had gone terribly wrong. The vehicle came to a screeching halt in front of the house. Their doors flew open as the rubber stench in the white cloud caught up with the skid marks. With weapons drawn, they moved up the walkway in assault positions. The front door was wide open.

"Hold up," said Tom, turning his powerful flashlight toward an odd shaped mound under the hedges bordering the front yard. They changed direction and put their gun sights on the dark mass. They crossed the yard quickly. The mass took a human shape as they approached.

"It's Patrick," said Michelle, reaching down to check for a pulse. "He's dead."

Tom leaned down to check the pulse on the body of another one of Steve's men lying behind Patrick. The two holes in the back of his head made checking unnecessary. They turned their attention back to the open front door.

"Let's go," ordered Michelle.

They entered the dark house using their flashlights and quickly cleared the first floor. Two more bodies were in the living room. Michelle was the first to reach the bottom step of the staircase. She silently moved up with Dallas and Tom close behind.

———

"Okay," exhaled Ryan. "First things first. I need some of your blood."

"Now who's the freak?" asked Derek.

"I have a scientist who's helping me find some answers," explained Ryan. "We have a little plan of our own to expose what happened at the lab, but they need a few things. One of those things is a sample of your DNA. Another is your medical records from the beginning of the Didache Project. The third part of that equation is finding a local lab for them to examine both. The funny thing is, we thought the most difficult part would be getting your blood."

"Who's the scientist helping?"

"I'm sorry. I can't answer that right now. Their identity and location needs to stay hidden. How do you want to handle Joshua?"

"We'll keep the schedule of me going up to the hideout. You can wire me up, but you'll need to stay away. If you're anywhere near the place, he'll know."

"You're going to take him into custody yourself? It doesn't sound like a simple or smart plan."

"I'm not taking him into custody, Ryan. I'm going to kill him."

"That's not how this is going to work, Derek. We don't assassinate suspects. We try to detain them. Remember that little piece of paper called the Constitution? It's what separates us from the animals. Even Joshua has a right to face his accusers at a fair trial. I'm not a bleeding heart liberal, but I still believe in the process."

"You don't know shit about him, do you? That position might work on the Colonel, but not Joshua. He goes beyond any law man created. He needs to be removed from the planet, and unless you have a spaceship, we're going to have to kill him to stop him."

"Give me one day, Derek. Let me work on a plan. If you still think it's impossible, then we'll talk about doing it your way, okay?"

"One day, Ryan. If you don't convince me, then I go get him alone. It's just the way it has to happen. None of us are safe as long as he's out there."

"Agreed," said Ryan. "We'll talk about what we're going to do with Colonel Brown tomorrow as well. How do I reach you?"

"I'll tell you when you leave," said Derek, glancing over at Jennifer.

"Looking at the hour, it needs to be pretty soon," said Ryan, feeling his hip for his phone. "I'm surprised nobody's – shit! That explains why nobody's called." He stood up and looked around. He walked over to the destroyed dining room table and picked up the pieces of his phone. "That's not good. I need to run to my car and grab my other cell."

"Let's call it a night," said Derek. "I'll walk you out and let you know how to reach me tomorrow."

Everyone stood and walked into the kitchen. Jennifer stopped Ryan and gave him a hug. "I can't even begin to tell you how much better we feel."

"I can't begin to tell you how happy I am you're letting me walk out of here," said Ryan with a smile.

"Believe it or not," said Jennifer, "I knew you'd listen. You're a good man. You both are. That's why I know we're going to be okay. Thank you, Ryan. Thank you for proving Derek wrong."

"The jury is still out, babe," said Derek. "But if you feel good about this, then so do I."

"I do," said Jennifer.

Derek walked out of the house with Ryan so Jennifer couldn't hear their conversation. They both instinctively walked slowly looking in every direction before leaving the carport. When they stopped at Ryan's car door, Derek moved in closer to the FBI agent sent to hunt him down.

"If you've ever loved anything in your life, then you might understand a fraction of how much I love her," said Derek. "She doesn't easily give her trust, but she's given it to you. Because of her, I'll give you mine as well. But you'll know the exact second when I take it back because it'll be your last on earth. I shit you not."

"I believe you, Derek," said Ryan, moving in even closer to the man that could kill him with little effort. "I really do, but you need to know something. I'm trusting you as well. My people are out there right now risking their fucking lives to help you. You and I need to drop the bravado bullshit and end this mess. You and I are going to end this so we don't have to worry anymore about the people we care about getting hurt. Can you do that, Marine?"

Derek looked at the ground for a moment and then fixed his eyes on Ryan. "Yes, I can. Come back here tomorrow morning after 8 a.m. when Jennifer leaves for work. I'll be here. I'm always here. Just walk up to the creek bed in the backyard."

"Okay, Derek, I'll see you tomorrow. Thanks for not breaking my neck."

"Thanks for not shooting me in the face."

Ryan sat in his car and watched Derek re-enter the house. He backed out of the driveway absorbing the intensity of the last few hours. He went from seeing old friends over dinner and drinks to being set up by a good friend to be attacked by one of the most dangerous men on the planet. He thought about how lucky he was to be alive. As he drove away from the house, he reached down and picked up his untraceable cell phone. There were nine messages. The last message, *"We're on our way to the safe house,"* made him stand on the gas pedal and fire up the blue lights.

It took him less than ten minutes to arrive. He parked his car next to the sedan that had skidded to a halt on the sidewalk. There was no movement outside. He popped the trunk and bolted out of the vehicle. He grabbed his automatic rifle and leaped up the stairs to the front porch with one step. He lowered his weapon when he entered the kitchen. He saw Dallas sitting at the table with his head in his hands. Dallas slowly lifted his head and looked at Ryan with swollen eyes.

"I fucked up, Boss," said Dallas. "This is all my fault. I really fucked up."

"Where's Tom and Michelle. Are they okay?" asked Ryan in a calm voice, noticing the numerous bullet holes in the walls.

"Tom's on the back porch. Michelle is upstairs."

Ryan had never seen Dallas so distant and disconnected. He was relieved to hear Tom and Michelle's location, but he needed to put his eyes on them. He slowly walked up the stairs. He saw more bullet holes in the hallway leading to Kristina's room. He turned the corner and saw Michelle sitting on the bed. She lifted her head and looked at him and then turned her eyes to the bathroom. Ryan felt an unusual pain in his chest. He knew what might be in there but tried to clear the thought from his head.

He put his hand on her shoulder as he passed. He stood in the bathroom doorway and deflated. Lying against the bathtub, Scott Wilson with a back full of bullet holes was covering another body. They were sitting in a large pool of blood. He took a step inside to get a better look at the body he had been protecting. As if they were frozen in time, Ryan saw Kristina wrapped in Scott's arms. She was dead.

The wall of the small bathroom kept Ryan from falling to his knees. Kristina's face was covered in Scott's blood as well as her own. He could see a large bullet hole in the top of her head. Several more holes among the blood spatter were in the tile wall behind them. The men who killed them wanted to make sure the job was complete. There was no mercy.

He slowly slid down the wall until he was sitting motionless next to them. Kristina's head was cocked to the side with her eyes still open. She was looking right at Ryan with a question. "Where were you when I needed you?"

"I'm sorry, sweet girl," whispered Ryan with a tightening chest. Lying next to her hand in the pool of blood was her copy of *Treasure Island*. He wiped what he could off the book with a towel. It only took a few moments before the tight feeling in his chest turned to anger. He stood, cleared his throat, and walked out of the bathroom to Michelle. "Why is Scott here?"

"The real question is why you weren't," said Michelle defiantly. "We've been trying to reach you for over an hour." She stood up with tears in her eyes.

Ryan lowered his eyes to meet hers and asked her again, "Why is Scott here?"

"He told us Colonel Brown and Alex knew where she was and they were planning to take her tonight. Donaldson ordered us to an assault briefing because they had a location on Derek and Joshua. We told Steve's men to move her and then we went to the briefing to maintain your facade, but there was no briefing. We were set up by our own fucking boss, and Scott led them straight to her. He obviously was in over his head."

"Scott brought them?" asked Ryan, confused.

"Yes, he brought them," said Michelle, gritting her teeth. "Since you don't believe me, go ask Tom."

Ryan left the room and found Tom staring off into the backyard. Tom didn't notice him walking up behind him. He put his hand on his shoulder, startling him.

"Ryan," said Tom, "Glad to see you're okay. I thought the worst. I thought we were going to find you here as well when we couldn't reach you."

"Michelle said—"

"Oh, yes, here," said Tom, handing him a small GPS transmitter. "They always make a mistake. They always leave something behind letting us know who they are. I found this on Scott. He led them right to her, Ryan. He played us."

"I'm tired of getting played, Tom," said Ryan, fighting back his emotions. "The gloves are coming off and I'm not putting them back on until this is over."

21

ALL foR ONE

HOLDING THE BLOODY COPY OF *Treasure Island*, Ryan stood alone on the front porch. He was thinking about the story he overheard about Kristina's father beaming with pride while his little girl was reading to him when he was sick. Ryan didn't have any children, but he imagined all the hopes and dreams her father must have had for her. Hopes and dreams any father would have for his child. He had never met the man, but Ryan felt an overwhelming sense of guilt for letting him down.

He had only known her for a few weeks, but he couldn't ignore the significance of the impact she had on him. It was obvious she was highly intelligent and driven in her career, but what he remembered most was her walking into the bookstore in Baltimore with a beaming smile and childlike excitement. There were very few days Agent Ryan Pearson wished he didn't work for the FBI. The day he met Dr. Kristina Anderson, he very much wished he was just a guy in a bookstore running into a beautiful face.

As he rubbed the dark red stain on the leather binding of her book, Ryan did his best to try and keep himself at a safe distance from the rage. He knew the emotion had claimed the lives and careers of many before him. It was critical for a man in his position to remain objective at all times. The moment he wavers will be the moment he puts everyone else in danger and gives the men responsible exactly what they need. And what the Colonel needed was for Ryan to become angry, confused, and to make mistakes. He knew the agent was already on his heels. He also knew killing Kristina would put him on his knees. Ryan's untraceable phone alerted him to an incoming call.

"Are you at the safe house?" asked Steve.

"Yes," said Ryan. In spite of the deaths, both men knew work needed to be done immediately.

"First things first. More of my guys will be there in a few minutes. They're going to recover the men I lost and sanitize the house. Do you want them to take Kristina and the rat?"

"No," said Ryan, trying to maintain his composure. "Recover your men, but I'm leaving Kristina and Scott where they are. As soon as your team is gone, I'm going to call the murders in to my boss."

"I'm not following you. He's going to wonder why you're there in the first place. If you stay, you're basically telling him you've been hiding a fugitive. Didn't you say he sent another FBI team to find her?"

"Even though he's dead, Scott's going to help me one more time," explained Ryan. "I'm going to tell my boss Scott found out where she was hiding. I'll say my team and I were on our way to verify her location and set up surveillance. When we arrived, we found them dead. Unless he wants to implicate himself, he'll have to play along."

"Not bad. It'll explain why your team's fingerprints are all over the place."

"How long will it take them to figure out the blood inside the house is from your men?"

"I seriously doubt they'll ever find out. My guys operate on the fringe. We make a point to erase any fingerprint, DNA or military files associated with any of my men. I basically turn them into ghosts when they start working for me. I hate to say it, but I do it for situations just like this."

"Okay," said Ryan, pausing. "Steve, I am sorry about your men. I know you guys are a pretty close group."

"It's okay, Ryan. This is the way our world works. Most of the time we hurt the bad guys, but every once in a while we have to pay the piper. If anything, I should be apologizing to you for failing the mission. I know she was more than a material witness to you."

"Is the mission over?" asked Ryan.

"That's your call. You know where I stand. I will tell you this: My mission isn't over until I put six feet of dirt on every prick making the choice to kill my men. The real question is, where do you stand, lawman?"

"I'll tell you when you get here," said Ryan. "But I need you to bring someone with you. We're going to need a rat of our own to get inside the Michaels Lab."

"I read you loud and clear. I'll see you in a few hours," said Steve, ending the call.

Several cars and SUVs pulled up to the house as Ryan put his phone in his pocket. Without the need for much conversation, Steve's men quickly removed their fallen comrades and cleared anything from the house that would identify its occupants. They were finished and gone in less than fifteen minutes.

Ryan asked Dallas for his cell phone and notified Deputy Director Donaldson that they had found Kristina dead. The deputy director's only question was if his team was okay. He even made the comment that it probably was Joshua or Derek who killed her. Ryan took a moment to think about what he would do when he finally came face to face with the man that was helping Colonel Brown. He handed Dallas his phone and sat at the kitchen table with his friend.

"This wasn't your fault, Dallas," said Ryan, breaking the uncomfortable silence. "I should've moved her the first time they tried to take her. We've been played since this mess started and –"

"Don't even, Boss," said Dallas, standing. "I'm smarter than this. There's no fucking excuse for what I did. That woman is lying up there dead because I was an idiot. I should've seen it coming. I really am smarter than this. I fucked up. Plain and simple."

"Sit down, Dallas," ordered Ryan. "I need you to listen to me, okay?"

"I'm listening."

"Is your head clear? Are you still with me?"

"Of course I am," responded Dallas. "I just know you cared about her and I –"

"That isn't what I asked," said Ryan, cutting him off and leaning in closer. "I'm asking if you're still with me on this, or are you done?"

"I'm with you," said Dallas. He'd been with Ryan long enough to know when he was going to step into the grey area between the laws of man and the laws of nature. He had no idea what Ryan was planning, but he welcomed the opportunity for redemption by the man he respected above all others.

"More feds will be here any minute," said Ryan as Michelle and Tom entered the room. "I'm telling them I received a call from Scott pointing us to this house as Kristina's hideout. When we arrived, we found them exactly as they are upstairs. Are there any questions?"

"Where were you?" asked Michelle again.

"I'll tell you later," said Ryan, hearing the arrival of the agents looking for Kristina.

They were questioned briefly by the investigators before being allowed to leave. It was business as usual and nobody suspected Ryan had been hiding her for almost three weeks. He knew it would be the last time he would ever see her face, so Ryan slowly walked upstairs as his team waited outside in the front yard. He knelt beside Kristina and took her hand in his. He looked around to make sure no one was near. He stared into her lifeless eyes, allowing his rage to feed. It only took a few moments to take him to the dark place he needed to find.

With his resolve galvanized by his anger, he finally lowered his guard. It was his last chance to talk to her.

"I'm not sure if you have any idea how beautiful you are," whispered Ryan. "I was hooked the second you walked into the bookstore. Even though you were dressed down with your hair up and glasses way too big for your face, nothing could hide that smile. It was brilliant. For a few seconds, I actually forgot why I was there.

"It's always been difficult for me to think about having someone in my life. But with you, it was easy. I even practiced how I was going to ask you to dinner after all this was over. Crazy, huh? I was positive you were going to say no, but I had to at least try. I'm so sorry I let this happen to you. I'm sorry I wasn't here to protect you."

Ryan swallowed hard, trying to force down the lump in his throat. He didn't realize he was crying until he looked down to see one of his tears fall on her arm. He watched as it slowly rolled off her skin and splashed into the pool of blood on the cold tile floor.

He closed his eyes and forced himself to imagine her terror and fear as men who knew nothing about her brought unthinkable violence. He pictured her scared and trembling on the bathroom floor, powerless to stop the advance of the monsters standing over her. He squeezed her hand while he thought about her last breath before the bullets exploded into her body. He wanted to feel every ounce of the fear they forced into her. He wanted to feel every ounce of the pain they inflicted on her. He wanted to remember every detail. He wanted to remember so he'd know exactly how much to give back to them.

———

Cautiously walking around the perimeter, Joshua arrived at the hideout east of Atlanta. He had a feeling Derek wasn't there, but he knew he was close. The intuition he felt with his fellow mutated Marines was the strongest of the group, but it still only brought him to their general location. It wasn't like an internal GPS system, but it was good enough to allow for little effort to pick up their trail.

He settled in a thicket of woods less than fifty yards from the front door and waited. The sun would be rising soon, and he didn't want to expose himself until he knew it was safe. Whatever Derek had recently experienced, Joshua knew it was an event powerful enough to elevate his level of awareness. He knew something was wrong.

——

The team arrived back at the FBI house with little conversation during the short trip. Michelle immediately separated herself from the group and went upstairs to her room. The men entered the kitchen and Tom grabbed three beers as they each took a seat around the table.

"How are you holding up, Boss?" asked Tom.

"I'm okay," said Ryan, "But I'm a little concerned about Michelle. She seems very angry."

"Would you care to hear my opinion about why?" asked Tom.

"Please."

"She's taking this hard because she lost a friend tonight," said Tom. "She'll probably deny she was getting close to Kristina, but I could tell. I can't help but think she may feel somewhat responsible."

"I'll talk to her and make sure she knows it wasn't her fault," said Ryan.

"I don't know if that's a good idea right now."

"Why?"

"Because she's also blaming you," explained Tom. "When nobody could reach you, she felt like you left us on our own to deal with some pretty heavy issues. I know you have a legitimate reason for being gone, but we needed you here. Dallas did the best he could trying to sort it out, but they really had us running in circles. He wasn't sure how to handle orders coming directly from Donaldson."

"Don't make excuses for me, Tom," said Dallas. "I screwed it up on my own."

"Calm down, Dallas. We agreed with the plan. We all screwed this up."

"Don't tell me to calm down."

"Guys," interrupted Ryan, "We can't start coming apart now. We all took a beating tonight, and it was nobody's fault but theirs. If we start doubting ourselves, then we don't have a prayer against them. We're all we have right now. They've had us on the defensive since this began, and it's time to change that. If we're going to stop them, we have to stay strong and stay together."

"Stop them?" asked Dallas. "Kristina was the only chance we had to figure this out. How do we prove it now?"

"You couldn't reach me because my phone was destroyed," said Ryan. "And it was destroyed when Derek Mathews put me through a table."

"Say again?" asked Tom.

"I had dinner with a friend from high school," explained Ryan. "She received a phone call from her security monitoring service that an alarm was tripped. I went to her house to clear it, and Derek was waiting there for me. I was set up. But he wasn't there to kill me. He was there to ask for our help. And we're going to give it to him."

"Just when I thought this couldn't possibly get any weirder," said Dallas.

"You and me both, brother. But we have him now, and we're going to use him to find Joshua and expose the Didache Project. I just have to figure out how."

"He just let you walk away?" asked Tom.

"Yep," said Ryan. "He's a pawn in this game just like we are. And just like us, he's had enough."

Ryan explained the details of his encounter with Derek and Jennifer. Tom picked up on the situation immediately, but Dallas was having issues trusting a murderer. But he did trust Ryan, so he was onboard with coming up with a plan. Ryan told them to brainstorm how they could capture Joshua instead of letting Derek kill him while he went upstairs to talk to Michelle. He knocked on her door and she let him in without making eye contact or saying a word.

"Tom said this would be a bad idea, but I'm out of time," pleaded Ryan.

"You're out of time?" asked Michelle condescendingly. "No, you have plenty of time. Kristina is the one out of time, or did you already forget about her?"

"Michelle, I'm –"

"Don't you dare say you're sorry! Don't you dare. You're the one who dragged her into this. You're the one who took her away from her happy life and threw her right in the middle of this shit storm," said Michelle, unable to restrain her anger, "You uprooted everything familiar to her and shoved her into a hole where she couldn't even see the light of day. You had me and your watchdogs babysit her while you ran around chasing your monsters. Well, Ryan, the real monsters got to her. She trusted you. She believed you'd keep her safe. I believed it, too."

Michelle stood and walked across the room and looked out the window. She didn't want Ryan to see her crying.

"You were bigger than life to her," said Michelle quietly. "She talked about you all the time. Christ, it was like a teenage sleepover whenever I stayed. I'd go out and get us a couple bottles of wine, and we'd sit for hours talking about how crazy our lives had become. But the conversation would always turn to you."

Michelle turned around, not caring anymore if Ryan saw her tears. She walked back over to him and sat on the corner of her bed.

"It's no secret I'm a hard ass," said Michelle, "And I forgot how to cry years ago. And I sure as shit didn't want you to be the first person to see me when I remembered. But she reminded me that it was okay to still be a woman while trying to do what people consider a man's job. She reminded me that it was okay to cry. Maybe not in front of you jerks, but somewhere where I felt safe and secure. She felt safe and secure with us. She knew we'd do whatever it took to protect her. She was wrong."

"I am sorry, Michelle. I didn't know you two had become close."

"We spent almost a solid week together. She made it very difficult not to become friends, and trust me, I tried. I knew it was a bad idea, but I couldn't help it. There's just something about her that disarmed me."

"You weren't the only one disarmed," said Ryan. "She did it to me the moment I met her. I instantly turned into a cliché. You know the whole at first sight thing."

"Really? You?"

"Yeah, me. I knew it was a bad idea as well, but like you said, you couldn't help it with her. I even thought about how I'd approach her after this was over. Because you're right, I did turn her life upside down. I did drag her all over the country and leave her to be watched by strangers.

And I did let her down, Michelle. I cared about her and I let them kill her."

"I'll be damned," said Michelle. "Dallas was right."

"About?"

"You having feelings for her."

"It was that obvious?"

"Apparently to everyone else but me. I'm sorry, too. I'm just angry and tired, Ryan."

"It's okay, Michelle. You have every right to be angry. But I don't think it'd be a good idea to tell Tom and Dallas about our conversation."

"Don't worry, I didn't plan on it. But you still haven't answered my question. Where were you tonight?"

"I was with Derek."

"Derek Mathews?"

"I'll explain everything downstairs," said Ryan, "But you need to answer a question as well."

"What is it?"

"Steve will be here in a few hours. He's going after everyone who had anything to do with killing his men. I'm going with him, Michelle. And I'm not going as an FBI agent. Do you understand?"

"I don't think I want to do this job anymore," said Michelle, "But I'm going to finish this one. So if your question has something to do with me helping, the answer is yes. Hell, yes."

22

MY BROTHER'S KEEPER

RYAN OPENED HIS EYES AND immediately sat up in bed. He was in an anxious place of waking, unsure of where he was or what he was supposed to be doing. He looked around, becoming more familiar with his surroundings. For a brief moment, he thought Kristina's death may have just been a nightmare, but quickly deflated when he realized it wasn't. She was still dead.

He managed to find three hours of sleep, but it wasn't nearly enough. He wondered if Steve had already made it into Atlanta, but the majority of his thoughts were about his meeting with Derek. He had a better understanding of the Marine's desire to end the lives of everyone involved. Ryan's original plan of convincing Derek to take the high road and try to avoid bloodshed was nowhere to be found. He headed downstairs for a cup of coffee and found Tom and Dallas already sitting at the table.

"Did you guys get any rest?" asked Ryan.

"No, we figured we'd hit the sack after you left to meet Derek," said Tom, yawning.

"Steve should be here shortly," said Ryan. "He's bringing us some intel on the layout of the Michaels Lab. I want you guys to figure out the best way to get in undetected. If we're going to face Alex, it's absolutely critical we get the drop on him. When he figures out we're there, it has to be too late for him to do anything about it."

"We can definitely work that out."

"I knew you could, buddy."

"So we're going to Maine?" asked Tom.

"Steve, Dallas, and I are," said Ryan. "You and Michelle are going to stay here."

"Are we done?"

"No, the exact opposite of done. I need you two for the other half of the operation."

"I can't wait to hear it," said Tom.

"I'll go over everything with you when I get back. Seriously, I want you guys to get some sack time. We're going to be pushing hard and fast from here on out. No telling when we're going to find time to sleep once this ball starts rolling."

The lead agent downed his first cup of coffee and grabbed a second for the road. He poured a cup for Derek, not knowing exactly what kind of fuel a super soldier required. He pulled into Jennifer's driveway and walked to the creek bank as instructed the night before. The Marine highly skilled in camouflage seemed to materialize out of thin air.

"You look like shit," said Derek.

"I had a rough night," said Ryan, handing him the cup. "Are we going to talk out here?"

"No, let's go inside. Thanks for the coffee."

"You're welcome. I take it she doesn't know you're hanging out in the woods behind her house every night?"

"No, she doesn't," laughed Derek. "It would be too distracting for the both of us. Plus, I can see anyone or anything approaching the house from out here. So what happened?" asked Derek, taking a seat in the living room.

"Colonel Brown discovered the location of our scientist last night. He and Alex killed her, the men protecting her, and another civilian helping our cause."

"I told you he'd do anything to preserve Didache," said Derek. "Are you starting to understand my apprehension about letting them live?"

"Yeah, I am," said Ryan.

"Was this scientist a friend of yours?" asked Derek, picking up on the tone and speed of his response.

"Yes, she was," answered Ryan, confirming Derek's suspicion.

"She," said Derek. "Was she more than a friend?"

"That really doesn't matter."

"That answers my question, and yes, it does matter."

"Are we here to work on a plan or talk about our feelings?" asked Ryan.

"Wow, you were more than friends."

"Derek, seriously, drop it," said Ryan, becoming irritated.

"Sorry, just trying to –" paused Derek, leaning back into the couch and raising his hands to his face as if he was in prayer. "Kristina? Those motherfuckers killed Kristina?"

"Yes, they did," answered Ryan. "And Scott Wilson."

Derek leaned forward and sat motionless with his head in his hands. His eyes were shut tight, and his jaw tightened as he clenched his teeth. Ryan could see the pain in his face.

"She was a very sweet girl, Ryan," said Derek, coming out of his trance. "I take it you knew her well."

"I didn't, but we were working on that," said Ryan, opening up slightly. "It was a little difficult considering our situation, but I agree with you. She was a very sweet girl. She certainly didn't deserve a bullet in her head."

"Fuck!" said Derek, standing in anger. "I'm going to kill Colonel Brown slow. As soon as I take out Joshua, that evil son of a bitch is next."

"We need to get to him first," said Ryan. "If he hasn't given the order to destroy every file on Didache and kill the other three scientists, he'll do it soon. We need to go get him now and I need you to come with me."

"That's not going to happen," said Derek. "I told you the only way I'm leaving Jennifer is if I'm going after Joshua. There's no fucking way I'm leaving her behind with him out there. He's here, Ryan. I think he came into town last night."

"What do you mean he's here? Joshua? You said he'd be hiding out in the mountains for a few more days."

"I can't explain how I know or exactly where he is, but he's close. I can feel him."

"Why is he here?"

"His intuition is much stronger than the rest of ours," explained Derek. "He always picked up on our stress, pain or fear better than we did. I'm not saying he can read minds, but he can feel when something significant changes. There's no way I'm leaving her, Ryan. Not now. I'm sorry, but you're on your own with that one."

"I need you to take Alex," said Ryan, pleading his case. "I can get us in the lab, but I don't think I can get us past him. I need you. As soon as we remove him and the Colonel, we'll focus every asset on finding Joshua."

"That's not good enough. I'm not leaving her. End of story."

"I told you I'd come back with a plan and I have one," said Ryan. "At least hear me out. If you still think Jennifer will be in danger, then I'll press on without you."

"You have my attention," said Derek.

The two men talked for half an hour before Ryan left alone. He still wasn't sure if Derek would commit to the idea of going after the Colonel first, but he couldn't waste valuable time trying to convince him it was the best approach. He understood why he wanted to stay behind and protect Jennifer, but the head of the snake needed to be cut off before anyone involved would be safe again.

He pulled into the driveway of the FBI house and noticed two unfamiliar SUVs parked on the curb. He heard Steve's voice in the kitchen when he walked through the front door.

"Speak of the devil," greeted Steve. Tom and Dallas were sitting beside him at the table.

"It always amazes me how fast you get around," said Ryan, shaking his hand.

"I tend to move a little more quickly when I'm pissed," said Steve. "Your package is upstairs with a few of my guys. We managed to get his teeth fixed while he was a guest at our facility."

"Hopefully he'll cooperate and keep them."

"Oh, I don't think you're going to have a problem with him. He's been extremely helpful giving us intel on the layout of the lab. I didn't have the heart to tell him he's actually coming with us."

"I'll take care of that," said Ryan. "We need to move fast on this. When can we have everything in place and everyone geared up? I'd like to leave this afternoon."

"This afternoon?" asked Steve. "I guess that's doable. How about you and I have a little chat?"

"Sure, we can talk after I go over the plans," said Ryan, missing the hint.

"No, I think you and I need to talk now. The deck?" asked Steve, less as a question and more as a demand.

"Five minutes, Steve. We need to get rolling."

The two friends walked outside, and Steve wasted no time starting the conversation. "You don't have to do this."

"What are you talking about?" asked Ryan, cocking his head.

"You don't need to go with us," continued Steve. "We've got a way inside, and we can get to Alex before he knows we're even there. I don't care how fast or strong he is, he's not bulletproof. Once he's out of the picture, the Colonel will be easy picking. I hope you don't take this wrong, but we don't need you."

"Don't underestimate his abilities," said Ryan. "But I'm not going with you because you need me; I'm going because I need to end this."

"Do you need to end this or end him?"

"You can't do one without doing the other," said Ryan. "You know that."

"I agree, but why do *you* need to do it?"

"This conversation is about over, Steve. I'm going. When did you become so philosophical about killing bad guys?"

"I'm not, but I'm also not an FBI agent. And you won't be either if you do this."

"It has nothing to do with me being an FBI agent. I suspect my days or even hours are numbered before the deputy director pulls the plug on my team and my career."

"But you don't know that for a fact, Ryan. If he's dirty, then he can be exposed. And if you're the guy doing the exposing, then your career stays intact. You won't be very popular, but you'll still have your principles."

"What's this really about, Steve?" asked Ryan, becoming impatient.

"It's about crossing that line and never being able to step back. It's about you risking everything you've worked your ass off to achieve since you joined the Marines."

"Haven't you been paying attention?" asked Ryan. "I didn't cross it, they did. They've been using me and my team the second I accepted the assignment. All of this has been orchestrated by Colonel Brown and my boss. We were never supposed to take any of them alive. They simply used us as government assassins to secure a billion dollar investment. This isn't about trying to expose a conspiracy anymore. This is about –"

"Revenge," interrupted Steve.

"Justice," replied Ryan. "Justice for Peter, Richard, Kristina, Scott, and everyone else who died at the hands of the real monsters. Their answer to the problem they created is to kill anyone that threatens the project. And they're obviously not going to stop because of my efforts. The victims will never have justice if Colonel Brown is alive."

"Once again, buddy, I don't need you to accomplish that goal. I'm just trying to figure out why you need to be the one to kill him. Is it because they killed Kristina?"

"Ah, now we're getting to the real reason for this little chat," said Ryan. "You really think I just want revenge for what they did to her?"

"Like I said, when you cross that line, you can't step back. I know you two had feelings for each other, but is that enough of a reason to do this? When the dust settles, you may be the one in jail. Where's the justice in that?"

"I'll admit to you, Steve, I want to make him pay for what he did to her, but it's not the reason he needs to die. He'll beat the system I'm normally willing to accept as flawed. He has a good chance of walking away from this without a scratch. I simply can't accept that. He's destroyed too many lives for him to keep his."

"I'm just worried the last one he destroys will be yours," said Steve. "Maybe I'm not willing to accept that."

"I appreciate your concern," said Ryan, "I really do. But you of all people should know why I need to be the one."

"Oh, I know why. That's not what bothers me. What bothers me is what happens after. You and I have spilled the same blood in the same mud, but we did it as Marines. It was our duty. It may not have made it easier to kill another human being, but it did make it easier for us to justify it to ourselves. What you're about to do is different. Very, very different."

"You don't need to protect me from the ugliness of taking a life, Steve. Like you said, we've been there before."

"You're not listening to me," said Steve. "I've been where we're about to go many times, but you haven't. I'm not saying I built my security company on body counts, but in order to make it successful, I've had to operate outside the boundaries of the law. You've never done that. You've always relied on that clear-cut line between the ones who enforce it and the ones who break it. All that goes away when you come with me. Are you ready for that? Are you ready to operate in that gray area?"

"Absolutely," answered Ryan.

"Okay, just don't come looking for a job when this is over," said Steve, smiling. "You're too high profile."

Even though the genetic enhancements made him keenly aware of his surroundings, Derek was still human and just as susceptible to sleep deprivation as anyone. The many sleepless nights lying awake and vigilant in the foxhole behind Jennifer's house were catching up with him. As he walked through the front door of his hideout several miles away, he didn't notice the man sitting in the dark corner of the blacked out living room.

"Good morning, sunshine," greeted Joshua, causing Derek to stumble backwards into a table.

"I almost shit myself," said Derek. "What the hell are you doing here?"

Joshua stood and moved in closer to Derek. "What happened?"

"What do you mean?"

"I'm not here because I wanted to take a sixty-mile walk, Derek. I'm here because I felt something was wrong. You know I'm quite sensitive to that."

In spite of being face to face and alone, Derek knew he couldn't kill him. He couldn't even think about it and run the risk of Joshua sensing his aggression. The sociopath always carried a weapon, and Derek's gun was in another room. If he were to have a chance, it needed to be a complete surprise. But even then, he'd have to find a way to clear his mind and ambush the seasoned predator. Derek told Ryan it would be as simple as walking up to him and putting a bullet in his head, but he knew differently. He was still the best weapon the feds had against Joshua, but the strongest of the four UA Marines would also be the hardest to kill. The only thing Derek could do in the hideout was try to redirect his anger, but more importantly, to not think about Jennifer.

"Everything is fine," replied Derek. "I went to check on my sister. I spent the night in the loft of her barn. While I was there, Ryan and his team showed up to ask her some questions. They started looking around the property including the building where I was hiding. I was about two seconds away from having to kill them when my sister called out and they left the barn. I was a little stressed."

"A little stressed?" asked Joshua. "You were more than a little stressed. Did your sister know you were there?"

"Of course not. I just needed to put my eyes on her. She worries about me. In fact, I check on my other sister and parents whenever I'm here. None of them know."

"I can't begin to tell you how stupid that is," said Joshua. "Checking on your family is an urge you can actually control. And you need to control it. We're too close to a resolution to make idiotic mistakes now."

"Easy with the idiotic and stupid comments. You've done a few things to draw unnecessary attention to yourself as well, so enough with the lecture. I'm going to continue checking in on my family, Joshua. In fact, I'll be looking in on my parents tonight. Don't worry, everything is fine."

"Is it?" asked Joshua, as if he knew differently.

"Yes, it is."

"Really? I only ask because I've been waiting here for you since yesterday. Where did you spend the night? I'm getting the sense you were somewhere you don't want me to know about."

"Why does it matter where I was?" asked Derek. "I have no idea what you do or where you go when we're separated. And I don't really care. Why are you so concerned about where I've been?"

"I told you I sensed something was wrong," said Joshua, moving even closer to Derek. "I just wanted to make sure you were okay."

"As you can see, I am."

"I don't understand why you're being so hostile towards me," said Joshua. "I came here out of concern."

Derek lowered his head and took a deep breath. He filled his mind with thoughts about Peter, Richard, and Joshua during better days, the early days of the project when they all felt more like brothers than volunteers for research. He took a seat and asked Joshua to do the same.

"I'm sorry, Joshua. I should be thanking you for checking on me instead of giving you shit. I'm just getting sick and tired of having to look over my shoulder 24 hours a day. I know I'm never going to have my life back, but any life has to be better than the one I'm living now. You're the only friend I have on this fucked up planet."

"I'm not your friend, Derek. I'm your brother. And I am my brother's keeper. This will be over soon, and you and I'll be sitting on some tropical beach living that better life, I promise."

23

CHOICES

DEREK AND JOSHUA SPENT THE afternoon going over their plan to assault the Michaels Lab in Maine. Less than ten miles away, Ryan and his team were doing the same.

"Do you think he'll show?" asked Steve.

"I hope so," replied Ryan. "I'd feel more confident going up against Alex with him behind us. It took a lot of bullets to bring Peter down, and we'll be using half the men we had at the farmhouse. Whether he shows or not, it's critical we get inside undetected."

"Our guy will pull through," said Dallas. "He's more afraid of the Colonel than he is of us."

"Okay, ladies," said Steve, looking at a message on his phone. "The plane will be here in thirty minutes. We'll meet up with my men at the hangar for the briefing. When is Red Team being picked up?"

"Paul said the Colonel chartered a plane that'll be here in about four hours," replied Steve. "We'll definitely beat them to Maine. He also said the Colonel wanted to see him as soon as he arrived. I thought the poor bastard was going to cry."

"Seriously, Dallas," said Ryan, "Is he going to be able to hold his shit together? If he breaks down and turns on us, we're all dead."

"He'll hold it together, Boss. I'm pretty sure he wants to keep his new teeth. The Colonel mentioned something to him about reassigning his men to perimeter security. He needs every man he can muster right now. Even if he thinks they're a bunch of fuck-ups, they can still pull a trigger."

"I agree," said Steve. "If he's not where we need him, we'll know before we get too far inside. I like this plan, Ryan. It's solid. Even if Derek doesn't show, it's still solid."

"Did Derek give you any idea when he'll let us know?" asked Dallas.

"Yeah, we'll know by tomorrow morning," answered Ryan. "Okay, let's gear up and head to the airport. We've got a plane to catch."

———

Joshua and Derek finished their discussion and planned on traveling to Maine in two days. Derek ate and caught a few hours of sleep before getting ready for his nightly vigil.

"Isn't your parents' place over thirty miles from here?" asked Joshua.

"Yeah, it's going to take me a little while to get there. I have a route that allows me to run along railroad tracks most of the way. It'll take me about an hour to get there."

"I still think you're taking an unnecessary risk going alone. Why don't you let me come with you? Four eyes and claws are better than two, my friend."

"I appreciate the offer, Joshua. But I enjoy the solitude. It's the only time I seem to be able to relax and clear my head. You're a bit of a talker," he said, smiling.

"True, it is a long time for me to stay silent. Be careful tonight, Derek. You know I can't finish this without you."

Derek looked around the dark and damp abandoned house. He covered the windows with heavy cloth so it would maintain the appearance of being unoccupied. The only source of light he could risk was a small candle in the main room. "I can't wait to be somewhere I can turn on a fucking light."

He left the house and headed for the railroad tracks leading to his parents' home. The old line crossed the road less than a hundred yards from the hideout. As he stood on the tracks, he stopped and looked around to make sure he was alone. When the coast was clear, he didn't follow the rail line. Instead, he continued along the road toward Jennifer's house.

Derek knew if Joshua discovered his relationship with her he would do everything in his power to end it. Joshua had a master plan to wreak havoc as an unstoppable team. They'd need to be light on their feet and able to travel anywhere at any time. They couldn't tolerate being held back by anyone without their abilities. Once they eliminated the ones that could stand in their way, they planned on moving freely to satisfy their urge without fear of discovery or interruption. It was Joshua's plan, but never Derek's.

He needed to appease Joshua by agreeing to partner with the sociopath. He wanted his revenge on the people who destroyed his life as much as Joshua. When Jennifer convinced him there was hope of a way out, everything changed. He knew Joshua wouldn't allow him to be with her. He knew he'd take her life to end the relationship and regain control of him.

As he approached Jennifer's house, he could see the deck illuminated with Tiki torches and candles. He could hear the music and see her dancing. He passed over his foxhole, crossed the creek, and slowly made his way to the first stair leading up to the deck.

Joshua maintained a safe distance while following Derek. He crept down the path and noticed the hole Derek used as cover for watching the house. He looked across the yard from the creek bed and watched as the two embraced. He knew he had been betrayed.

Derek sat holding her hand and talking with her for nearly two hours. Joshua sat motionless replaying in his head how he was going to kill her. He refused to let a simple woman drive a wedge between his fantasies of ultimate domination and the only person who could help him achieve it.

His anger rose to an apex as he watched them embrace again and hold a passionate kiss long enough for him to realize where Derek's loyalties truly lay. Derek turned away from her and started back towards the woods. Joshua silently moved farther down the creek bed to avoid detection. He watched her extinguish the lights and music as Derek assumed his post for the night in his foxhole. Joshua moved quietly back into the thick brush and took a position less than fifty yards away from the traitor. For the remainder of the night, he stared coldly at Derek, who never took his eyes off her house.

As dawn began to push back the cover of night, Joshua made his way back to their hideout and waited for Derek to return. He sat alone in the dark room trying to subdue his anger. He didn't want to tip his hand that he was aware of the relationship. Instead, he focused on the pleasure he would obtain snuffing the life out of the woman jeopardizing everything. After sitting alone for three hours, he heard footsteps approaching the front door. Derek was home.

"An uneventful evening?" asked Joshua from his chair in the corner of the room.

"Very," replied Derek, taking a seat across from him. "I have to admit I nearly ran into the house when I started smelling my mother's fried chicken. Good Lord, that woman can cook. I can't tell you the last time I sat at her table and ate a home-cooked meal."

"Are you going back tonight?"

"Not to my parents'," said Derek. "I'm gonna grab a couple hours of sleep and then head to my sister's place. She lives further away, so I'll probably head out as soon as I wake up."

"Sleep well, my friend."

———

Paul walked slowly down the hallway leading to Colonel Brown's office. He breathed deeply as he entered the last place on earth he wanted to be. Standing in front of the Colonel, Paul was silent while his boss finished a phone conversation.

"Enjoy your vacation?" asked Colonel Brown.

"It was no vacation, sir," replied Paul. "It was pretty much hell on earth where they kept us."

"Oh, no, son," said Colonel Brown, walking up to the nervous team leader. "You have absolutely no idea what hell on earth feels like. But I'll make you feel it if you screw up again."

"I won't, sir."

"I really didn't want to hear that," said Colonel Brown, standing with his arms crossed only a few inches away from Paul's face. "I should've left you and your team to rot in your cells, but I need you here."

"My team is ready, sir."

"Explain to me again why they let you just walk out of there? If it were me, I would've buried you out in the desert."

"I believe that was the original plan," said Paul, trying to stay calm.

"But after what happened to the doc and his men, the guy running the show had had enough. He's worried about a federal investigation and losing his business. More killing would've brought more attention. I think he's done helping Ryan."

"I wouldn't be so sure," replied Colonel Brown. "I did some digging, and those two have been friends for over fifteen years. I imagine both of them are pissed right now. They're probably looking to come here and get some answers and a little revenge. It'll be the end of Ryan's career and Steve's company if they do, but it was my intention to force them to make mistakes. Coming here would be one of those mistakes."

"Where do you need my team, sir?" asked Paul, attempting to change the subject.

"You and your guys are going to be on the perimeter. Alex is running the show and volunteered you to be the initial line of defense against an assault. He figures, even if you do screw up again, they'll waste bullets and time chewing through your men first."

"We'll be ready," said Paul. "They won't get by us. My guys and I are looking for a little payback."

"So are they."

—

Four large SUVs were parked outside a small airplane hangar at a private airstrip twenty miles from Bar Harbor, Maine. Ryan, Dallas, Steve, and his men were checking their gear and going over the final details of the assault on the lab.

"Still no word from Derek?" asked Dallas.

"Not yet," answered Ryan. "He has a few hours left to decide. We're moving forward as if he's not going to show."

"You know, I can't really blame him," said Steve. "We did a lousy job trying to protect Kristina. I don't imagine he has very much confidence in our ability to protect Jennifer."

"We can't worry about it now," said Ryan. "We need to take this one step at a time, and the first step is shutting down the Colonel."

"In order to do that, we have to get past Alex," said Dallas. "Any ideas?"

"He's not bulletproof," said Ryan. "None of them are. I'm not saying it's going to be easy, but if they have no idea we're there, it won't be as hard. We focus on quietly finding him first. After he's incapacitated, we can go loud on the rest of the troops."

"The lab will be practically empty tonight except for the security force," said Steve. "Even if there's a skeleton crew of employees, they'll be easily distinguishable in their white coats. I handpicked my guys. They're some of the best in the world. I don't see us racking up a civilian body count."

"Good," said Ryan. "Being a Friday night will also help us. Everything shuts down in there on the weekends. As far as Alex, our eyes on the inside should pinpoint his location for us. The Colonel may be the head of the snake, but Alex is his fangs. We eliminate him and the rest of the security force will fold."

"What about the Colonel?" asked Dallas.

"I'll be taking him," said Ryan. "I need him alive. At least long enough to answer some questions."

———

Derek lay in his bed staring at the ceiling for nearly two hours. He had no intentions of falling asleep with Joshua in the next room. Knowing he was so close to Jennifer made him nauseous, but he had to control his level of distress and fear. Joshua was highly sensitive to any fluctuation in his level of anxiety. Thinking about bringing the nightmare to an end helped him ease his mind. How it was going to end was still a slight mystery. He had no other option at that point but to trust Ryan.

He looked at his watch and realized it was nearly time to leave. The plane waiting for him at the airport wouldn't be there much longer. He walked out to the living room and discovered Joshua sitting in the same dark corner.

"Good morning, princess," greeted Joshua.

"Do you ever sleep?" asked Derek.

"I slept like a baby right here in this chair. How was your nap?"

"I could use a few more hours, but I feel pretty good. I need to get moving, though. What are your plans today?"

"Funny you should mention that," replied Joshua. "I've been sitting here thinking about what you're doing."

"What am I doing?" asked Derek.

"Putting your eyes on people you care about. I'm thinking maybe I should do the same."

"Good for you," said Derek. "It does help knowing for sure they're okay. Even if you can't let them know you're there, it helps."

"I agree."

"Who are you going to see? I didn't know you had family around here."

"No, I don't. But there is one woman in particular I'd like to check in on. She's an old friend I've always had a thing for."

"Really?"

"Yeah, but don't worry. I wouldn't risk exposing myself to talk to her or let her know I'm here. I know it would ruin everything we've worked to achieve. I wouldn't let anything or anyone come between you, me, and our mission. I couldn't do that to you."

"I appreciate that, Joshua, I really do. I think you should go see her. Who knows, when all this is over, you may have the chance to tell her how you feel."

"I seriously doubt that."

"Never say never," said Derek.

"You seem pretty optimistic today. Do you know something I don't?" asked Joshua.

"I'm not sure what you mean."

"You said when this is all over," continued Joshua. "This will never be over for us, Derek. Do you understand? There is no cure for what they gave us. We'll never be the men we were before they did this. The sooner you come to grips with our reality, the sooner you can stop the ridiculous dream of being normal again. It simply won't happen."

"We don't know anything about what we are," said Derek. "We don't know for sure if our condition is irreversible or permanent. We don't know if it'll ease up over time or become more intense. The only thing we do know is that we don't want to be this way. After we make things right with the assholes that started this, I have to keep looking for a way to get my life back. Why is that so hard for you to understand?"

"Because it's a fucking dream and nothing else," said Joshua, becoming angry.

It was exactly what Derek wanted. He wanted to get him as angry as possible before he left.

"It's not a dream," said Derek. "It's just hope. If I lose that, I have absolutely nothing left. Nothing. I have to believe there's at least a chance.

I don't want to kill innocent women anymore. I don't want to accept I'm going to be a monster for the rest of my life. To me that's not a life worth living."

"It's not about accepting you're a monster," said Joshua. "It's about accepting the things you can't change. And we can't change what happened to us. Peter and Richard had hope, and look what happened to them. They were murdered by the same people who created us. We're not the monsters, they are. Damn it, Derek, you're all I have left and I won't let them take you. I won't let anyone take you. We deserve to live. It may not be the life you hoped for, but at least it's a life. If you hold on to that dream, they'll kill you for it. I'd rather live and fight than hope and die."

"I'm with you, Joshua, I really am. We do need to fight. We need to make sure they never do this again to anyone else. But after, I need something to keep me going. I don't know exactly what that's going to be, but I have a good idea."

"I know you do," said Joshua.

"You do?"

"Yeah, I do. But I also know, in the end, it'll let you down. The only thing we can rely on is each other. Nobody else on the planet knows what we've been through. Nobody else on the planet will ever truly understand us. They'll always look at us as murderers. They couldn't care less about why we did it. Whether we wanted to or not is irrelevant. Someone has to pay, and it'll be us."

With Joshua's last statement, he didn't need to push him any further. For a brief moment, he actually felt sorry for him. The feeling was quickly subdued when he thought about the inconceivably evil actions of a man he once thought of as a friend.

"You're probably right, Joshua. Our lives are never going to be the same. Nothing we do or say will ever make them understand. If it has to be you and me against the world, then so be it."

"Make no mistake, it is you and me against the world."

"Okay. I need to get going. I'll make it a short night. We have a long day ahead of us tomorrow. I'm looking forward to finally getting my hands on those motherfuckers."

Derek made it to the airport with less than an hour to spare. The pilot of the aircraft notified Steve and Ryan that he was onboard.

24

RAIN

IT WAS LATE AFTERNOON WHEN Derek arrived at the airfield in Maine. Ryan and Steve were the first to greet him when he walked into the hangar housing the assault team. Dallas was asleep in a small office adjacent to the building.

"How was your flight?" asked Ryan with a handshake.

"I've never been the only passenger on a plane," replied Derek.

"I apologize for no in-flight movie," said Steve, holding out his hand. "We didn't have much time to prep."

"Derek, this is my good friend Steve."

"So you're the man I need to thank for the ride," said Derek, shaking his hand. "You're also the guy making sure Jennifer is safe, correct?"

"On both counts, yes," said Steve.

"You have a very difficult and important job, Steve."

"One I take very seriously."

"For everyone's sake, I hope so."

"Let me get you caught up on the details of the mission," interrupted Ryan, sensing Derek's apprehension. "We have a room next door we've set up for the briefings."

"As soon as I'm done here, I'm back on that plane," said Derek. "Do both of you understand?"

"We do," said Ryan. "The plane doesn't leave the runway unless you're on it."

"Okay," said Derek, "I'm all yours."

Ryan and Derek had to walk by nearly every man on the assault team. They had heard about his abilities, and each tried to size him up as he walked past. Derek didn't make eye contact with any of them. He was focused on doing the job as quickly as possible and getting back to Atlanta before sunrise. He was already starting to worry he had made a mistake leaving Jennifer.

———

As soon as the sun went down, Joshua was on the move. He didn't waste any time in returning to the woods behind Jennifer's house. Cloaked in darkness, he made his way to the foxhole Derek had created as a place to watch and protect her. He climbed inside and pulled the camouflaged tarp over his head. He saw her shadow through the curtains as she moved from the kitchen to the living room. He felt a sense of urgency to kill her, bury the body, and get back to the safe house as soon as possible.

He knew they'd be leaving for Maine in less than twelve hours. Joshua was already devising plans to postpone their return to Georgia indefinitely. He'd keep them on the move so Derek wouldn't be able to easily check on Jennifer. He figured after a few weeks, or possibly even a few months, Derek's connection to his girlfriend would become weaker. But in the off chance he discovered she had been killed, he already had a story created that would point the finger of blame at Ryan and the feds.

After lying in wait for nearly an hour, she opened the back door and began to light the Tiki torches and candles. She turned on the music and sat down with a cocktail. Joshua breathed deeply, taking in the moment during his favorite phase of the hunt. He enjoyed knowing what they didn't. He enjoyed knowing he would soon be taking his prey from a peaceful night on the deck into an unimaginable nightmare. He reveled in the silence before his attack. It was as if he were allowing them to have a few more moments of serenity before he would introduce sheer terror into their world. A world they'd no longer be a part of when he finished. He gave her the moment and then slowly climbed out of his hole.

———

Ryan finished giving Derek the details of the assault on the lab. He'd be going in with the Alpha Team consisting of Ryan, Dallas, and Steve. Their mission was to quickly get to Alex and engage him with maximum violence. Two other four-man teams would breach the lab at separate locations and converge at the highly secured Didache section of the building. Their assignment was to take out any security forces they encountered along the way and seal off possible exits the Colonel could use to escape.

They had four hours until the assault. Ryan took Derek to the small office Dallas was using as a bunk room to grab a few hours of sleep. Dallas didn't budge as Derek spread a few blankets on the floor in a corner of the room. He was nearly asleep before Ryan killed the lamp and closed the door. He found Steve talking to some of his men who were re-checking their gear.

"He may be as strong as four men, but he went down like a baby when I turned out the lights," said Ryan, motioning Steve to join him at a nearby table.

"I'm guessing he's had a busy couple of days as well," said Steve, walking with Ryan. "But I'm actually a little surprised he can sleep as uptight as he is about leaving Jennifer."

"Yeah, he didn't seem too confident in our ability to protect her," said Ryan, taking a seat beside his longtime friend.

"Like I said, I don't really blame him with our track record," said Steve.

"It's a little different now," said Ryan. "I'm not playing by their rules anymore."

"Speaking of which," said Steve, "Are you ready for this?"

"Of course I'm ready."

"No, you know what I mean. Are you ready to cross the line? You're not going in there serving a warrant and identifying yourself as a federal agent. You're going in there looking for revenge."

"Aren't you?"

"Fuck yes, I am. But my situation is considerably different from yours. I'm already on the other side you're looking to join. I know what the consequences are going to be of my actions tonight. You have no idea how you're going to react when we finish this. And to be perfectly honest, I'm a little concerned you may hesitate to pull the trigger without the usual warrant or without identifying yourself."

"What are you saying, Steve?"

"Look, I'm not questioning your ability or courage. You know that. But what I am saying is, you may want to hang back until we secure the facility. Derek can do the job of a four-man team by himself. He's got everything to lose if he doesn't go in there like a bat out of hell. I say we turn him loose, follow the bodies after they hit the floor, and watch his back. I'll make sure we put the Colonel on ice and wait for you. That way you don't get your hands dirty. Well, too dirty."

"I'm leading Alpha team inside with you, Derek, and Dallas behind me," said Ryan, narrowing his eyes at Steve. "I'm staying on point until we clear the building and reach the Colonel. Am I clear?"

"Okay, okay," said Steve, holding up his hands and backing down. "I just feel like I'm turning a Boy Scout into a pirate. I'm not exactly comfortable sitting idly by and watching you flush your career down the toilet. But I'll respect your wishes and I won't bring it up again, okay?"

"Thank you."

———

He silently slithered down to the creek bordering the edge of Jennifer's backyard. The normally ankle deep water was up to his waist after a series of afternoon thunderstorms. Even with his enormous strength, Joshua had to concentrate on his footing or be swept downstream. When he made it to the bank on the other side, a solitary bolt of lightning flashed its warning of another storm beginning to form in the pitch black summer sky.

Joshua slowly raised his head above the creek wall, expecting to see her scrambling to extinguish the candles and return to the false safety of the house. Instead, she sat motionless as if in a daydream. He imagined her thoughts were of the future with Derek. He knew she was the one filling his head with lies about a return to normalcy. He grew angry at the audacity of her believing she had more power and control over Derek than he did. It was time for Joshua to cut the ties that bound him to her. He scanned the backyard one last time, making sure they would be alone when he took her.

He lowered himself from the steep bank and took two steps back to the water's edge. The six-foot muddy wall was slippery, and he needed room to launch himself to the grassy yard above. Joshua knelt by the torrent as another bolt of lightning lit up the night sky. A sharp clap of thunder indicated the fast-growing storm was also preparing to unleash chaos onto her world.

He took a deep breath as the transformation caused every nerve in his body to electrify. He opened his mouth wide to allow the fangs to push through his gums. The rustling trees masked the sound of the bones cracking and popping in his fingers as they grew into hideous claws. His face turned pale, and the blue veins under his skin pulsated with each accelerated heartbeat. As another bolt flashed in the sky, he uncoiled from his kneeling position and cleared the bank with several feet to spare. Joshua landed on the grass at the edge of the backyard and prepared to hurl himself at top speed toward her. He still had over thirty yards to cover before he reached the deck. As he planted his back foot like an Olympic sprinter ready to fire off the line, he slipped.

He assumed the ground was waterlogged from the earlier storm as a large divot of grass flew into the air behind him from under his boot. He looked up to see her still unaware and undisturbed sitting in her chair staring into the darkness. The building storm was helping him remain concealed from his prey. In the slippery yard, he wouldn't be able to reach his top speed of forty miles per hour as he started running to close the distance between him and the first stair of the deck.

Joshua was only able to propel himself less than twenty feet before she launched out of her chair, dropped to one knee, and raised her weapon at her confused attacker. It was Michelle. As he planted his foot to stop his advance and maneuver out of her line of fire, he quickly realized the water soaked yard had not been created by an earlier storm. The team had effectively eliminated his advantage of inhuman speed and agility.

At that point, Joshua wasn't terribly concerned with his inability to maneuver at full capacity. He knew she would probably miss her first shot as he pulled his weapon, knowing he wouldn't miss his. But before he was able to level his gun sights, the entire backyard was bathed in intense white light. The team had also effectively eliminated his advantage of inhuman accuracy and rate of fire with a weapon. At that point, Joshua became concerned.

Michelle squeezed the trigger, and as he suspected, her first shot missed but only by a few inches. What Joshua didn't know was the first shot was a signal. Before he could regain his footing and return fire, every window on the back side of the house exploded outward as the large caliber bullets cleared a path to their target. The first projectile traveling at 3,000 feet per second to impact Joshua was fired from Tom's sniper rifle. The .50 caliber round tore through his hip, nearly severing his left leg from his torso.

Two three-man teams concealed in the hedges flanking Jennifer's house added to the chorus of bullets. Joshua fell to the ground, stunned, while firing blindly into the white light. The wet ground around him erupted into dozens of tiny volcanoes as all twelve guns aimed at the same man delivered their payload.

Earlier in the day when Michelle and Tom received word from Derek that Joshua had returned to the hideout, they started setting the trap. They'd been working on a plan for days, trying to figure out how to even the playing field. Joshua's strength wasn't as much a factor as his speed, agility, and accuracy with a weapon.

Jennifer had been put on a plane two days earlier and was resting comfortably with Steve's wife and children at an undisclosed tropical location. They knew Michelle would pass as Jennifer at a distance with a wig transforming her brunette hair to red. What they didn't know when they started working on the trap was how to slow him down. The answer came with the first storm. As Tom was walking through the backyard mapping out firing positions, he noticed there was little traction in the slippery grass. He realized the house was built on a flood plain and was one more downpour away from becoming a marsh. He immediately dropped two hoses in the middle of the yard and left them running for hours.

Dallas came up with the idea of installing high-powered floodlights with the purpose of instantly blinding Joshua when the shooting began. Tom covered nearly every window on the back side of the house with a tinted film which would allow Steve's men to see out, but would obstruct Joshua from seeing in. It gave them the advantage of taking their time lining up gun sights on the target. Each man was behind a heavy weapon mounted on a tripod for stability and increased accuracy. As a backup, two teams were concealed in positions flanking the house and would advance on Joshua during the attack. They'd also give chase in the unlikely event he survived the first round of fire and attempted to escape through the woods. As insurance, a third team was stationed along the path leading to Jennifer's backyard which cut off his only way out.

Joshua managed to roll away from the initial hail of bullets but didn't get far before Tom fired another round from the sniper rifle. The huge bullet ripped a large hole through his abdomen, flipping him onto his back. The only movements afterward were his arms extending up to the sky as if he were reaching out for something to help him get back on his feet. Several more shots were fired into him before his arms dropped and, he lay motionless in the middle of the yard. As if on some kind of celestial queue, the sky answered by releasing a heavy downpour of rain. The order to cease fire was broadcast over their radios. The two teams stationed at the sides of the house cautiously approached the downed killer. They stopped less than ten feet away from him.

"He's still alive," said the lead shooter, hearing the gurgling sounds emanating from his wrecked body. "I don't know how, but this piece of shit is still alive."

Michelle coolly walked up to Joshua who was spitting up blood with every agonized breath. He slowly opened his eyes and stared blankly at her as she removed her wig. He narrowed his gaze and managed a slight smile as he coughed. She calmly raised her gun and put the front sight between his eyes.

"The only regret I have is that I can't make this hurt more," said Michelle. "But I'm glad the last thing you'll ever feel is a woman killing *you*."

She stared back into his eyes for a brief moment before gently squeezing the trigger and ending him.

——

"Rise and shine," said Ryan, waking Dallas and Derek. "Time to go to work."

"Five more minutes, mom," yawned Dallas, rolling away from the light.

"Derek," said Ryan, "Steve's holding a phone call for you. You're going to want to take it."

Dallas, hearing Derek's name, nearly snapped his own neck flipping back over to face him.

"Is Jennifer okay?" asked Derek, quickly getting to his feet.

"She's fine. Steve's outside in the hangar," said Ryan.

Derek left the small room and Dallas stood motionless, glaring at Ryan.

"What?"

E.E. Borton

"You left me in here unconscious and alone with him? Are you nuts? He could've drained me in my sleep."

"He's on our side, remember?"

"For now, but who knows when that'll change again. I can't believe you did that to me!"

"Calm down, Nancy. You're not his type," said Ryan with a smile as he left the room. He walked over to Steve who was putting the phone call for Derek on speaker.

"Are you sure?" asked Derek.

"Very," said Michelle. *"I'm standing over him right now. I thought you'd want to know as soon as we got him."*

"Could you do me one more favor?"

"Sure."

"Shoot him again," said Derek. "As a matter of fact, if you have any bullets left, use them all on him now."

"Okay, Derek. We'll take care of it. Listen, we handled our end of the bargain. It's time for you to handle yours. Good luck to you."

"For what it's worth, thank you," said Derek.

"You're welcome. Piece of cake."

Steve ended the call as Derek dropped his head and exhaled. "I've got to tell you, Ryan, I didn't think you guys could pull it off. He was one truly evil sonofabitch."

"You can thank this guy for that part of the plan," said Ryan, putting his arm around Dallas, who was still groggy and irritated.

"I can't thank you enough," said Derek, holding out his hand. "It's like I can breathe again for the first time in months. I owe you a big one. All of you."

"My pleasure," replied Dallas, shaking his hand. "Thanks for not chewing my face off in my sleep."

"Don't mention it," said Derek, laughing. "I'm starving. Is there any grub around here?"

"Yeah, I'll get you set up over there," said Dallas, walking away with Derek.

"I take back all those things I said about you not being able to cross the line," said Steve. "Nice work on Joshua."

"It's easier for me than you think, Steve."

"Apparently, but why do I have this funny feeling killing Joshua was the easy part?"

"I'm not sure, buddy. But I have the same feeling."

25

OPTIONS

VERY LITTLE WAS SAID AS the men mounted the vehicles that would take them to the Michaels Laboratory. Their destination was a forty-five minute ride. It was Ryan's last chance to change his mind and find another way to stop Colonel Brown and his super soldier hitman Alex Tifton. But aborting the mission was the furthest thing from Ryan's mind. He'd been lied to, manipulated, and used by men who believed they were untouchable. After Kristina's murder, he was more than ready to reach out and touch everyone involved.

The vehicles pulled into a wooded area bordering the west side of the lab. From the cover of the trees, it was only a short distance to the ten-foot chain link fence around the perimeter of the complex. Cameras and motion detectors covered every inch of the large campus. The men exited the vehicles and checked their radios and gear for the last time before the assault. When everyone was set, they took a knee and waited for Ryan's command. He was already positioned with Steve, Dallas, and Derek in a shallow ditch along the deserted road.

Inside the lab, Paul, leader of Red Team, made his way to the security hub. It was a small room located just outside of the entrance to the Didache Project section of the large four-story building. In the hub, two men monitored the electronic sensors and remotely controlled access to every gate outside and every door inside.

Around the perimeter of the campus, there were three entry points along the fence. Each was manned by two heavily armed security personnel from Paul's Red Team. Four more of his men were stationed at the main entrance to the building. Two-man teams guarded the three other access points. All of the security personnel in position to be the first to respond to an assault were under Paul's command.

The Blue Team consisted of twenty men. They were assigned to internal building security. The men inside the security hub were from Blue Team as well as the six on station inside the Didache section. Four others were split into two patrols which constantly roved through the entire complex. The remaining ten were in their bunks and would relieve other team members in the morning. Alex was asleep in his room, which was two doors down from the Colonel's office and sleeping quarters. Both were located within the tightly secured Didache section.

"Good morning, troops," greeted Paul, walking into the security hub. "This sure beats walking around outside sweating my ass off and getting sucked dry by the mosquitoes. When is the last time it got above ninety around here?"

"I can't remember," said Frank of Blue Team, "When I first got here two years ago, I didn't even know there were mosquitoes in Maine."

"Same here," said Paul. "I'm from Florida. I thought this place would be frozen year round."

"No kidding," said Frank, scanning the numerous screens in front of him.

"What time do you have, Frank?" asked Paul.

"Three a.m.," responded Frank.

"That sucks for you guys," said Paul, raising a silenced pistol to the back of Frank's head.

"Why do you –"

Paul squeezed the trigger, spraying Frank's blood and brain matter over every screen in front of him. He fired another round into the side of Frank's partner's head before he knew what was happening. He locked the security hub's door and pushed Frank aside. He typed furiously on a keyboard in front of a screen identifying all the secured access points. One by one, the red indicator lights showed locked positions turning green. On one of the cameras, he watched the service entrance gate on the west side of the complex roll open. A few seconds later, he saw the camouflaged men rise out of the ditch and run towards the open gate. Paul's men assigned to the gate dropped their weapons and placed their hands high in the air. It was the prearranged position all his men would take when they were approached by Ryan's team. He was using the same playbook as Colonel Brown and turned his own security force against him.

The three assault teams quickly covered the distance to the main entrance of the lab. The four men from Red Team guarding the doors dropped their weapons and raised their hands when they saw Ryan approach. They stopped at the front desk and waited for Paul's instructions from the security hub.

"Eagle, this is Alpha," said Ryan, talking to Paul over his radio. "We're in position."

"*Roger that, Alpha,*" responded Paul. "*First patrol is on the second floor moving east to the stairwell. They'll be heading up to the third floor. Second patrol is on the fourth floor and will be taking the west stairwell down to the first.*"

"Understood," replied Ryan.

"Bravo Team," said Steve, "Take ambush positions at the stairwell and wait for the second patrol to exit. Charlie Team, take the elevator to the fourth floor and wait for the first patrol to show up. Move fast."

Both teams acknowledged and snaked down the corridors to lie in wait for the security patrols. Ryan's men were equipped with silenced automatic weapons to minimize alerting others who were still loyal to the Colonel.

Ryan, Dallas, and Steve turned and headed for the opposite stairwell which would lead them to the basement floor. It was the location of the security hub and the Didache section.

The Didache labs consisted of nearly the entire basement floor. They were divided into three sections. The middle section held all the treatment areas and equipment used for research. It resembled a large hospital intensive care unit with glass front rooms surrounding a central administrative kiosk. It was the most secure with four of the six guards assigned to the basement. Ryan's team would be entering one of the two flanking sections holding most of the offices used for daily tasking by the scientists and technicians. It was the smallest of the three rooms and the least likely to have security guards. The Colonel and Alex were sleeping in their quarters in the opposite section, which also held his office and two large conference rooms. One of the conference rooms had been converted to a bunkroom for the three scientists who were the brains of Didache.

"*Colonel Brown and Alex are still in their quarters,*" radioed Paul. "*Four

Blue Team guards are in the lab, and two are posted outside of his sleeping quarters."

"Got it, Eagle," replied Ryan. "We're moving down now."

As the stairwell door closed behind Ryan, the door on the opposite side opened. The two men on security patrol didn't have time to react as Bravo Team opened fire as soon as they stepped through the doorway. Their Kevlar body armor did nothing for their unprotected heads as the volley of bullets hit their marks.

"Alpha, this is Bravo," said Derek, leading the team.

"Go ahead."

"Patrol is neutralized."

"Understood. Take your position down at the basement entrance and stand by for our signal."

"Moving now," replied Derek. He was leading Bravo Team because they'd be the first to reach Alex's quarters. The other three men on his team were there to take out the two security guards posted at the Colonel's door. If Alex were alerted to the assault, he'd easily be able to kill all three before they reached their goal. Derek was there for one reason: Terminate Alex before Alex terminated all of them.

The elevator doors opened on the fourth floor, and Charlie Team spilled out into the corridor. They hugged the wall as they moved toward the stairwell door. The second patrol would be coming through in a matter of seconds. They took their ambush positions as the knob turned. The first man walked through with no expectation that four heavily armed men would be waiting on the other side. When he appeared in the doorway, Charlie Team opened fire. The security guard's head snapped back as the first of many bullets impacted his face. He fell into the second guard, momentarily blocking the volley of rounds. It bought him enough time to squeeze off one round before he was riddled with bullets. Even though they were on the fourth floor and Alex was in a deep sleep in his basement quarters, it woke the Marine with genetically enhanced hearing and alerted him to gunfire. Derek heard it as well.

The plan was to wait until Bravo and Charlie Teams eliminated the patrols before entering the basement. It would allow them to enter in full strength against the large number of security guards located in the largest section of the lab. The plan changed when the muffled sound of the single shot echoed down the stairwell.

Derek knew the most effective way to eliminate the super soldier was to catch him off guard. He also knew Ryan may have been oblivious to the sound of gunfire four stories above his head. If he didn't hear it, he wouldn't give the order to enter until Charlie Team joined them in the stairwell. Derek turned and told his team they were going in early as he pushed open the door.

The two Blue Team members stationed in front of the Colonel's quarters glanced over at the opening door, expecting to see their own security patrol. Instead, they saw Derek with three shadows behind him bolt into the corridor. Before they could focus on the intruders, all four opened fire and cut them down before they fired a single shot. Derek shouldered his weapon and burst down the hall at top speed. His three teammates were over twenty paces behind him when he arrived at Alex's door.

Alex sat up in bed, instinctively knowing something was wrong. He reached over and grabbed his pistol from the nightstand. Wearing only his boxers, he flung open his bunkroom door. The last person he expected to see was Derek. Before Alex could twitch a muscle to aim his pistol, he was blinded by a lightning fast punch which sent him crashing into the far wall of his room. Disoriented, he felt the pistol being ripped out of his hand. Derek quickly removed the slide and magazine, rendering the weapon useless. Alex held his arm up in a defensive position as his vision began to clear, but it wasn't enough to prevent Derek from delivering another bone-crushing punch to his ear. The blindness returned along with a deafening ringing in his head. With two powerful and accurate strikes, the super soldier was nearly incapacitated.

Ryan's radio sprang to life with chatter from Bravo Team as they entered the basement from the opposite stairwell. Ryan's team immediately entered the basement and found no resistance in the office section, just as they had suspected. They moved quickly to the door separating them from the four security guards posted on the other side. A small window at head level gave them a clear view into the heart of the lab. Ryan peered through the window and saw the four guards on their feet looking in the direction of Derek's position.

"They're moving away from us," whispered Ryan.

"They probably heard Bravo make entry," said Steve.

As the first guard looked through the window, the door separating them from Bravo Team exploded in their faces. Derek used Alex as a projectile and launched him down the hall and through the heavy steel door. Two of the guards went down with Alex and the door on top of them.

"They definitely heard that," said Steve.

"On me," ordered Ryan as he made entry into the lab.

With his weapon already sighted on one of the two standing guards, Ryan ordered them to drop their guns. The two men spun around with panicked eyes. Ryan instantly knew they weren't going to follow his commands. He squeezed the trigger and the first round found its mark, snapping the guard's head back. The second guard managed to find cover when Steve's first round only grazed his shoulder. The lab erupted in gunfire.

One of the guards taken down by the door recovered to his knees and began firing wildly in Ryan's direction. Alpha Team dove for cover as the rounds peppered the wall behind them. The gunfight ended quickly as Derek calmly came up behind each guard and killed them at close range. Each man on the assault team, including Steve, jumped to his feet, but none of them lowered their weapons. From his cover position, Ryan could only see their shocked faces. He slowly rose and made eye contact with what was not allowing Steve or his men to stand down. It was the first time any of them had witnessed the transformation.

Breathing heavily, Derek stood alone in the doorway with the security guard's blood dripping from his elongated fingers. He didn't say a word as he turned his attention toward Alex lying a few feet away, broken and bleeding. Ryan walked slowly toward Derek, who was looking down at his former friend.

"How could you kill them?" asked Derek with blue veins bulging through his pale face. "Did you know they were going to do the same thing to you that they did to us? Peter and Richard were just scared and running for their lives."

"They were rapists and murderers" wheezed Alex. "Just like you."

"Joshua was the only one raping," said Derek. "But you're right, we did kill them. Not that it matters now, but they did this to us. They made us kill and we couldn't stop ourselves. But you killed because you were following orders. The same man who did this to us turned you into a murderer as well. The difference is, you killed your brothers."

"You're not my brother, Derek. You're a fucking abomination. You all are. You're all going to burn in hell."

"Right again, Alex, but I'll be sending you first."

Derek raised his hand high above his head and drove each razor sharp claw into Alex's throat. With his other hand, he punched deep into his chest, forcing out his last breath. When Alex stopped moving, Derek picked up his body and started walking towards the Colonel's office. Ryan and Steve quietly followed.

Before he entered the lab, Derek directed the three men on his assault team to secure the Colonel's office and quarters. The door was unlocked and the Colonel was sitting at his desk adorned in his Marine dress uniform. When the men entered, he stood slowly and handed over his service pistol without firing a shot.

Derek coolly walked past his team and dropped Alex's body on Colonel Brown's desk. "One more for your collection," said Derek as the Colonel took a step backwards.

"They really fucked you poor bastards up, didn't they?" said Colonel Brown, cocking his head and staring at Derek's mutated face. "They said it was impossible, but here you are standing in front of me exactly how they wanted to build you. Fascinating."

"And who would 'they' be?" asked Ryan, walking in the room with Steve and Dallas.

"Ah, Agent Pearson," said Colonel Brown with a smile, "The gang's all here."

"Answer my question, Colonel."

"They would be the young men cowering in one of the rooms you passed getting to me. Those are the ones responsible for Derek's condition."

"Dallas."

"I'm on it, Boss," responded Dallas, leaving the room to find the scientists.

"And you must be Steve," said Colonel Brown.

"I am. I want to thank you for the opportunity to kill those sorry assholes who jumped my men. I enjoyed it thoroughly."

"I take it you're the one who turned Paul against me."

"I had a little something to do with it," said Steve. "Kind of sucks not knowing who to trust, doesn't it?"

"Oh, I never trusted him. I actually thought you'd kill him and the others before you got to me. The fact that he survived is of no consequence. It's all been factored in the final solution."

"The final solution?" asked Ryan.

"Oh, yes, Agent Pearson. Do you think I'd leave myself without options?"

"From where I'm standing, I don't see any."

"On the contrary, there's always an option. And if you take a moment to think about what I'm going to tell you, you'll understand my option will be the only one for you as well."

"Humor me," said Ryan.

"You see this sorry pile on my desk that used to be Alex? Well, he's the one responsible for killing Peter and Richard and trying to kill Joshua and Derek. When he found out his brother Marines turned into serial killers, he saw no other course but to defend the honor of the Corps and try to salvage all the hard work conducted here at the lab. While under no direction from me, he ran a side operation shadowing your agents. When you caught up with Peter and Richard, he simply moved ahead of you and killed them. He also came in behind you and contaminated all the evidence linking them to the Didache Project."

"So, your plan is to frame Alex for all the people you wanted dead," said Ryan.

"The deaths were senseless. But in Alex's deranged and altered mind, he viewed them as a threat to Didache. Just as he viewed you and your team as a threat."

"That's your story?" asked Ryan. "Alex is responsible for everything?"

"He is," said Colonel Brown, handing Ryan a folder. "I finally broke through to him yesterday. He volunteered to sit down and produce a sworn statement documenting every step he took since Derek and the other three went UA. He showed a great deal of remorse and was contemplating turning himself in to the oversight committee. The same oversight committee and federal law enforcement officials who received my report yesterday. But it seems he changed his mind and tried to kill Derek and your team."

"You're a very sick man," said Ryan, reading the fake documents handed to him by the Colonel.

"Really?" said Colonel Brown. "Well, then you won't mind showing me the warrants. The warrants giving you authority to trespass on private property, kill my men, and arrest me. If you don't possess any warrants, then killing my men becomes premeditated murder. And I know you don't have them because Deputy Director Donaldson, your boss and my longtime friend, didn't authorize any. Now, once again, you need to pay attention to what I'm offering.

"Alex takes the fall for the killings. He resisted arrest and was subsequently gunned down by your team which arrived after my call for help. You see, I had no idea he was out there trying to cover up the mistakes made by the project scientists."

"And what happens if I don't agree to jump in bed with you?" asked Ryan.

"The other FBI team arriving here shortly, sent by your boss after my request, will be arresting you and your men. I'll still be submitting Alex's confession to the committee and walking away with a slap on the wrist. The reality is, they'll probably shut down the Didache Project for a few months while they conduct an investigation. And when they find it was a horrible series of uncontrollable mistakes made criminal by your actions, I'll be back at the helm before the end of the year."

"What fucking planet are you on?" asked Ryan. "Didache is finished. Even if you manage to separate yourself from Alex, when what you did to Derek and the other three Marines goes public, the doors on this place won't be opening again."

"God, you are naïve, Agent Pearson," said Colonel Brown. "The U.S. Government has spent millions of dollars backing the Didache Project. Do you really think they're just going to close the doors because of one mistake? Do you really think, because a few people died while I created the perfect weapon against terrorism, they'll simply throw it away? If you do, then feel free to arrest me. I'll come peacefully. And before the ink dries on your paperwork, your own boss will set me free and throw your irritating carcass under the fucking jail."

"You arrogant prick," said Ryan. "One of those people who died was named Kristina Anderson. She was a sweet, intelligent, beautiful woman who didn't deserve to die on a cold bathroom floor with a bullet in her head. But you decided the Didache Project was more important than her life. That's where you fucked up, Chief."

"Enough of your dribble, Agent Pearson," said Colonel Brown, defiant. "Read me my rights so we can get this over with. I have a ten o'clock tee time with the Lieutenant Governor tomorrow, and I won't be missing it."

"God, you are naïve, Colonel," said Ryan. "You actually think I'm here to arrest you."

Dallas pushed the three young scientists to the floor when he heard the single gunshot from the Colonel's office. He drew his weapon and rushed through the doorway. He lowered his gun when he saw Colonel Brown leaning back in his chair with a large hole still smoking in the middle of his forehead.

26

GREEN-EYED MONSTER

Dallas stood silently behind Ryan. Derek moved into a corner of the office as his claws and fangs painfully retracted into his body. Steve walked past everyone and moved out into the hallway to check on his men. The death of Alex and Colonel Brown signified the death of the Didache Project.

Ryan wasn't thinking about the consequences of his actions. He was thinking about Kristina. For a brief moment, he wondered if she would have been disappointed in him. He wondered if she would understand his solution. Colonel Brown was an evil, manipulative, and extremely dangerous fanatic who needed to be removed from the planet. He felt there were no other choices.

"You okay, Boss?" asked Dallas, not sure what to say.

"I am. You?"

"Yeah. Listen, don't go second-guessing yourself on this one. He had it coming. Nothing will convince me otherwise. I just wish you would've let someone else do it."

"Did you find the three super geeks?" asked Ryan, quickly changing the subject.

"Yeah, they're shitting themselves in the hallway."

"We don't have time to talk to them here. This place is going to be crawling with feds shortly, and we still have some work to do. Have them grab up every file and piece of paper relating to Didache. Let them know they're in the middle of a shit storm, and if they hold anything back, I'll pull their fingernails off."

"Sure thing," said Dallas with a smile.

"Steve," said Ryan, getting his attention.

"Make it happen," said Steve into his cell phone and then ending the call. "I take it we're not sticking around?"

"No. Is anybody hurt?"

"Nope, my guys are good."

"We have about five minutes to get what we need and get out of here. Are the planes ready?" asked Ryan.

"Yeah, just called the pilots. Both aircraft are fueled and waiting by the hangar. This may be an odd question, but where are we going?"

"I'm taking Dallas, Derek, and the scientists back to Atlanta. You and your men are going home. I don't know how long I can keep my boss chasing his tail. Eventually, you may be getting a knock on your door, so go home and be with your family until then."

"You did the right thing, Ryan," said Steve, putting a hand on his shoulder. "Just so you know, if you hadn't shot that animal, I would've."

"If you're worried about me losing sleep, don't," said Ryan. "But this isn't over until I deal with the deputy director."

"Whoa, partner, taking out the Colonel is one thing. You're not thinking about –"

"No, Steve, I'm not going to kill him. What I am going to do is make sure everyone knows he's a rat. Ruining him will be enough for me."

Dallas and the three motivated scientists worked feverishly to collect as much data as possible. Ryan thanked Paul and the rest of Red Team for playing possum during the assault. He reminded Paul he needed to find another line of work. He agreed.

They left the Michaels Lab shortly before a convoy of federal vehicles descended like locusts. The chaos of the scene would keep them busy long enough for Ryan to initiate the final phase of his plan. The phase unknown to everyone except Ryan.

With everyone safely on board the aircraft, Ryan and Steve parted with a handshake. He and his team were heading home to New Orleans. Ryan and his group were going back to Atlanta. He boarded the plane and sat quietly as the aircraft lifted and reached cruising altitude. He unbuckled and walked back to where the newest members of the team were sitting. When they saw Ryan approach, each sat up in his seat with wide eyes and increased heart rate. When Derek approached, Ryan noticed they all held their breath.

"My name is Ryan Pearson. I'm a special agent with the FBI," he said, producing his credentials.

"I take it you know who this is," said Ryan, looking at Derek. "And you three are the microbiologists assigned to the Didache Project. I know the names Jeff, Stewart, and Randy from conversations with Dr. Kristina Anderson. Are the names correct?"

"Yes, sir," said Jeff. "And we do know Derek. We know him very well."

"He wants to kill us," said Randy.

"He did," said Ryan. "And I don't blame him. But he's not going to hurt you. Well, not unless you withhold any information from me. At that point, I won't be able to guarantee your safety. Do you understand?"

"Absolutely," said Jeff. "We'll tell you anything you want to know. I just want this to be over with."

"We have that in common, Jeff," said Ryan. "And it will be for you as soon as you answer my questions."

"I'm sorry, Agent Pearson," said Stewart, "But we can't openly talk about Didache or anything that took place in the lab. We could go to jail for the rest of our lives. We signed government documents that don't expire for seventy years. Would you mind telling me where we're going?"

"We're going to Atlanta."

"Why?"

"That's classified, Stewart," said Ryan, motioning Dallas to join them. "Dallas, would you take Stewart into the other cabin? He's not feeling very cooperative."

"My pleasure, Boss," replied Dallas, separating Stewart from the other two.

"He seems a little overly defiant considering the circumstances," said Ryan, returning his attention to Jeff and Randy. "Any idea why?"

"Yes," said Randy, "Because all this is his fault."

"All of this?"

"Why the Marines are the way they are," said Jeff.

"That's a good place to start, Jeff. Why were Derek and the others intentionally made into killers?"

"Jesus Christ, Agent Pearson," said Randy. "Do you think we did that to them on purpose?"

"I know very little about why any of this happened," said Ryan. "All I do know is that there are too many dead bodies lying in the wake of what you did. I need to know why, Randy."

"Stewart did it to them alone," said Randy, talking fast. "It was because he got dumped by his girlfriend. And really, she wasn't even his girlfriend. They went out on a couple of dates, and Stewart acted like they were going to get married. He found out she was sleeping with another guy at the lab, and he went fucking ballistic."

"Randy, I need you to slow down a bit," said Ryan. "What does an ex-girlfriend have to do with Didache?"

"Everything," said Jeff, speaking in a much slower tempo. "She had everything to do with this. Her name is, I mean was, Bethany. She was an intern –"

"I know who Bethany was," interrupted Ryan. "She was the first victim. The Colonel had us believe she was random and killed near the campus of Syracuse University. But we know she was killed near the dorms."

"They lied to everyone, Agent Pearson," said Jeff. "We tried to speak up one time to the Colonel and he went through the roof. He said we'd never make it to jail because Derek and Joshua were coming back to kill us for what we did. He said he was the only person on the planet who could keep us safe. That's when he basically locked us up in the lab. We've barely seen daylight since this thing started."

"These past few months have been very confusing," said Ryan. "You and I need to sort this out. Tell me about Bethany's involvement."

"She didn't do anything," continued Jeff, "It was Stewart. When he found out about the other guy, he swore he was going to pay her back for cheating on him. I mean, he was really out there."

"Focus, Jeff, please."

"I need to tell you a little bit about what we did at the lab first, okay?" said Jeff. "You'll understand why very shortly."

"I'm all ears."

"I don't know the extent of your knowledge, but –"

"Feel free to dumb it down for me, Jeff. I won't be offended."

"We created extremely detailed computer models of the Marine's physiology. The software programs we use are more advanced than anything else in existence. They were constantly being fed by biomedical devices attached to each man. In essence, we created exact virtual replicas of them. It's so detailed and sensitive, that whenever they ate a meal, we could track where each nutrient went by monitoring the virtual replicas. We could monitor which cells were being replenished and which ones died. Are you with me?"

"I am," said Ryan. "You created a carbon copy of each Marine in the computer program."

"Correct," said Jeff. "What it allowed us to do was alter their physiology through genetic experimentation without affecting a single cell in the real Marines. We'd introduce a round of gene therapy in the virtual Marine and then monitor how it affected the virtual body. If the changes were within specific parameters and deemed safe, then we'd take the next step and introduce the mutated gene into the real Marines. And one hundred times out of one hundred times, the real Marines reacted in the exact same way as the computer models. The science and technology involved is light years ahead of any published research."

"I'm still with you, Jeff," said Ryan.

"We're able to tinker with any area of the human body including the brain. Uploading genetic mutations to certain areas of the brain can alter behavior. That's where things really become interesting. It's also where Colonel Brown wanted us to focus most of our efforts. It became almost elementary to change the physical capabilities of the Marines, but the Colonel wanted to control their behavior. But behavioral modification is still in its infancy stages.

"There aren't as many controls set up to monitor how it could adversely affect them. In fact, there are no controls in the virtual Marines at all. The only thing we could do was verify if there was any damage to the brain matter itself. We couldn't tell him how they'd actually react in real life, but it didn't sway his position. He pushed us every day to find a solution.

"We created another virtual model that we could attach to the existing version which gave us very basic tools to alter behavior genetically. That's when Stewart created the Vampire model."

"Okay, now you're losing me," said Ryan.

"He was fucking around and created a virtual model which would turn them into vampire like soldiers. He basically uploaded genetic mutations and made them hunt down and kill Bethany. It was his way of getting revenge on her for cheating on him."

"You're saying he programmed them to murder his girlfriend?"

"Only in the virtual models," said Jeff. "It's important you know that. He never intended it to actually be injected into them. It was an accident."

"An accident," said Derek with a growl. "Do you have any idea how many lives you've ruined because of your accident?" He stood up and moved closer to Jeff. Derek's face began to turn pale. "Do you have any idea how many women have been murdered?"

"Women?" asked Jeff confused. "Bethany wasn't the only one?"

"We believe as many as twenty," said Ryan, putting his hand on Derek's arm to calm him down. "They've been taking victims exactly six weeks apart to the day. They couldn't stop themselves."

"Stewart told us he dated her for six weeks before she cheated on him," said Jeff, making the connection. "He must have programmed a loop in computer models. I didn't know. I swear to you, I didn't know."

Derek closed his eyes and lowered his head. The color began to return to his face and he took a seat next to Ryan. "I can't believe we've been through this hell because of a relationship gone bad. He may not have known about the others, but I still want to tear him out of his skin."

"Easy, Derek," said Ryan. "We need him in his skin to answer a few more questions. Jeff, continue. So this was all an accident."

"I think so," said Jeff with a shaky voice. "When he found out the technicians mutated the genetic material and gave it to the Marines, he freaked out. He just walked in circles slapping his head and said how stupid they were for not verifying the order."

"The order?"

"We create the recipe, we don't cook it."

"Okay, you may have dumbed it down too far," said Ryan.

"Sorry," said Jeff. "We build the schematic which a different department follows to create the real genetic material. We're not hands on. When we complete an order based on what the military medical team requested, they take what we created on paper and alter the actual genetic material. They're the ones that put the material into the Marines.

"Stewart never should've been fucking around in the program, but none of us thought it would work. When the computer model indicated that it had a chance to succeed, we put it on ice until we could do further testing. Not because we wanted them to kill Bethany, but because we discovered how to genetically modify behavior. Do you have any idea what a monumental breakthrough that is? For science geeks like us, it would be like finding life on Mars."

"You didn't find life on Mars, Jeff," said Ryan. "You just managed to end a bunch of them here on earth. Nearly thirty people have died because your buddy was pissed at a girl."

"I'm sorry," said Jeff. "It was a stupid thing to say. I'm just a little nervous."

"You should be," said Derek. "It doesn't matter how this happened. Just because we know why it happened isn't going to change the end result. All I know is, day after tomorrow, I'm not going to be able to stop myself from killing again. I get to look forward to being a monster for the rest of my life."

"Joshua didn't tell you?" asked Jeff with a puzzled face.

"Tell me what?"

"The mutation is completely reversible."

"Reversible?" asked Derek, needing clarification.

"Joshua was in the room when we told the Colonel," continued Jeff talking faster. "He said he wanted to be the one to tell you guys the good news. The next thing I know, the Colonel tells us you went nuts and took off. He said you just snapped and threatened to kill everyone involved, starting with us."

"No, he didn't tell us," said Derek. "Joshua did tell us you were planning on spiking our next round of therapy with potassium chloride. Of course we ran."

"That's very good news, Derek," said Ryan. "How do we make it happen, Jeff?"

"Well, the easiest way would've been back at the lab, but you seemed to have removed that option."

"Thank you for the observation, Jeff," said Ryan. "What are our other options?"

"You said we're going to Atlanta?"

"Correct."

"That gives us a couple options," said Jeff. "We have the material and the knowledge. The CDC or even Emory University has the equipment and staff. Do we have access to either?"

"Not at the moment," said Ryan. "But we will. How long will it take?"

"Five to seven days before he feels any effects," said Jeff. "He should be in the clear after a few weeks."

"Looks like you're still going to be taking that long nap, Derek," said Ryan.

"Actually, that's a good idea," said Jeff. "If he's unconscious and paralyzed during the peak, it should pass in a day or so."

"That's the day after tomorrow, Ryan," said Derek. "Where and when do you plan on sedating me? And then after, how do you plan on getting us access to the CDC? In case you forgot, you're pretty much a fugitive like me."

"Don't worry," said Ryan with confidence. "I have a plan."

"Are you going to share it with me?"

"Sure, as soon as we land. I have a couple phone calls to make."

"Ah, as soon as we land. Again, this is the part when you tell me I'm just going to have to trust you?"

"That's worked out pretty good so far, hasn't it?" asked Ryan.

"So far," said Derek with a weak smile.

The plane landed at an airstrip outside of Atlanta. Ryan was relieved when they walked off the aircraft without an army of federal agents waiting for their arrival. The welcoming party consisted only of Michelle and Tom.

"How was your trip?" asked Tom, greeting Ryan with a handshake.

"Productive," responded Ryan. "Nice work with Joshua. You made a believer out of Derek."

"I really can't thank you enough," said Derek, joining the reunion. "I really don't care what happens to me at this point. Jennifer being safe and not living in fear is all I wanted."

"You're welcome," said Michelle. "She's going to be staying put for a little while, but you'll be seeing her soon. Tomorrow's going to be a very interesting day."

"He doesn't know," said Ryan.

"Oh, this is going to be fun to watch," she said.

"What does that mean?"

"She means telling you about my plan."

"Well?" asked Derek, staring at Ryan.

"The only way we're going to get access to the CDC and get you better is to bring you in."

"This is what I get for trusting you?" asked Derek, perplexed at Ryan's idea.

"Hey, it's you and Jennifer who opened my eyes to the effectiveness of the simple plan."

"Simple, not stupid," said Derek. "And I have to tell you it sounds stupid. You're going to hand me over to the deputy director? He's one of them. I'm a dead man if I go into custody."

"You're not going into custody," said Ryan. "I said I'm bringing you in. What I mean is, we're going to the Atlanta field office and meet with the agent in charge. I've known him for years and I trust him.

"Think about it, Derek. You're still wanted for rape and murder, and they're going to have a few questions for me about assaulting a military lab and killing a Marine Colonel. Those are fairly considerable weights hanging over our heads. If we run, those questions won't get answered, and the deputy director will still be in control. Not to mention you won't get the help you need."

"We can figure out another way to reverse the effects," said Derek. "We have the scientists; we just need to find a lab. It can't be too hard after what we've been through."

"What about after?" asked Tom. "What do we do after? Join forces and live our lives on the run? I agree with Ryan. We do what isn't expected."

"And if they don't believe us?" asked Derek.

"We shoot our way out."

"That's the only thing about this plan that makes sense."

"I'm joking, Derek. I've put a little more thought into it than that," continued Ryan. "We'll have an exit strategy, but we won't need it."

"How can you be so sure?"

"The Colonel and the director almost succeeded because it was contained within their offices," explained Ryan. "Exposure is what they feared the most. They used their power to keep a lid on everything. We'll use ours to blow the lid off. Even if the Atlanta office can't wrap their heads around what happened, they'll be asking more questions than the deputy director can dodge. After all, even he has a boss. A boss who coincidently worked in the Atlanta field office before moving to Washington."

"You're thinking you can beat this by using the same system that sent you to kill me? I wish I could see the positive results as clearly as you. And don't tell me to trust you on this one."

"Okay, I won't," said Ryan. "But I know you do. I know you've got to be tired of running. I've only been doing it for a few days and I'm ready to stop. We accomplished what we set out to do. Maybe not in the way you thought of a few months ago, but Didache is dead. No one else is going to get hurt. Let's go put the spotlight on the deputy director and watch that prick dance."

"I'll tell you right now, I'm going to regret this in the morning," said Derek.

"You mean in a few hours," observed Tom.

"Let's try to get a little sleep," said Ryan. "We're all going to need it."

27

TRUE BELIEVER

NOBODY SLEPT. EACH SPENT THE hours looking back at the past few months, but from different angles. Tom was worried it was the end of the team and the end of the only family he knew. Michelle had already made up her mind it was her last assignment in the field. When Kristina was killed, she not only lost a witness under her protection, but a rare friendship. Dallas worried about his boss. He had an uneasy feeling the man he greatly respected had crossed a line, changing him forever. Derek imagined himself sitting on a beach with his arm around the only person in the universe who mattered.

Ryan simply wanted it to be over. He wanted everyone involved who had survived to be shielded from the consequences of his actions. The veteran agent was prepared to shoulder the blame for every move made outside of the law. He knew he'd face criminal charges for going off the grid and killing the men responsible without due process. What worried him the most was that he didn't care.

Dawn was breaking, signaling the continuation of a long day which seemingly had started weeks earlier. Ryan went over the details of his final plan and relayed his last orders to the team. If it all fell apart, Michelle and Tom would be waiting close by to cover Derek's escape while Ryan covered theirs. But in the back of his mind, he really wasn't worried about a shootout with federal agents. Derek's speed would put him out of harm's way before anyone could put cuffs on him.

A sedan pulled up to the hangar, and one of Steve's men approached

Ryan, carrying a garment bag. Inside was a pressed Marine uniform complete with a duty belt and service pistol. Derek wanted to be in his dress blues when he turned himself in to the feds.

Not much was said when Ryan and Derek were dropped off at the marble stairs of the Federal Building. They calmly walked inside and passed through the security checkpoint with no interference from the posted guards. They took the elevator to the third floor and stopped at the door with the large brass nameplate. Ryan put his hand on the knob leading to the office of Special Agent in Charge (SAC) Gregory Archer.

They walked in to see Archer standing beside his secretary's desk in the waiting room. "Well, look what the cat drug in," said Archer in a slight southern accent. "Good Lord, Ryan. How long has it been?"

"About two years, sir."

"Two years? Really? Time slips by me faster and faster every day. I would've sworn on a stack of Bibles you left this office no longer than two months ago, let alone two years."

"It is getting harder to keep track," said Ryan, holding out his arm to bring Derek closer. "Sir, I'd like you meet a friend of mine. This is Captain Derek Mathews."

"An honor to meet you, sir," said Derek.

"Honor is mine, son," replied Archer, gripping Derek's hand. "I was Navy, so I hold a special place in my heart for Marines. Which unit are you with?"

"The 2nd Marine Special Ops Battalion out of Camp Lejeune."

"A fine unit," said Archer. "So, what brings a Special Agent from Virginia and a Marine from North Carolina to my front door?"

"Sir, may we speak in private?" asked Ryan.

"Absolutely. My morning brief doesn't start for another half hour. Will my office do?"

"Yes, sir," said Ryan with a smile. "It will."

As they entered the office, both Ryan and Derek took a deep breath before making themselves comfortable in the chairs opposite Archer. Ryan had been in the same seat in the office several times in the past. His eyes gravitated to a framed photo of Deputy Director Donaldson shaking Archer's hand during an award ceremony. He was hoping Derek didn't notice the picture.

"How's DC treating you, Ryan?" asked Archer with the first round of small talk.

"The traffic is ridiculous, but I don't spend much time in the city."

"That's right," said Archer, remembering the new assignment, "You're with a fugitive recovery unit."

"Yes, sir," answered Ryan. "It's why I'm here. I don't mean to be rude, but Derek and I are working under the gun. We don't have very much time."

"Okay," said Archer. "Am I to assume you're not here to catch up on old times?"

"That would be correct. I'm here because I trust you, and I also need your help."

"You have my attention."

"I've been on assignment for the past three months under orders from Deputy Director Donaldson," stated Ryan. "Those orders were to hunt down and recover four Marines who went UA from their post. The four Marines are Peter Arrington, Joshua Bell, Richard Elliot, and the man sitting beside me. They were there as volunteers for a classified research initiative identified as 'The Didache Project.'

"They were basically human test subjects for genetic therapy. I won't even begin to try to explain the science behind the project, but I'm in contact with three young men who can. They can be here in thirty minutes if you decide not to lock me up in a mental hospital."

"Let me help you cut to the chase, Ryan," said Archer. "Why did you bring Derek here, and what are you asking of me?"

"Yes, sir. Derek is here to show you the results of the genetic therapy. I couldn't see you believing my story if I didn't bring him. What I'm asking of you is to bring in the Special Counsel for your office so we can give a sworn statement."

"I don't have to remind you of FBI protocol regarding affidavits, Agent Pearson. That can happen anywhere. Why did you feel the need to sneak up on me with this? I need you to drop the cryptic shit and tell me why you're here."

"Like I told you, sir," said Ryan, "I'm on assignment from the deputy director, and I believe it was his intention for me to bring in these four fugitives dead instead of alive. I also believe he's responsible for the murder of a witness who was under my protection."

"I believe the cheese has just slipped off your cracker, son," said Archer. "Agent Pearson, tread lightly. I've known Boyd Donaldson for twenty-five years. I argue there isn't another man with his level of integrity and honor in this Bureau. Whatever you think he's done or said, I can assure you there's a legitimate explanation."

"I very much wish that to be true, but I almost killed this man sitting beside me thinking he was a violent fugitive," said Ryan, holding his ground. "He's not a fugitive, sir. He's a victim."

"You have an impressive service record," said Archer. "But this behavior and what you're telling me is flat out baffling. The only thing keeping me from picking up the phone and having you thrown in a cell are those years of dedicated service. I've always thought of you as a good man, Ryan. That's going to buy you about one hour with my Special Counsel, but that's just to get this insane accusation on the record to cover my ass. I have a very strong feeling you just fucked up."

"What happens to me after this is the least of my worries. I'm sorry to say I'm confident it'll be the least of yours as well," said Ryan.

"You can give your statement here in my office," said Archer. "I'll have my counsel, John Kramer, here in less than an hour. You go ahead and get your scientists and anybody else you need."

"Thank you, sir. We need to give those statements on video as well to record the physical mutations."

"Mutations?" asked Archer. "No offense, but he looks like a standard Marine to me."

Ryan looked over at Derek. It was time to make Archer a believer.

Derek stood and took off his shirt. He neatly folded it and placed it on the seat of his chair. Reaching up to his mouth, he gripped his two front teeth and with a slight jerking motion removed what resembled dentures. He placed them in a plastic container and put them in his pocket. Archer shook his head with a slight smile as if he were about to be the victim of a prank.

"Agent Pearson, I'm sorry, but this is borderline ridiculous. And this little show isn't helping. I'm thinking maybe I need a psych evaluation if I let this continue. Both of you just sit down and let me get in touch with Donaldson before this goes too far."

Derek closed his eyes and started to hyperventilate. Archer immediately stopped talking, leaned back in his chair, and narrowed his eyes.

"He's turning pale," observed Archer. "Is he going to pass out?"

"No, sir, that's how it starts."

"The mutation is his skin color? That's not exactly what –"

Before Archer could finish his sentence, pulsating veins resembling chaotic blue lightning bolts shot to the surface of Derek's face and neck.

"My God," whispered Archer, mesmerized by Derek's transformation. Ryan's eyes were fixated on Archer's face because he knew what was coming next would radically change his expression.

Derek began to move his head around in circles like someone trying to stretch a sore neck. He pressed his lips together in obvious pain and produced a low throaty groan. He abruptly stopped the rotation and threw his head back, opening his mouth wide. He strained to open it wider until Archer heard a disturbing popping noise. He assumed it was his jaw dislocating. Archer instinctively stood up and drew his weapon when he saw the source of the noise.

With his head tilted back, two fangs pushed out of his gums and locked into the spaces previously occupied by the fake teeth. Blood sprayed on Archer's desk when the fangs broke through a thin layer of recently healed tissue inside his mouth.

Archer aimed the weapon at Derek's head, but the Marine never took an aggressive step towards him. Ryan reassured Archer he was in no danger. It seemed to offer him very little comfort.

Derek slowly raised his hands to his chest. During the mutation, his fingers extended two inches past their normal length. His fingernails added another inch as they thickened into intimidating claws. As the fingernails transformed, they ripped through the sensitive skin, adding to the pain of the event. Blood began to trickle down his palms and forearms. Archer's hands were shaking as he kept the sights of the pistol on Derek's disfigured face.

"This is what they did to me," said Derek in a distinctively lower voice. "They did it to all of us."

"Derek," said Ryan in a calming voice. "I think he understands now."

"I don't think he does," said Derek, glaring at Archer.

"Bring yourself back, buddy," said Ryan, slowly moving his hand to Derek's shoulder. His earlier reassurance to Archer that he was in no danger wasn't exactly true.

"Talk to me and I promise to help you, son," said Archer, lowering his weapon. "I want to know who did this to you, Marine. I want you both to tell me everything."

After Derek mutated in front of Archer and then returned to his normal human appearance, he truly had his undivided attention. Archer summoned his Special Counsel who took their sworn statements. After receiving the signal from Ryan, Michelle and Tom sent in the three Didache scientists who gave their statements as well. Everyone was gathered in a conference room in front of a bank of microphones and video cameras.

The meeting was in its sixth hour when the door to the conference room opened, causing Derek to jump to his feet. Ryan rose slowly beside Derek after the Marine recognized the man in the doorway. Ryan wasn't surprised when Deputy Director Boyd Donaldson walked into the room.

"I expected this," said Ryan, attempting to calm Derek.

"I didn't."

"I made the call when we were setting up the room," said Archer. "Listen to what he has to say, Ryan. You need to hear it from him."

"Keep the tapes rolling," said Ryan.

"Of course," replied Archer.

Donaldson took a seat at the table across from Ryan. Derek reluctantly returned to his seat, never taking his eyes off the man who wanted him dead. Donaldson had anticipated the cold welcome and deliberately made his movements as slow and non-threatening as possible. He was aware of Derek's ability to kill him in less than a second, but was more wary of Ryan's disposition.

"The only way to do this was in person," said Donaldson. "I can only imagine what's going through your head right now."

"No, you can't," said Ryan. "If you did, you'd be doing this over the phone."

"This is exactly why I'm here. You'd be less inclined to believe me if I chose that option."

"I trusted you," said Ryan, "Every word. You used your position to further your own agenda, and it cost the lives of innocent people. Whatever you told Archer to bring him to your side won't be enough. It may not happen today, but I swear I'll be the guy putting the match on the pile that burns you at the stake."

"Ryan, you walked into my office asking me for help," interrupted Archer, "And I'm giving it to you. Nobody is going to put a hand on you or Derek. You have my word. You're both going to walk out of here today."

"With all due respect, sir, I don't give a shit about that. There's no doubt in my mind that Derek is walking out of here. But I'm not going anywhere. I'm not going anywhere until he's in a cell."

"I betrayed your trust, Ryan," said Donaldson, "And I'll resign my position if you still feel the same way at the end of our conversation. All I'm asking for is a few minutes. Will you allow me that?"

"You may have swayed Archer. You won't sway us, but go ahead and start dancing."

"I betrayed your trust because I trusted Colonel Brown," started Donaldson, "And it was a mistake that'll haunt me for the rest of my life. Before this mess, he was a respected leader and a vital component to a program with unprecedented potential to save lives in combat. The more I learned about the Didache Project, the more I believed in it. The results were extraordinary and the applications were sound. But the lengths he was willing to go to insure its survival weren't. He betrayed all of us, Ryan."

"You're telling me you had no idea what was happening?" asked Ryan. "I can't accept that. I can't accept you simply took his word that we needed to kill Derek and the others."

"Ryan, even you were taken in by the need to stop them before they killed again. Neither one of us knew why. We just knew we couldn't let them continue. The Colonel manipulated the evidence and the situation to make us believe they were murderers on a rampage."

Archer interrupted again. "Before the deputy director left Washington, he sent me the transcripts and recordings of every conversation he had with Colonel Brown and you. When you hear them, I think you'll have a better understanding. For what it's worth, I have very little knowledge of what happened, but the tapes are compelling. The Colonel motivated nearly every move the Bureau made. And we now know everything coming out of his mouth was a lie."

"We started to suspect he was playing us when we discovered he authorized the destruction of Joshua's juvenile criminal records," continued Donaldson. "I immediately put a team on investigating the nature of the offenses. It didn't take them long to put the pieces together proving he was a true sociopath. We still didn't understand why Derek, Peter, and Richard jumped on Joshua's killing bandwagon, but it raised enough red flags for me to put the brakes on accepting the Colonel's request for support. Unfortunately, you had already uncovered the truth about his intentions. When we couldn't contact you, I knew something was wrong. After he sent Alex's fake confession to the oversight committee, there was no doubt in my mind of his true nature. When I sent the agents to Maine, they didn't go to protect him. I sent them to help you. Obviously, you didn't need it."

"I killed him," said Ryan, "And Alex. That needs to be made perfectly clear. It's all on me. And Joshua was killed while he attempted to take another victim. It was a clean shoot for Michelle and Tom."

"I have no doubt, Ryan," replied Donaldson. "I'm sorry you thought you were out there alone on this. From what I've heard so far, and for the record, the Colonel was barricaded in the lab and resisted arrest. His was a clean shoot as well. The U.S. Attorney's Office concurs. We have a mountain of paperwork to complete, but at this point no criminal charges are being filed against you or any member of your team. After you finish the reports I'll be helping you with, you're going to take a very long vacation while I sort out the details. I'm sorry, but there's no way to avoid putting you on administrative leave until this case is closed."

"Administrative leave is the least of my worries, but what about Derek?" asked Ryan.

"It's a little trickier for him," said Donaldson, who turned his attention to Derek. "Regardless of why, there are still a number of families out there wondering what happened to their daughters. We have to answer to them. There's no way to avoid it."

"He helped us end this, sir," said Ryan, becoming irritated. "As crazy as it sounds, they programmed him to kill those women. There was no premeditation or natural urge. I understand the families need closure, but there has to be another way. Derek doesn't deserve to go to prison."

"Ryan," said Derek in a disarming tone, "You know he's right. I have to answer for what I did, in spite of the reasons. There's no way around the fact that I murdered them. When I walked in here with you, I was ready to tear these walls down if they tried to take me into custody. But the truth is, it's the only way."

"No, it's not, Derek," said Ryan, standing. "I won't let them do this."

"Hold on, Ryan," said Donaldson. "We're not going to take him to jail. He's going to walk out of here a free man, but we do have to process him into the system. If you'll agree, I'll release him into your custody. You'll stay with him while we take care of our legal obligations to the victims and their families. I'm going to handle it personally. But first, we need to get him well. How long before the urges take over, Derek?"

"It'll probably start tomorrow, sir. I need to be sedated and locked up for at least three days."

"How would you feel about it happening back at the lab in Maine?" asked Donaldson. "We'll send the scientists with you to start the reversal therapy immediately. I don't think they'll have a problem with getting back to work for our side. Actually, they don't have a choice."

"I don't care where it happens," said Derek, "I just want this out of me."

"As of now, I'm reinstating the Didache Project for one purpose," said Donaldson, "To get your life back. When it's complete, those doors will never open again. I'll put the locks on myself."

"We shot up the lab pretty good," said Ryan. "I don't know how long it will take to repair the damage."

"From what I saw, most of the equipment we'll need is still intact," said Stewart, sitting at a table in the conference room with the other two scientists. "I won't sleep until I make this right. I swear to all of you, I'll work non-stop until he's better. All of this is my fault."

"Thank you," said Derek. "I know you didn't do this on purpose." With a smile he added, "If you did, you'd be with the Colonel right now."

"He'll have to answer to the murder charges, Ryan," continued Donaldson, "But the U.S. Attorney has already agreed to speak to each family and explain the circumstances. They feel strongly most will be satisfied with the actions already taken against the men responsible. And I'll be with him every step of the way. But first things first, let's get both of you back to Maine."

The technicians shut down the recording equipment, and nearly everyone in the room grabbed a phone to begin making all the necessary arrangements. Ryan and Derek sat quietly at the table as most of the occupants left the room.

"Well, that turned out a little better than I expected," said Derek, finally breaking the silence.

"I'd have to agree," said Ryan. "I also have to tell you I didn't think we'd be walking out of here free men. Shit, I actually think I still have a job."

"Looks like it, buddy."

"I have a plane waiting to take you to back to Maine," said Donaldson.

"I won't be joining you just yet. I need to get back to Washington to start moving the mountain of paper. Are you two going to be okay?"

"Yes, sir," said Ryan. "We're going to be fine. Just one more thing."

"Whatever you need."

"I'm sorry I thought you betrayed us," said Ryan. "I'm glad you proved me wrong."

"I'm the one who's glad, son. Judging from what happened to the people who did betray you, I'm very glad," said Donaldson, leaving Ryan and Derek alone in the room.

"Well, you ready for your nap?" asked Ryan, slapping Derek on the back.

"I really am."

"Listen, I may not be there when you wake up."

"Where are you going?"

"I have promises to keep."

28

BENEFITS

DEREK AND THE SCIENTISTS BOARDED their plane and headed back to the lab. Ryan walked up to the ticket counter and, for the first time in over five years, bought his own seat. His plane landed at Shenandoah Regional Airport where he rented a car and headed for Harrisonburg, Virginia. He arranged to meet Sheriff Bill Parker the following morning.

Ryan slept hard for nearly seven hours before the alarm jolted him awake. Shortly after, a knock on his hotel door signaled the beginning of another long day. He opened it to see Sheriff Parker standing with a smile and two large cups of coffee.

"It's not moonshine, but it's not far from it," greeted the Sheriff, handing Ryan a cup.

"You're a life saver, Bill," replied Ryan, taking a sip. "How have you been?"

"I've aged about ten years in the past couple of months, but other than that I'm good. The real question is, how are you holding up?"

"How far is the drive to the first house?"

"About forty-five minutes."

"That's not nearly enough time for me to answer your question, but I'll try."

"Unfortunately, we have three other homes to visit today," said Bill. "We'll have plenty of time to catch up. But I want to make sure I tell you now how much I appreciate you keeping your word. You didn't have to come back here and do this. That says a lot about your character."

"I can't take all the credit for being here," said Ryan. "You can be somewhat persuasive yourself."

"Let's get out of here before we start hugging," said Bill.

Both men sat in the car for a moment after they pulled into the driveway of the first house. They mentally prepared to face the parents of Laura Ackerman. She was Peter Arrington's first victim in Virginia. The job didn't get any easier when they visited the second, third, and fourth families. Ryan didn't return solely to try to give closure to the families of the victims. He needed to find it as well.

He didn't immediately leave Harrisonburg after he finished the somber task of explaining to the parents how and why they lost their daughters. It was more emotionally exhausting than he anticipated. The Sheriff graciously offered his isolated hunting cabin amidst the serenity of the Shenandoah Valley. Ryan spent two days alone with his thoughts for the first time since he had accepted the assignment. When he finally answered his phone, he quickly closed up the cabin and drove directly to the airport.

With each connecting flight, the aircraft grew smaller and smaller until he was sitting behind the pilot, occupying one of only four seats. Nearly ten hours had passed since he had left Virginia. The car waiting for him at Belize City Airport carried him to a large marina where he boarded a thirty-eight-foot speed boat. At seventy mile per hour, the driver took him to his final island destination in less than two hours.

They docked alongside a small pier and took a stone path to a large two-story Spanish villa overlooking the water. Ryan noticed two men in Hawaiian shirts walking along a sundeck on the roof of the house. Each was scanning the property with high powered binoculars with higher powered rifles slung across their backs. He identified two more armed men patrolling through the expansive manicured backyard among the palm trees and tropical plants. The stone path ended at the edge of a large pool deck with a cascading waterfall at one end and a Tiki bar on the other. He approached a laughing group of people sitting at the bar while a blender mixed another round of piña coladas.

"This is a bit nicer than any FBI safe house I could've put you in," said Ryan as Jennifer jumped to her feet and greeted him with an excited hug.

"Steve doesn't know it yet, but we're never leaving," said Jennifer, tightening her squeeze.

"When you told me you were going to lock her away somewhere safe,

I imagined a dark dank hotel room somewhere in Jersey," said Derek, shaking his hand after Jennifer loosened her grip.

"Believe me, I had no idea either," said Ryan. "I'm not sure how you were able to leave the country, Derek. But Steve doesn't seem to play by anyone's rules but his."

"No, my handlers actually know I'm here. But if they ask, I came down with you," said Derek with a smirk.

"I take it everything went well at the lab?"

"I woke up feeling great. I have to head back in a few days for more reverse therapy, but all indications to this point are very good. I can't voluntarily force the mutations to happen anymore."

"I couldn't be happier for you. The both of you."

"How could I possibly thank you enough?" asked Jennifer, making no attempt to hold back her tears. "You made our dreams come true. I wasn't too thrilled about Derek kissing Michelle on my deck, but I know it had to look real for Joshua to believe it was me."

"You're very welcome," said Ryan. As Michelle and Tom joined them at the bar, he added, "Glad to see you guys decided to take a break."

"We're not going back either," said Tom. "This place is fantastic. The island is practically deserted."

"Did Dallas come with you?"

"Yeah, he's inside having an interesting conversation with Steve. You probably need to check in on them."

"I heard you're both going back to Behavioral Sciences at Quantico. Is that true?"

"More than likely," said Michelle, "But I agree with Tom. I may never leave this place."

"Nobody would blame you," said Ryan, heading for the house and leaving them to their next round of piña coladas. Dallas met him as he was walking up to the back door.

"Hey, Boss, perfect timing. Steve's up those stairs," pointed Dallas, wearing a ridiculously loud tropical shirt.

"Nice threads."

"There's a closet full of them upstairs. When you finish, put one on and join me at the Tiki. You and I are going to get hammered tonight. Don't even try to say no."

"Deal," said Ryan, taking the stairs to meet Steve.

"You have no idea what you've done," said Ryan, joining his friend on the second-story balcony overlooking the pool.

"What's that?"

"I really think they're staying."

"They could," said Steve, "And so could you."

"I wish that were true. We all needed this little getaway and thank you for offering this place, but I have a little explaining to do back on the mainland."

"You have a lot of explaining to do if you plan on trying to keep your job. But if you decided to resign, I don't think anyone in Washington would try to stop you. In fact, I'm sure they'd prefer it. You're about to blow the lid off a project they've sunk almost a billion taxpayer dollars into. You may even win a few favors with some powerful Congressmen if you just quietly went away. Favors which would come in handy for a guy like, oh, I don't know, me."

"After everything that's happened, you want me to keep my mouth shut about Didache?" asked Ryan.

"Easy, rejuvenated lawman," said Steve, handing Ryan a cocktail. "It wasn't too long ago you turned your back on the system and kicked in a few doors. And I must say you're pretty good at it.

"Listen, you and I both know Didache is finished. But we also know another program just like it will sprout wings in a matter of weeks or less," continued Steve. "You close that ugly door behind you, and a bunch of other ones are going open. And I'm one of those doors."

"You really do want me to come work for you, don't you?" asked Ryan.

"I really do. And now so does Dallas."

"Dallas?"

"Yeah, he's looking forward to having you as his boss again."

"And you're looking forward to being mine?"

"I wouldn't be your boss. We'd be more like partners."

"I had a funny feeling you'd pull something like this. I mean, getting me and my team down here to taste the good life. Giving Derek and Jennifer their dream vacation, proving to me we did the right thing by crossing the line. You're very predictable and very diabolical, my friend."

"Did I mention we have a great dental plan?"

"When can I start?"

LaVergne, TN USA
31 March 2011
222298LV00005B/38/P